RUIN OF THE ORIGINAL
CONSERVATORY
OF MUSIC

TEMPLE OF
HEROES OF
SUPERLATIVE
CHARACTER

HALL OF THE
EIGHT PRECIOUS
VIRTUES

HALL OF LILTING
RADIANCE

BOYS' AND GIRLS'
DORMITORIES

COURTYARD
OF SUPREME
PLACIDNESS

BRIDGE OF
SERENE HARMONY

TEMPLE OF SAGACIOUS
MONK GOOM AND CHINGU

GALLERY OF
PARAGONS OF HONOR

EASTERN HEAVEN
DINING HALL

GREAT GATE OF
COMPLETE CENTRALITY AND
PERFECT UPRIGHTNESS

PEARL FAMOUS
ACADEMY of
SKATE AND SWORD

RAIL-GONDOLA
TOWERS

PEASPROUT CHEN

FUTURE LEGEND OF SKATE AND SWORD

PEASPROUT CHEN

FUTURE LEGEND OF SKATE AND SWORD

HENRY LIEN

HENRY HOLT AND COMPANY
NEW YORK

Henry Holt and Company, *Publishers since 1866*
Henry Holt® is a registered trademark of Macmillan Publishing Group, LLC.
175 Fifth Avenue, New York, New York 10010
mackids.com

Library of Congress Control Number: 2017945045
ISBN 978-1-250-16569-5

Our books may be purchased in bulk for promotional, educational, or business use. Please
contact your local bookseller or the Macmillan Corporate and Premium Sales Department at
(800) 221-7945 ext. 5442 or by e-mail at MacmillanSpecialMarkets@macmillan.com.

Book design by Carol Ly

First edition, 2018

Printed in the United States of America by LSC Communications, Harrisonburg, Virginia

1   3   5   7   9   10   8   6   4   2

If I learned just one thing,

Then the year has not been wasted.

If I traded one illusion

For a revelation,

If I kept just one friend,

Then the year has not been wasted.

May we meet here in the new year.

May we meet here in Pearl.

—"PEARLIAN NEW YEAR'S SONG"

CHAPTER
ONE

I commit this venture to the imperium of Shin!

I commit this venture to the radiant Empress Dowager!

I commit this venture to . . . well, perhaps I can come back later to complete the eighty-eight honorific hailings. At this moment, it's hard to think of anything except that today I, Chen Peasprout, sail into the city of Pearl.

The city that looks as if it were made of milky porcelain.

The city that looks as if it were poured, not built.

The city that is always busy with racing, jumping skaters, from the smooth white boulevards to the sweeping white roofs.

I, Chen Peasprout, a girl from the village of Serenity Cliff in Shui Shan Province, of the shining empire of Shin, sail today into this city of legend. As the ship heaves toward Aroma Bay, the city of Pearl appears to rise before us out of the sea like the stage of an opera, all creamy sweeps of roofline and slender pagodas.

Today, I begin my studies at Pearl Famous Academy of Skate and Sword, where I, a girl of just fourteen years, shall become a legend of wu liu, the beautiful and deadly art of martial skating! I shall finish this year with first ranking and win the lead in the Drift Season Pageant! The Empress Dowager would be disgraced if I achieved anything less, for I am the first student from Shin to attend the finest academy under heaven devoted to the only form of kung fu that is performed on bladed skates! A form that was invented by a Shinian, the legendary Little Pi Bao Gu! A form that I—

"Peasprout, what are you doing?" My little brother, Cricket, tugs at the sleeve of my academy robe.

I unclench my fist and uncross my arm from my chest.

"Nothing," I say. "What is it?"

"I'm going to get last ranking at the academy. I know it." Cricket twists in his skates like he always does when he's nervous.

"Let go; you're creasing my sleeve," I say.

"Oh, I'm sorry!" He pets the cuff of my silk academy robe as if it were a wounded animal.

In the fables we grew up hearing, princes who flew on dragons to their palaces on the moon wore silk. This is what every student at the academy wears. To Cricket, the academy must be as unreal as a palace on the moon. My little Cricket, with his chin buried in his breast, his hands wringing each other, and his big elbows sticking out, is nothing like me. But he will be. I'll see to that.

"Cricket, it doesn't matter how much older or bigger anyone is than you. The Empress Dowager of Shin, the greatest empire under heaven, selected us as her emissaries in the goodwill exchange of wu liu skaters! No one else at the academy can say that."

"The Empress Dowager only included me because Pearl sent two siblings to Shin," Cricket says. "Do you think the Pearlians will take us hostage?"

Ten thousand years of stomach gas. You stamp on one of Cricket's fears and two more spring up. He tries to take a deep breath but chokes on his saliva.

"Cricket. You have no need to be afraid of this place. None of those little brats at the academy has journeyed three thousand li. None of them has sacrificed what you sacrificed to study wu liu."

I can't let him hear my voice shake. If I cry, he cries. I must collect my emotions. Ever since our parents disappeared, Cricket has been my responsibility. I might be an orphan now, but I'm not going to let him be one, too. "All those spoiled Pearlian students will reincarnate as fleas, and you'll reincarnate as a hero. Their names will be forgotten. Your name will be long-lived."

Cricket's eyes widen and he nods like he's reminded of some great destiny. "I will reincarnate as a hero. My name will be long-lived."

As we sail deeper into Aroma Bay, the dazzle of the sun's reflection off the creamy architecture becomes painful. Cricket and I put on our smoked spectacles bought specially for our arrival. Two weeks' worth of rice is a lot for a pair of lenses, but it's hard to see anything in the city without protection for the eyes.

The ship docks at a jetty made of white filigree. Cricket and I shoulder our pouches, and I make sure the reed basket of soaps that we brought as gifts for our teachers is secure. We skate down the disembarking rail with the other passengers.

Everything here is made out of this substance that they call "the pearl." Even though the whole city is ribboned with waterfalls and fed with canals, the pearl itself is dry and never melts. As I skate, my blades bite into it, but the pearl smooths itself behind me. The sensation is delicious. We have nothing like this back home. In Shin, we have to skate on rinks made of ice preserved in caves until it's ridged and yellowed like bad toenails, and even then it's gone by the fourth month of the year at the latest. The inventor of wu liu might have come from Shin, but our country hasn't advanced conditions for wu liu training in two hundred years.

The wu liu skaters here in Pearl can train all year long. That means that the other first-year students at the academy could have had a total of several years more training than I have had.

So what? I was a Peony-Level Brightstar. Before that, I was wu liu champion for all of Shui Shan Province five times before the age of ten. And the Empress Dowager chose me for this goodwill exchange because Pearl sent the mayor's sons, Zan Kenji and Zan Aki, the lead skaters of the New Deitsu Opera Company. Who cares if the other students train year-round? They probably spend the extra time on purely ornamental moves, like bowing and hand flourishes. I can do hand flourishes just fine. My hand flourishes are legendary.

"It's like pools of poured tofu!" says Cricket. He crouches to touch the pearl. He pops his finger into his mouth.

"Cricket!"

He pulls his finger out of his mouth and says, "It's salty. Maybe the pearl comes from the sea."

"We're not here to study architecture or work for the pearl-works company, so it doesn't matter. Come on, we have to find our way to the rail-gondola towers." The academy scroll says that the gondolas are the easiest way over the sea to the string of islets on which the academy sits, but we have to board them before they stop running at sunset. The sun looks like it's only an hour from setting.

We have to arrive on time. We can't disgrace the Empress Dowager.

Cricket and I are blocking the main path of the boardwalk, so we skate off to the side and huddle next to a series of pungent vats that must belong to some sort of stinky vinegar-tofu factory.

I notice two boys in official-looking uniforms watching us. Cricket digs his nails into the back of my sleeve and says, "Don't talk to them."

"Cricket, how do you think we're ever going to succeed if we're afraid even to talk to the people here?"

The boys skate over to us. They're not much older than I am, but they wear uniforms that remind me of the ones that government officials wore back in Shui Shan Province. The logograms on the boys' sashes are too small to read while they're moving around. I bow and say, "Hail, brothers."

"Brothers?" they say together, then laugh.

What is there to laugh at?

"Shinian, neh?" says one, a compact, square-shaped boy. How does he know we're from Shin? I speak perfect Pearlian. It must be Cricket's accent. I've told him ten thousand times that no one curls their tongue when speaking Pearlian. Make me drink sand to death!

"You've come to study wu liu?" the square-shaped boy asks. "Which school?"

"Pearl Famous Academy of Skate and Sword."

The boys look at us as if for the first time. I know this look on their faces. It's envy. Well, they should be envious. The square-shaped boy reaches inside his coat and brings out a small clay tablet and a stylus.

"Name," he says to me.

"I am called familial name Chen, personal name Peasprout," I answer. "My little brother is called familial name Chen, personal name Cricket."

"Peasprout, neh," he says. "*Kawai*." Is he mocking me, or does he really think that my name is cute? And why is he using an Edaian word like *kawai*? The empire of Shin is no longer at war with the empire of Eda, but that doesn't mean we're going to just forget the war.

"Please," I say. "We have to get to the rail-gondola towers before the sun sets."

"You're not going anywhere until we approve your papers."

I hand him our scrolls confirming acceptance into the academy. "No good," he says, handing them back to me. "No seal."

"What seal? Nobody told us we needed to get a seal."

"No seal, no admittance farther into the city."

"Where do we get a seal?"

"If you're Shinian, you have to get the seal from the office of the Minister of Culture for your province."

"Where might that be?" I ask, trying to keep my voice even. We're going to miss the last gondola. The academy will turn us away and say that Shinians are too ignorant to tell time.

The boy squints at the setting sun. "If you start swimming now, you might get back in time to see the rest of your class graduate."

This can't be. The Empress Dowager would've provided us any necessary documents. I knew that Pearlians would be unfair to us. Two hundred years later and they still blame us for the damage caused to their city by the Great Leap of Shin.

"Peasprout, look at their sashes!" Cricket whispers.

The writing on their sashes is so small, but Cricket always did have eyes like an owl. I pick out the words: *Number-One Best Quality Auspicious Golden Dragon Discount Wu Liu Academy and Noodle House*.

My heart fills with a thousand throbbing fists.

These boys are only students as well, not officials. They've been making us stand here like fools while the sun sets over the gondolas. I want to teach them a lesson, but I know we should just skate away.

"How many Shinian feng shui masters are needed to take care of a tree blocking the front door of a house?" says the square-shaped boy to the slighter boy in a loud voice meant for us. "Eighty-one. One to yell at the tree and eighty to push the house."

I whip into a combat stance. "Show some respect! I am the emissary of the Empress Dowager!"

"Meaning you're her spy? What's in the basket—bombs?"

The boy grabs for the basket. I push Cricket far from the combat radius. We didn't bring these gifts across three thousand li just to have some harbor scamp steal them. I enter into the single-toe butterfly spinning leap, ending with a diagonal toe kick that connects with the boy's forearm. The force of my kick sends his hand slapping against his own shoulder.

The pearl here is so smooth, so responsive. I stand with my skates biting deep into the surface, my palms crossed in blade position, ready for more combat. I toss the basket of soaps to Cricket. He plucks it from the air and skates far away to keep it safe.

The boys circle out to either side of me and then charge. I launch into a defensive move, the iron parasol spin. I dive onto my fingertips and split my legs above me, my skates rotating in a deadly circle that spins faster and faster. The boys scrape backward from my flashing blades, but they've built up too much momentum and now they're sliding toward me. When they're about to meet the steel, I pull in my skates, channel the gathered Chi energy of my spin, and use my knees to knock them back.

The boys land on the edge of the vat of stinky tofu. They spiral their arms and peddle their feet wildly to keep from falling into the stew. I leap up, balance my skates on the edge of the vat between them, and grab the fronts of their robes in my fists.

On the horizon, the bottom edge of the sun is nearly touching the water.

"Where are the rail-gondolas to the academy?"

The boys answer only with sneers.

"I'm going to ask each of you where the rail-gondolas are. And you'd better say the same thing, or you're both going into that vat. Now, whisper it in my ear."

I bend my ear to the slimmer boy. "You first."

He says, "It's to the east, just past the dolphin embassy's water court."

I bend my ear to the square-shaped boy. He spits out, "Your ancestors leaked out of rancid turtle eggs, Shinian pig!"

I release the boys, straighten my robe, and perform a double-jump double-knee tornado kick. I send them both flying into the vat of stinky tofu.

CHAPTER
TWO

The sun is now half covered by the sea. If those two nasty boys are any indication of how Pearlians treat Shinians, the teachers will probably ship us back home if we arrive late.

I search for the rail-gondola towers from atop the vats. In the far distance, something that could be a water court glimmers in the light. I look for the thin rails stretching across the open sea, but my view is blocked by the plumes of water that spray up from all the canals and pools throughout Pearl. It's the Season of Spouts, after all. I calculate the distance using finger geometry. The towers are thirty li away! It will take us an hour to skate there!

"Peasprout, let's leave the street level so we won't lose sight of the towers."

We skate our way atop a high bridge rail and leap upward. The pearl surface bounces with us as we jump, launching us into the sky up to roof level. The new skates that the Empress Dowager sent us have filigree blades in the shape of a dragon. The tail curls up and spirals under the heel to serve as a wonderful spring.

The roofs are designed to be skated on. They form another complex of streets above the streets below, like a second city floating above the first one. I'm proud of the fact that a Shinian invented the art of wu liu, but Pearlians have built a whole city made for it.

The sun is now three-quarters covered by the water! However, we can keep the towers in view from up here. The ornamental curves at the edges of the roofs send us lifting into the air. We cross the city, striding left and right, skipping off the structures as if we were leaping from stone to stone in a pond.

At last, we reach the towers. Only a sliver of the sun remains above the water. A group of tourists from the Shin mainland is gathered at the scenic overlook point between the towers.

"Witnessing the sunset in the legendary city of Pearl produces feelings of serenity and quietude!" shouts the touring group's guide through his hollering cone.

There aren't any rail-gondolas at the foot of the towers. A small scroll at the base of one tower informs us that we've missed the last gondola to the academy. I almost panic until I notice there's still a portion of sun left above the water.

"Customs are different in Pearl. Even their sun sets differently!" shouts the tour guide to his group. "In Pearl, it is sunset when the bottom edge of the sun first touches the edge of the water!"

Ten thousand years of stomach gas. Why didn't I read anything about this in *The Imperial Anthology of the Pearlian Colloquial, Vernacular, and Obscurely Idiomatic?*

The tourists from Shin look at me and whisper to one another. Two girls from the group skate toward me. Their movements are terrible, exactly as you would think Shinians on skates for the first time would look. I don't want to be seen with them. Luckily, there are no Pearlians nearby.

"Everyone, look!" squeaks one of the girls. "It's the Peony-Level Brightstar Chen Peasprout!"

The others in the touring group make their way over, all of them appalling skaters. Some even use snow poles to balance.

The tour guide bows deeply and says, "We're all so proud of you. All hail the Peony-Level Brightstar Chen Peasprout, emissary of the Empress Dowager!"

An old man and woman at the back of the group tuck their heads in and bow shyly when I catch their gaze. They look at each other and unfold two identical fans with my face painted on them. They look like my maternal grandparents.

I can't be ungracious to these people. My people. And we're already late anyway.

I lose a tenth of an hour returning their bows, thanking them as they praise me, and brushing my autograph on their merchandise. I'm just glad that none of them has one of those mortifying paper dolls of me, especially the one with me dressed like a silly assassin or the one with me toppling an entire pagoda with a flying side kick of my skates. When I become a legend of wu liu here, I'm going to use my money to buy every last one of those and burn them.

At last, Cricket and I climb up the steps of the towers and hop onto the thin rails atop them leading over the water.

I warn Cricket to skate cautiously due to the winds and the waterspouts. We work our way across, leading with one skate and pushing with the other. It's an unnerving sensation to be skating over open sea balanced on a slim rail.

At last, the islets of the academy come into view. In the fading light, the campus is profoundly beautiful. There is one central island composed of terraces, great sweeps of plazas, and roofs. It's ringed with smaller islets, all of them connected by rails. Everywhere there are banners fluttering and snapping. Canals atop the structures send water flowing down their sides. The roofs shimmer in the twilight, their edges and spines weaving across the campus in exuberant curls like dragons nested with each other. We reach the landing and leap off the rails.

We pass under a vast arch in the form of milky sea horses meeting snout to snout, garlanded with flowers and carved with the words *The Great Gate of Complete Centrality and Perfect Uprightness*.

"That's the first new structure that Cloud-Tamer Zwei built after the Great Leap of Shin!" cries Cricket.

"Cricket, what did I say? Don't talk about the Great Leap!"

We skate through the gate and up to the entrance of a crystalline hall with a roof wider than I thought was possible in this world. A prefect stands at the door, clutching a scroll of what I assume are the names of new students. She lifts her arm and flaps her hand at us. "Come, come, come! The Feast of Welcoming is almost done!"

Cricket and I hand her our academy scrolls for inspection. We bow, apologize for our lateness, and beg her not to turn us away. The girl smiles with an Enlightened One's face of kindness and says, "No troubles. You missed Supreme Sensei Master Jio's speech. That's a good thing. Now, in you go before all the hot food and all the cold food swap temperatures! And happy Year of the Dolphin!"

It seems that not all Pearlians are like those boys from the discount academy. I wish we could go to our dormitories first to put away our belongings, but we're already very late, so we skate in.

The hall is a wide, open structure lined with rows of milky tables and benches, filled with laughing students. Strange, gelatinous lanterns hang everywhere. One wall is covered by a great curtain of silky white.

This is our first chance to meet some of our fellow academy students. We have to make a good impression as the first students from Shin ever to attend the academy.

Heads turn toward us. Girls whisper to one another. Are they laughing at us?

Cricket and I take a little of every dish offered at the central serving table onto our trays. I don't recognize a single food. No pickled chicken feet or sheep intestines or any of the other comforting home-style foods we have in Shin. And there's no one to stop us from taking too much. Is food so plentiful here that they don't have to control portions?

We look for a place to sit, but everyone is packed together, deep in their conversations and private jokes. I feel like I'm skating straight into a cold sea.

No one sits alone except for one girl, at the end of the hall. Her hair is a long black waterfall. On a technical level, I admit she's slightly more beautiful than I am. However, she stares at the table in front of her in a very unattractive way.

The girl lifts her face and meets my gaze. I turn away quickly.

When I glance back, she's still looking at me! Pearlians have no manners. In Shin, we never look people in the eyes, unless they are speaking to you and they are at the same social level.

"Peasprout," says Cricket, tugging on my robe in the way that I hate. "Everyone's almost finished, so let's not bother them. Let's eat at that empty table."

Ten thousand years of stomach gas. As if it were not hard enough to make new friends here without Cricket isolating us at every opportunity. I scan the rows and see two boys sitting at a table by themselves.

I can do this.

I was wu liu champion for all of Shui Shan Province five times before the age of ten.

I was the Peony-Level Brightstar.

I am the emissary of the Empress Dowager.

I skate toward them. I look back to Cricket and urge him to follow, but he only shakes his head.

When I reach the two students, I see they're very handsome. I flash my famous smile, which everyone loves, even if they haven't seen it on the posters and paper dolls. I cast each of them a flirtatious look. Then I notice that the two boys are holding hands across the table. They unclasp hands, bow their heads to me, and politely ask me to join them as my neck and face flood with embarrassment.

I catch their names as Ong Hong-Gee and Song Matsu. Beyond that, I can barely hear the polite questions they're asking me between the sound of the blood beating in my ears, the heat on my face, and my attempts to eat more quickly than I've ever eaten in my life. All the strange foods are bland, as if Pearlians didn't use any salt, and I can't tell if some of them are sauces or dishes.

The boys, kind souls that they are, ask me please not to rush, as they were just about to get second servings themselves. I protest that I'll be finished shortly, too, but they won't allow it. By the time they come back to me with full plates, I *am* finished. Then it's my turn to sit and watch while they eat food that they don't want to eat.

Thankfully, the torture is interrupted by Supreme Sensei Master Jio, the head of Pearl Famous Academy of Skate and Sword. He skates to a great dais, rubbing his belly like the Enlightened One and laughing as if hearing the best jokes in his life one after another, although no one else is saying anything. "Ahihahaha, sweet little embryos! Now the second- and third-year students shall welcome you to Pearl Famous with a demonstration of Pearlian opera. For as you shall learn when you attain sagehood, the shadow they cast is the you that you shadow."

A student skates out and unfurls a scroll that reads, FIRST-YEAR STUDENTS: DO NOT ATTEMPT THIS YOURSELVES WITHOUT THE SUPERVISION OF A SENSEI! ALWAYS SKATE RESPONSIBLY!

The great curtain of white silk covering one side of the hall is drawn aside. We gasp as we see that there is a vast white stage set behind it built in the image of the whole city of Pearl in miniature.

The older students enter into the cityscape. They sing as they skate, while strumming or pounding or drawing bows across instruments. I know the song. It is "The Pearlian New Year's Song," sung throughout the month of the New Year's festivities.

"If I learned just one thing, then the year has not been wasted!" they cry.

They skate faster and faster and then begin to leap up and down from the rooftops to street level, flipping from bridge to balcony. The miniature cityscape is alive with a dazzle of figures dressed in ravishing pearlsilk brocades that swirl and flip like petal-fall in a wild wind.

"If I traded one illusion for a revelation," they sing.

The stage riots with color and motion and the flash of blades. Skaters in scarlet and skaters in black robes spin and fly at each other in one-on-one duels like dark, metallic parasols.

The voices crescendo, and I feel a ball of emotion grow inside me as they sing, "If I kept just one friend, then the year has not been wasted!"

The hall quakes with Edaian *taiko* drumming over the sound of skates whisking on the pearl like bladed blossoms.

"May we meet here in the New Year!"

Skaters bear down hard toward the curling rooftops to the left and right edges of the stage. They whip into the curves and go hurtling back toward one another with their arms spread like eagle wings. They fly through the air until their skates clash and shower sparks onto the crowd. With each strike of metal on metal, we roar with joy.

"May we meet here in Pearl!"

With the last note of the song and the last strike of the drums, the skaters stamp their skates, toss their chests out, and punch their fists in the air, like statues of heroes from legend. The hall explodes in applause.

This is all I have ever wanted.

At last, at long last, I am finally where I belong.

And I do belong here. Because Little Pi Bao Gu was Shinian, and she invented this beautiful art form. So no one is going to make me feel that I belong here any less than anyone else.

After the performance, the two boys invite me to come and tour the campus with them sometime. I learn that they're second-year students. They tell me that you can distinguish year by the trim on the front seam of a student's robes: silver for first-years, gold for second-years, various colors for third-years depending on their conservatory. I burn with embarrassment, because second-year students don't spend their time with first-years. There are kind people here in Pearl as well.

I look for Cricket, but I can't see him. He must have skated off to hide in his dormitory chamber with no evenmeal. His hands tremble very badly when he doesn't eat. Why did I leave him?

As I head toward the boys' dormitory, I see two people sitting inside one of the rail-gondolas stationed at the towers at the academy entrance: Cricket and a boy I don't recognize.

The gondola hangs from the rails, bluntly snouted like the lip of a walnut shell and swaying gently. I climb the tower steps to them.

They're eating noodle soup with mushrooms and bright vegetables. The boy who is sitting with Cricket is handsome but smiles too much. Boys who have dimples overuse them.

He smiles. "Ah, Disciple Cricket, we have a guest!" He smiles again. "You must be Disciple Peasprout." Another smile.

I press my hands in a bow and sit on the gondola bench beside Cricket.

"Joyful fortune to make your acquaintance. I am called familial name Niu, personal name Hisashi."

What kind of name is Hisashi? Not Pearlian. Certainly not Shinian. Another Edaian name? Why are the Pearlians so obsessed with Eda?

"Thank you for feeding Cricket," I say.

"You didn't actually eat that stuff they serve in Eastern Heaven Dining Hall, did you?" he asks. He laughs. He has a nice laugh, as if he's remembering something amusing while trying to clear bean jam from the roof of his mouth.

"Why didn't you eat in the dining hall?" I ask.

"I don't like crowds. And everything they serve has meat or other things taken from animals in it. The architecture is magnificent, though."

"Disciple Hisashi said that he thinks I have the hands of an architect!" says Cricket.

What does that matter to him? Cricket has as much focus as a puppy.

"You're too kind," I say. "But Cricket is here to study wu liu. We are the skaters sent in the goodwill exchange with Chairman Niu Kazuhiro of New Deitsu Pearlworks Company."

He tenses when I mention the Chairman of New Deitsu. Why is he acting like— Wait, the familial name. Niu. He must be the Chairman's son. This boy is the son of the man who controls the company that manufactures and sells most of the pearl in existence. So why is this rich boy from a powerful family out here alone with Cricket?

"Tell me, friends"—Hisashi smiles, breaking the silence—"what has your impression of Pearl been so far?"

This boy's big eyes have a way of turning into merry little crescent moons when he smiles.

I take time to think. When someone asks a question like that, it's stupid to answer with something that anyone could say, like "It's very nice here." I want to make a startling observation about the culture here and the experience of a five-time wu liu champion skating on a city made of the pearl. I want to say something he'll never forget.

"It's very nice here," answers Cricket. "Everyone is very friendly."

Ten thousand years of stomach gas. "Cricket—" I struggle to control my irritation. "That's not what he's asking. And not everyone has been so well-mannered in Pearl as Disciple Hisashi."

"Just Hisashi. Did you meet any trouble?" His concern sounds sincere.

"No trouble I couldn't handle. But not everyone's been as polite as you. There was a girl eating alone in the dining hall. With hair like a waterfall. She stared straight at me without turning away."

Hisashi stiffens.

"Have I said something?" I ask.

"That girl is my twin sister. Doi."

"My apologies, Hisashi. I didn't know."

Heavenly August Personage of Jade. I've just met this boy and he was kind to Cricket and me, and I've already made him uncomfortable twice by talking about his family.

I steal a glance at him in the awkward silence. I can't see any resemblance between him and his sister. Before I can stop myself, the words are out of my mouth. "If she's your sister, why was she eating alone?"

Sometimes I think I should just bite off my own tongue and swallow it.

"She and I . . . avoid each other."

I've upset him. That's three times now. There's clearly some secret sadness in their family. I want to let him know that Cricket and I know all about sad family histories. I want to tell him about why our parents disappeared, but I don't trust my mouth.

After Cricket finishes his noodle soup, we descend from the rail-gondola. Hisashi says, "I hope to see you again soon, and you can tell me all about life in Shin." He bows and says, "May we meet here in the New Year."

"May we meet here in Pearl," I reply, bowing back.

He begins to skate away, but he stops and turns back. He smiles again, but this time the smile is deep and sad and wise and happy, all at once. This time, he looks a thousand years older and a thousand times gentler than any boy I have met.

"Yes, my sister, Doi, was sitting alone," he says. "But most people who do great things in this life know what it is to be alone."

He turns and skates softly away.

CHAPTER
THREE

I don't want to cry during the first day of classes, but the ache in my chest is so great that I might. I watch Cricket being led away from me, over to the boys' side at the assembly at Divinity's Lap, the largest square on the Principal Island of the academy. Cricket, with his small build and his bewildered face, thrust among these noisy, confident boys, disappears in the sweeping expanse of this square, under a towering sculpture of the Enlightened One, into a sea of black robes, all jostling sharp shoulders, narrow torsos, long sleeves, scholars' collars, and trim pants. They look as hard as an army of crows. Cricket turns back to look at me as he departs, every stroke of his blades cutting sore little slices on my heart. Fifty first-year boys. Fifty second-year boys. Twenty-five third-year boys. And Cricket is the youngest and smallest one among them.

How is Cricket going to hold up against these huge, rough boys?

He only learned girls' wu liu styles with me. No one taught boys' styles in Shin. I had to teach him what I could read about in books. I can't help but feel like I've failed him. He's so unprepared.

I straighten my robe and pretend to rub at something in my eye under my smoked spectacles. I'm glad that our uniforms are black so that no one can see where I dry my fingers in the pleats of my skirt.

During the assembly, the first-years watch the older students to see when to stand up or kneel down. A couple of evil second-year boys keep pretending to stand up at the wrong point to trick us into standing when we should be kneeling. One student is left standing by himself twice as the whole school giggles. It's Cricket. I'm going to remember those evil older boys' faces in case I ever have an excuse to fight them.

The second- and third-year students separate to go to their classes. We're told that the first-year girls will be taught wu liu by Sensei Madame Liao and the boys by Sensei Master Bao. I'll have to get used to calling my teachers by the Edaian title *sensei* instead of *shifu* like we did in Shin.

In the gathering of first-year girls, I see the girl with the waterfall hair. Hisashi's sister, Doi. I skate over to introduce myself properly and make a fresh start, but before I can speak, another girl cuts me off.

This second girl is not without beauty. But her hair is bobbed short and tucked behind the ear on one side, swinging loose on the other. This must be the fashion here, since she's followed by an entourage of other girls with identical haircuts. Why doesn't anyone besides me wear braids? This bobbed-hair girl says to Doi, "Nice hair. It looks like pearlsilk."

Her followers giggle behind their hands. One of them says, "Ask her how much she paid for it, Suki!"

"Don't think that we owe each other anything," Suki continues. "What happened at Pearl Rehabilitative Colony for Ungrateful Daughters meant nothing."

Pearl Rehabilitative what?

The girls go silent as Sensei Madame Liao skates to the front of our gathering. She has the sharp cheekbones that indicate a hunger for power. I can tell she's a cold woman. "Worthless, ungrateful daughters of Pearl—" She notices me and quickly adds, "And worthless, ungrateful daughter of Shin.

"The wu liu regimen here at Pearl Famous incorporates rigorous daily training; grueling Motivations; deprivation of food, shelter, and sleep; and whatever else it takes to achieve excellence. The effectiveness of our institution's curriculum is directly proportional to the misery of the student. That is why Pearl Famous is *number one* in helping each student attain the greatest joy possible in life, which is to bring honor to her esteemed parents."

She's just trying to frighten us. She doesn't know me. I don't know what sort of training these rich students in Pearl got, but I'm not afraid of hard work. I'm not afraid of disappointing my parents. I don't even know where they are. The only thing I'm afraid of is not winning. Let's get on with this.

"We will test just how completely without qualities you are. You will be examined in wu liu this year through six Motivations.

Today will be the first, Veneration of the Three Aunties. Three beacons have been lit on three different islets. It's not easy to see the beacons. It's even less easy to get to them. Touch the beacon on the Conservatory of Wu Liu, then the Conservatory of Literature, then the Conservatory of Music. You must not, for any reason, attempt to enter the Conservatory of Architecture.

"You will encounter water on this route, so you will need to step in the pit of tuber root starch powder to keep your socks from slipping.

"The girl who reaches all three beacons in the correct order and comes back first will receive top ranking.

"Any girl who fails to touch all three beacons or who falls off the rail will fail the Motivation."

So here it begins. All the years of training. They were all leading to this.

The chance to prove that I'm the best, that the Empress Dowager was right to choose me, that wu liu belongs to Shin.

I will place first.

I will make Pearl Famous Academy of Skate and Sword history.

I will be a legend.

Sensei Madame Liao turns from us, sits on a small stool, pulls a little scroll from her sleeve, and begins to read.

I assume that the race has started.

None of us is quite sure how to begin. Then one girl, with a friendly round face and a mole on one side of her chin, grins and begins taking off her skates to powder her socks.

The other girls see this and everyone else starts to take off their skates to step into the pit. These socks they gave us are terrible for skating, as loose and droopy as elephants' ankles. Why are girls made to wear inane, impractical, performance-hindering, accident-inviting things? For the sake of cuteness? Why don't boys have to wear them? At least we get to wear skirts, which we don't have to worry about tearing when doing splits, like boys' pants.

Doi looks at the pit, then looks at Suki and her entourage. None of them is taking off her skates to step into the pit of powder.

Instinct tells me that these are powerful girls, and if the powerful girls don't want to step into the pit, it's because they know something. I keep my skates on.

Suki hops on one of the rails connecting the Principal Island to the smaller islets, with her followers close behind. Doi watches them skate away. She leaps onto the rail after them. All the other girls put on their skates and follow.

We glide on the rail toward the islet where the Conservatory of Wu Liu sits. I look for a beacon as we speed along the rail over the open sea, but there are so many structures covered with pearlplate roofs that their rows seem like meandering, elbowed moon dragons. I'm grateful for my smoked spectacles, for the whole of the white academy blooms with glare.

Behind us, I see several girls stopped on the route. What is happening? Some of them are taking off their skates and banging them.

We skate on the rail curling around the Conservatory of Wu Liu. Fields of older students train below. Some are doing exercises in lines. Some are practicing weapons combat with staffs and dual katanas.

I flip off the rail onto the spine of one dragonlike structure and ride its undulations. I think I see a brightness that could be a beacon in the coils of its tail, but it's only a tower studded with little lounges and sitting rooms. What does the beacon look like?

A glimmer on the edge of the islet catches my attention. It's difficult to see in the full daylight, but the wind sweeps a spray of seawater in front of it, refracting it into a flash of wild colors.

The light issues from a pagoda topped by a mirrored bowl that has a blaze of torches in it. The beacon! How do I get up there? The structure is three stories tall. Sprays of seawater keep blowing at me.

I see how to reach the beacon! The hall next to the pagoda has a roof that sweeps up like a pumpkin vine. I can skate off that roof and leap up toward the tower next to the pagoda. I can kick against its side with a single-footed grasshopper move so that I spring back at a sharp angle, followed immediately by a hammer throw spin in midair. I'll come slinging toward the pagoda and land directly on the platform with the beacon. I have to be careful not to overshoot or I'll go sliding off into the sea.

As I prepare to execute these moves, two figures skate past me and do exactly what I planned. Suki and Doi. Ten thousand years of stomach gas!

I execute the moves. They work just as I thought. It feels wonderful to finally be doing these moves on actual buildings after doing them for so many years on just a training court. This is how it felt in my dreams.

I tag the beacon with my hand. The pearl forming the mirrored bowl is surprisingly cool. I look around for the next destination, the Conservatory of Literature.

The beacon there is easier to find because the conservatory is made of enormous sheets of the pearl formed into scrolls, unfurling out of the sea. Below the rails, students sit at desks in neat rows, working on the scripts of operas in open air. They look up and begin to applaud as the first-years pass over them. It's a joyful thing to be applauded by students of so legendary a school.

Ahead, Suki and Doi skate hard toward a curling sheet of the pearl. It sends them flying back toward the beacon. They execute a string of three backflips in the air, scissoring and snapping their legs closed at the end of each flip to sling themselves farther. I'll have to try that.

The backflips send them whipping up toward the pedestal on which the beacon sits. They each reach out a hand and tag the beacon. They grab the pedestal below the beacon with one hand and use the remaining momentum to whip around the pole twice. They sling toward the rail leading past the Conservatory of Architecture. I'm not far behind them. I tag the beacon and follow them onto the rail.

Ahead of me, Doi skates just an arm's length behind Suki. Suki turns around and takes an illegal swipe at her with one skate. What a vicious little snake.

Doi easily ducks Suki's skate. She even adds the insult of flicking her finger against Suki's blade as she dodges under it, as if she were testing the quality of a porcelain cup in a half-reputable shop. This has become personal.

I skate behind Doi and Suki on the rail that passes by the Conservatory of Architecture, where students design the strange and wild opera sets that the wu liu performers skate across. There's only one straight, ominous rail that leads to this conservatory. It passes through a little door in a high wall of the pearl rising out of the water, encircling the whole islet and blocking the operations within entirely from view.

As our path swings past it, I see that the wall is covered in adornments. There are fins, horns, paws, claws, tails, levers, prows, and masts erupting from the surface. Flowers and vines are carved everywhere. What do they do behind that wall?

Ahead on the rail, it's all-out war between the two leaders. Now Doi is in the lead, elbowing Suki aside. Now Suki does the seven-fingered somersault egret move and lands ahead of Doi. These girls are not without skill. Of course. They train here year-round. But I've trained harder.

As we skate down the rail to the islet of the Conservatory of Music, I hear humming and ringing. The halls of the conservatory are grafted with wind flutes. Trumpets that end in spread-mouthed blossoms streak up the sides of towers.

A troupe of drummers skates in single file along the perimeter of the islet, racing up and down the gentle hills that form the breakwaters, each drummer beating at the drum slung on the back of the person in front of her.

Singing breaks out. We look into the glassy pearl trees sprouting from the sides of the breakwaters. They're filled with boy choristers. They turn to watch us midsong, smile and wave, and make their song into a serenade for us.

We speed over the principal orchestra platform where spoon-fiddle virtuosos turn up their faces at the combat that's playing out above. Their conductress barks at them not to drop the tempo. The fiddlers saw harder at their instruments, and the frenzied melodies seem to give our skates wings.

I have to say, this is fun.

Doi and Suki each strike the last beacon with flawless round-house kicks. They jump onto parallel rails leading back to the finish line at the Principal Island, skating side by side. Each knows the other's moves well enough to perfectly dodge or block them. It's clear from the emotion in their wu liu that they've not only fought each other before, they're continuing unfinished business.

I slap the beacon and bear down hard toward them. If I keep this up, I'll finish third. I didn't come here to finish third.

As we ride the rails from the Conservatory of Music down to the Principal Island of the academy, we cross a great expanse of open sea. Here, the Season of Spouts makes itself most felt. All around us, we're misted with warm, gentle rain, but it's not rain, since it's falling upward.

The rails ahead of us end. The Principal Island lies before me, across a stretch of open sea too wide to jump across. How are we supposed to cross that? I slow so that I don't go shooting off into the sea before I solve the puzzle.

Doi and Suki are still too busy with combat to notice. When

they finally see the gap, they hop and skid sideways to make a sharp stop, right in front of me. The only thing I can do to keep from crashing into them is to plant a two-heeled sesame-seed pestle jump so that my skates pound down together on the rail below me and the dragon tails curled under my heels bounce me up and send me flipping over the girls' heads.

The next moments seem to pass so slowly, as if it takes days. I hang suspended in the air, skates above me, my braids swinging an arc under my head, the surprised faces of the girls watching me. I land and look behind me to see them clutching each other's collars, mouths melting open at the realization that they're not the only two in this race. In the distance, I see the banners that mark the finish line on the Principal Island. There's only a short stretch of rail ahead of me, and I know I won't be able to stop in time.

Three waterspouts grind slowly in the water in front of me, spewing water and fish toward the sky. Dolphins leap into the columns of wind and water, rise up, and go shooting out of the tops through the air.

I understand the solution to Sensei Madame Liao's puzzle. I end my slide with a single-footed forward flip, flinging myself off the edge and into a waterspout. The spout spins me higher and higher. I focus my mind and loosen all my muscles except my back muscles to center my Chi and make my body as sleek as a dolphin's. Like the dolphins, I go shooting out of the top of the spout.

I land in a crouch on the Principal Island so heavily that it bruises the pearl in a disk around me. I make sure to finish right in front of Sensei Madame Liao, in a one-footed landing, head thrown back, both arms fanning out behind me like a swan spreading its wings. Never let them say that Shinians have no style.

Suki and Doi land behind me. I don't know which one came in second and which in third. I don't care. Because I've finished first at our first Motivation at Pearl Famous Academy of Skate and Sword. I, Chen Peasprout from Serenity Cliff. I've only just arrived here and I've already started my rise to become a legend of wu liu.

Bring on the rest of the days. It's going to be a lucky year!

CHAPTER
LUCKY

After the Motivation is complete, I check my skate blades. They didn't suffer any damage. I didn't have to take many steps, and I could glide for much of the route since it was mostly racing and jumping. It's combat that eats up a lot of steps.

Many girls complain to Sensei Madame Liao that they were delayed because they had to stop to empty pebbles in their skates after stepping through the pit of tuber root starch powder. Doi, Suki, and Suki's entourage exchange glances. Somebody put something in the pit to sabotage the other skaters. After seeing Suki take an illegal swipe at Doi during the Motivation, I suspect it was her or one of her followers.

Sensei Madame Liao rakes the filtering comb through the pit but finds no pebbles. Nonetheless, she orders the pit to be scooped out and refilled with fresh powder.

Now the group of first-year boys takes over the course to be given the same Motivation. I look for Cricket, but I don't see him among them. Is he all right? I hope the other boys haven't been teasing him. And please, Heavenly August Personage of Jade, let Cricket not finish last.

I wanted to get the chance to see how Cricket does, but no. Sensei Madame Liao leads us to the far side of the Principal Island to the Courtyard of Supreme Placidness for what she calls "visualization exercises." As soon as we enter the walled courtyard, the sounds of activity from the academy become muted. The courtyard is made of eight rows of eight squares, all filled with sand. Sensei tells us each to sit in a square of sand, cross-legged in lotus position.

She lights sticks of incense in an urn and says, "Do not think yourselves skilled for your performances at the first Motivation. Your skills are trash. None of you has the excellence, discipline, and perfectly upright character needed to have a career in Pearlian opera yet. Now you will learn to harmonize your Chi after performing wu liu.

"You might think you understand Chi. Everything you know is trash. Chi is not some mystical force invoked in just meditation and acupuncture. Chi is energy. Energy drives wu liu. Energy is everything. Lift the palm of your hand to your face. Hold it in front of the point between your eyebrows without touching your face. Feel the energy from your hand interacting with your Chi."

I already know all this, but I do as she instructs. I feel a dull, aching pressure on my invisible Third Eye from the closeness of my palm.

"Wu liu practitioners who practice visualization of themselves successfully completing their moves improve their performances dramatically. Throw away your understanding of all laws of the visible world. Your understanding is trash. Now visualize yourselves performing better at the first Motivation. Except you, Chen Peasprout."

Everyone turns toward me. Doi looks at me with that hard, unblinking gaze. Suki practically has fumes curling out of her nostrils.

"You," Sensei Madame Liao says to me, "visualize yourself performing with the humility to remember that this was only the first of six Motivations."

Make me drink sand to death.

After we finish our visualization exercise and say prayers to our honored ancestors begging them for forgiveness for our worthless performances, Sensei Madame Liao tells us to go bathe and dress for the Osmanthus Banquet, the traditional feast held after the first Motivation.

After my bath, I wait for Cricket outside of the boys' dormitory, ready to comfort him. I only hope he didn't finish last. He will be devastated if he finished last.

"Peasprout!" Cricket skates up to me.

"I'm sure you did your best, Cricket," I say quickly. "Are you all right?"

"I didn't finish last! Most of the boys did the final leap, but about ten of us were too frightened and got stuck on the last stretch of rail that ended in open sea. One boy finally tried, but he messed up the timing and shot out of the side of the waterspout instead of the top. He was flung back and knocked us all into the sea. So we all tied for forty-first place!"

He beams like he was just given the gift of a baby dragon. My sweet little Cricket. But sweetness is not going to get him to his best possible future.

"Cricket, only half of the one hundred students in each class are invited at the end of the second year to devote to one of the conservatories. And the rest are kicked out. Only twenty-six are invited to devote to the Conservatory of Wu Liu. Twenty-six students, Cricket."

He tucks his chin into his breast. I wish he wouldn't do that; he looks like he's three years old. "I know, Peabird."

"Stop using baby talk!" He didn't stop confusing the *miao* in Peasprout with the *niao* in Peabird until he was five, and he reverts to my childhood nickname when I'm scolding him. "Never let anyone hear you calling me that."

"I won't, Peab—sprout."

As grateful as I am that Cricket didn't finish last, I can feel that his Chi is agitated and remind him to be calm at the Osmanthus Banquet. These appearances in front of other students are also performances.

When we skate into Eastern Heaven Dining Hall, Suki catches my eye. She motions me over to her table with a silly little flap of the hand that Pearlians must consider cute. Cricket and I skate to her.

She's wearing a white bandage around her head. We're not wearing our smoked spectacles because it's nighttime. She has a perforated metal patch cupping one of her eyes. I don't remember her being injured during the Motivation. All the other girls sitting around her are similarly adorned, with bandages, slings, and eye patches. One girl has even patted black and blue kohl powder around one eye.

Fashion. They're doing this as some ludicrous sort of fashion.

Suki says, "A glorious victory today." She smiles as if she's about to take something away from me. "You were lucky."

Here it is. I've made an enemy. Without even trying. Well, that's nothing new to me. You don't get to be the Peony-Level Brightstar without making some enemies.

She looks hard at me. I stare right back into her big brown eye. She laughs. "Calm down. I value lucky friends."

Lucky! It wasn't luck. She's lucky the Motivation didn't require her to fight me.

"Come sit." She flaps her hand at an empty chair beside her. I sit, and Cricket takes the seat next to mine.

"You can't sit there," says Suki to Cricket. She points to a stone tied with a cord that has been set on the chair. "They're ceremonial seats. Families buy them for their unborn children or children who have died." All the sacrifices Cricket and I endured to get here, and Pearlians can afford to buy places at the academy for children who don't even exist.

Cricket takes a different seat a few spaces down. I hope he won't embarrass us, so far away from where I can guide the conversation.

"We haven't formally met. I am called familial name Gang, personal name Suki," she says. "Although you may call me Your Grace, Radiant Goddess Princess Suki. I am Princess of the House of Flowering Blossoms."

"I am called familial name Chen, personal name Peasprout."

"Ah, *kawai!*" she cries, and all the other girls also squeak "*Kawai!*" Why does everyone here love using Edaian words so much?

"And that's my little brother, called familial name Chen, personal name Cricket."

"Disciple Peasprout, Disciple Cricket, welcome to Pearl Famous." Who is she to be welcoming me to the academy? She's a first-year, too. "Allow me to introduce you to my court. This is my first lady-in-waiting, Disciple Chiriko; my second lady-in-waiting, Disciple Etsuko; my first lieutenant, Disciple Noriko; my second lieutenant, Disciple Mitsuko; my first fan-bearer, Disciple Mariko; and the newest member of my court, my second fan-bearer, Disciple Yukiko. I had another second fan-bearer, but we no longer speak her name. I learned that last Glimmer Season, at the Immortal Ruby Tea Society Thousand Octopus Lantern-Viewing Party, she wore vermillion out of season. She could have destroyed me."

Why do they all have these ridiculous Edaian names? Pearl is part of Shin, and Shin and Eda were enemies. How is this not open treason?

"How do you all already know each other?" I ask. The girls look to Suki. Her face hardens. "Did you go to another school together?" No one answers. "Was that what you and Niu Doi were talking about? Pearl Colony for Rehabilitation of Unwanted Girls, or something like that?"

Suki scowls, then smiles sweetly. "I really liked your wu liu style. Especially the ending flourishes you added on to every single little move. Like what people used to do in our grandparents' generation. So quaint. The only thing missing was a pink peony tucked behind your ear." The girls all cover their teeth with their hands and giggle. What are they laughing at? *The Imperial Anthology of Wu Liu Style, Fancy, and Faddish Whimsy* says that ending flourishes and wearing pink peonies behind the ear are the latest fashion in wu liu. What do these girls know about style? They're wearing bandages and eye patches.

The great doors to Eastern Heaven Dining Hall are closed, and the windows facing out to the sea are opened. Mists from the waterspouts stream in. They're lovely in the lantern light.

Supreme Sensei Master Jio takes the dais, smiles, and laughs. "Ahihahaha! And now . . ." And then he starts intoning something with so much vocal modulation that I can't understand any word except for *tsunami*, which I think is the Edaian word for *tidal wave*, and *delicacies*. There are gasps of delight from all around. I hope Cricket doesn't ask what was announced.

The lines of serving girls come skating out in brown uniforms. I stiffen as I see that they're all Shinian. No one else here in Pearl wears twin pigtail braids. Except for me. Suki is going to say that I look like the servants. I wish I could unbraid my braids right now. They bring out the first course of the Osmanthus Banquet. I hope the Shinian girls don't recognize me and try to talk to me in front of Suki.

I have two things to say about this banquet. Number one is that people reveal more about their culture through their food than through anything else. Number two is that I'm grateful that academy tradition holds that we each attend this banquet only once a year, because I don't know if I could survive more than one Osmanthus Banquet a year.

Course Number One: "The Obscuring Mask of Lady Hu." These aren't too bad. The problem is that you're served a dish that looks like a crisp apple varnished with water. You bite into it, and instead of the fruit that you expect, it's chopped pork and lobster with scallions, ginger, vinegar, and sesame oil, covered in a glazed candied shell. At the center is a watery, bubbled egg seasoned with horseradish. Actually quite delicious but just not salty enough. Like all the food I've tasted in Pearl, it could definitely use some salt or soy sauce.

I'm not going to let this food and these girls make me feel out of place. "We have a very similar dish in Shin that's a meatball with egg inside," I say.

"Friendship between Shin and Pearl is very strong," says Suki. I can't tell if she's mocking me. "What do you call that dish from Shin?"

Stupid me, why did I bring up anything about Shin? "We call it . . . meatball with egg inside." Make me drink sand to death, Shinians are such peasants.

Course Number Two: "Clarity of the Moon." It turns out that shortly before the start of the school year, Pearl was hit with a tsunami that washed ashore all sorts of unusual creatures churned up from the bottom of the sea. The chefs of Pearl mobilized and harvested all of them before scholars of science could collect them for study. The sea creatures are so rare that they don't even have proper names.

The dish is served on a lovely porcelain plate that has a poem written on it in spidery black calligraphy. I can read the poem through the food because everything in this dish is bleached transparent in kelp vinegar. There's a blanket of wide clear noodle garlanded with cucumbers cut as thin as paper and slices of uncooked white fish. At the center, encased in a bubble of gelatin, is a translucent creature that I've never seen before. It's sealed in a dumpling made out of what looks like its own birthing sac, tied closed with its own pink intestines. The creature stares out at me from inside the sac with one great silver eye.

Then it blinks.

All the students begin to devour the dish.

Somehow, I manage to get this creature down my throat and make it stay there, but I don't like to talk about the experience. It's behind me now.

Course Number Three: "Geh-Hu." After conquering the translucent sea creature, I feel a swell of confidence. How much worse could it get?

The conversation is also going well. I didn't mean to insult Suki when I asked about Pearl Girl Detention Colony or whatever it's called. But I've managed to save the evening. My skills of conversation are very high. I know that sounds conceited. But words are power. Look at Cricket. He even speaks Shinian like a foreign language.

As I'm thinking this, they bring out the dishes of tofu. No, not tofu! I turn toward Cricket, but it's too late.

When he sees the tofu, Cricket says to Mitsuko in a voice loud enough for everyone to hear, "Oh, I can't eat tofu. I developed an allergy to my own saliva after I started my ivory yin salt treatments to improve my wu liu practice. Whenever I eat tofu, I salivate so much. When I have to swallow so much of my saliva, I cough. The coughing causes me to salivate more. Which causes me to cough even more. It always ends in violent vomiting."

Ten thousand years of stomach gas.

The girls giggle behind their hands. Mitsuko explains to Cricket, "It's not tofu. It's imitation tofu."

Etsuko explains, "It's made out of crabmeat. But it tastes just like the real thing."

Chiriko adds with reverence, "It's a new *hatsubai*." I think that means new product. "From Eda."

Suki says, "Of course."

"Of course," coo all the other girls in agreement.

Course Number Four: "The Cave of Jade." It's a rubbery cylinder, like a sea cucumber. The only features on it are four moist, glistening tubes growing out of its back, each ending in something that looks like a mouth with puckered lips.

The Shinian serving girl ladles seawater seasoned with

eight-horned star anise over the thing. She catches my eye. I think she recognizes me as the Peony-Level Brightstar. It looks like she wants to show me how to eat it, but the last thing I want is for Suki and the other girls to see me talking with the Shinian servants, so I pretend not to see her. She bows and turns away in silence.

I instantly feel regret. She's Shinian and she only wanted to be kind to me because I just arrived from Shin. And I dismissed her like a scrap of trash. I turn to her but only see the back of her head, braids bobbing as she skates away.

I watch the other girls. They take their eating sticks, insert them into one of the four tubes, and split them open. Green fluid leaks out. They each twist a tube off, dip it in the fluid, and eat.

Across the table, Cricket pokes his dish in the middle. It immediately deflates and shrivels.

"That's not how you eat it. You've ruined it!" cries Noriko. "Well, don't think you'll get another one. That creature's very rare."

I immediately spear mine through the middle with my eating sticks, too.

Course Number Five: "Tea Olive Pies." Finally, something that I recognize. I'm so grateful. Just sweet bean jam flavored with osmanthus in a moon cake crust. Nothing with blinking eyes or multiple tubes coming out of it. I savor every bite. I never want it to end.

Final Course: "First Kiss." The eating sticks are taken away by the serving girls. A blunt knife is brought out. Then we're each served a bristled tongue impaled on a stick.

I can't do it. I drop mine on the floor when no one is looking.

When the last of the dishes is cleared, Supreme Sensei Master Jio stands up to address us.

"Ahihahaha! So sweet to watch you eat, little embryos. But as you shall learn when you attain sagehood, nourish abundance to nurture perfectly." I'm starting to think that I simply can't understand anything that comes out of his mouth when he says, "And now, time to announce the next Motivations. The first-year girls' second Motivation will be Lady Ming's Hand-Mirror! And the first-year boys' second Motivation is Vertical Battlefield!"

Afterward, the students proceed to the Hall of Six Excellences for conversation and tea anemones. What a horrible drink. But everyone drinks it because most children our age aren't allowed it at home. Not even in Pearlian homes, I understand. Cricket and I join the river of students skating in a slow circle.

Suki and her court appear at my side. Chiriko is cupping something in her hands. It's a white chrysanthemum blossom, blushed with pink streaks. She offers it to me and says, "Her Grace, Gang Suki, Princess of the House of Flowering Blossoms, humbly begs you to confer honor on our house by accepting the title of third fan-bearer."

The whole circle of skating students slows as everyone watches to see what I'll do.

Why would I want to be some other first-year girl's third fan-bearer in some stupid club? This is a veiled insult. How dare she? I took first ranking. I'm going to make history here.

I know that I'm new here. I should be as slow to make an enemy as I should be swift to make new friends. But this girl could use a public bucket of cold water. Cricket sees my face.

"Peasprout, no. . . ."

"Shut up, Cricket." I smile at Chiriko. "Her Grace, Princess Soo-Kee" (I intentionally mispronounce it so that it sounds like the Pearlian word for *loser.*) "confers too great an honor on a worthless girl from Shin. I can't accept, because I was never sent anyplace like Pearl Penal Colony for Unbearable Girls, so I'm not rough and used to being banged up like all of you."

Suki scrapes to a stop right in the middle of the flow of students. "Infuriate me to death!" says Suki.

The friendly faced girl with the mole on her chin skates over and whispers to me, "Oh no, now you've really failed to keep the monkey pleased." All the other students giggle. I don't recognize the Pearlian phrase, but the meaning is clear.

Suki stares at me, her face a mask of sizzling hatred. She looks left and right.

She's confirming that there aren't any senseis around.

She wants to fight me. Right here. Right now.

All the students part the way between us like a tide.

She's trying to take off that stupid fake metal patch over her eye, but it's glued on. She scowls at me with her big brown eye. She doesn't want to fight me if she has a disadvantage.

I reach into the pocket of my robe and take out the cotton cloth that I carry to wipe my skates. I fold it in a triangle and tie it around my head, covering one eye.

Now I've brought myself down to her level.

Suki feels the insult. She is furious. She crouches into position to spring at me.

I pull my arm back, ready to receive her kick.

Cricket pulls on my arm. "No, Peasprout! You'll be disqualified from the next Motivation! Don't risk it! It was a perfect day!" I look down at his pleading face. "It was the favorite day of my life!"

"I think you have something on your arm," says Suki. "You'd better take care of it before it starts to cry. Mew mew mew!" All the students start to laugh. Suki turns and skates away with a strut in her step. She's acting like she won. But I know she was relieved that Cricket stopped us.

My good humor is all depleted, so Cricket and I retire.

In my dormitory chamber, I unroll my bed and cross my legs on it in lotus position to meditate before sleep.

The sound of the activity of the academy outside drops to a hum.

Despite all the struggle and strife of this past day, I end it with a peaceful heart.

Because I've ended this day on my own terms.

CHAPTER
FIVE

A terrible noise jolts me awake. It sounds like the walls of the dormitory are about to come down around me. It's an earthquake! I fumble with the paper shoji door to my chamber and accidentally tear a hole in it before sliding it open. I race into the middle of the dormitory courtyard in my underclothes.

No one else is awake.

One by one, the girls come out of their chambers wrapped in their bathrobes and with trays of washing materials. They look at me standing in the courtyard like a fool.

The girl with the mole on her chin walks over to me and takes my arm. She smiles and says, "I'm sorry. Do they not have this in Shin? Our walls are tunneled through with mazes lined with metal plates. They release steel balls into the mazes, and the noise is used as an alarm for emergencies but also to wake us up each morning."

"I know," I say, taking my arm back. "I just thought it was an emergency."

"Yes, of course. Oh, look. You've torn a hole in your shoji."

"It's fine."

"Let me help you patch it."

"It's all right, just one of the four corners got loose."

She winces. "*Aiyah*, don't say that!"

"What?"

"That number. We don't mention that number, because it sounds like the word for *death*. Say *lucky* instead."

Everything is so strange here.

While I take my bath, I remember that Cricket and I forgot, in the excitement of the first Motivation, to give our senseis the artisanal soaps. I don't want people here to think that we are so poor in Shin that we don't give gifts to our senseis at the opening of term. After I finish bathing, I pack up a basket of gifts for Cricket to take to his classes with the other boys.

As I'm skating to class, a low, hoarse voice says, "Don't bring those." I turn, and Doi is skating beside me, her waterfall hair swinging behind her.

I'm so startled by her rudeness that I don't know what to say. She reaches to snatch my basket of soaps. I slap her hand away. I scrape to a stop and glare. "Mind your own business!" I say.

"You'll be sorry."

"Is that supposed to scare me?"

I look straight into her face. How unlike her brother she is. The nose is the same; the mouth and the shape of the face are the same;

even their builds are the same. However, Hisashi is all dimples and laughing eyes. Perhaps his sister also has dimples and laughing eyes. I have no idea, because you can't see either of these things on a person who refuses to smile. I turn from her and skate away.

At the assembly, we are told that since our whole first day was taken up with the first wu liu Motivation, we only have architecture, music, and literature classes today.

Our first class is architecture. We're taught by Supreme Sensei Master Jio himself. We don't gather on the islet of the Conservatory of Architecture, as that's for third-years only. We are sent to the open square on one lip of the Principal Island of the academy. It is lined with desks. Supreme Sensei Master Jio hasn't arrived yet. I don't see other students with gifts. I wonder if they have different school customs here. The guidebooks said that students at wu liu academies in Pearl aren't required to attend class. They treat us like university students, because they hold us responsible for our own performances.

As I look around, the basket is clawed out of my hands! Etsuko skates with it to the back and delivers it to Suki. Suki rips off her smoked spectacles and peers into the basket. She unties the reed leaves and takes out the cakes of soap.

"What is this junk?" cries Suki. "Bleached rocks?" All the girls laugh. "No wonder you invaded us for our bamboo if this is what you eat in Shin."

"Give them back!" I say.

"What are they?"

"They're opening-of-term gifts for our senseis."

"Yes, but what. Are. They? Do you understand Pearlian? Does anyone here speak Shinian?" Suki asks. She's just trying to insult me. I speak perfect Pearlian and, anyway, everyone in Pearl understands Shinian.

"I do!" says Etsuko. "Oink oink oink!" All the vile girls laugh.

"They're distilled lard soaps," I say. "Number-one quality-grade artisanal soap."

"Artisanal soap! Does that mean you made it all by yourself in your little hut in Shin?"

Everyone laughs. What is there to laugh at?

"It's made from a thousand-year-old recipe!"

"*Wah*! Is the secret ingredient your grandmother's petrified bladder stones?"

I lunge for the basket of soaps, but the girls from the House of Flowering Blossoms block me. Someone kicks her skate under mine and I nearly stumble.

The students are silenced by the arrival of Supreme Sensei Master Jio. Suki skates to him. "Sage and venerable Supreme Sensei Master Jio," she says, bowing. "Chen Peasprout wishes to present to you a gift that she brought all the way from Shin." She skates back to me, wrapping a cake of soap back up in a reed leaf, and shoves it at my chest.

Everyone is looking at me, but why should I be ashamed of my gift? I skate to Supreme Sensei Master Jio and say, "I beg permission to present to you this worthless opening-of-term gift to express my gratitude for the honor of being your undeserving pupil." He opens the leaf and holds the cake of soap in his hand.

One of the students cries out, "Don't touch it. It's her grand-mother's bladder stone!"

The students erupt in laughter. Only one student isn't laughing. Doi. Probably gloating because she was right that I would be sorry. Or maybe she was the one to tip off Suki about my soaps, since she's the only one who saw me bringing them? She must hate that some Shinian girl beat her.

Supreme Sensei Master Jio's face fills with merriment. "Ahiha-haha, how sweet a sound, little embryos! For, as you shall learn when you attain sagehood, children's laughter, greatly promoting."

This sensei is a fool.

During architecture class, he doesn't teach us anything about actual architecture. Instead, he gives us little dexterity puzzles. He asks us to feel our teeth with our tongues and mold scale models of them out of clay. He gives us vision tests with optical illusions. He asks us strange ethical questions about whether we'd choose to save the last surviving copy of the *Five Transcendental Classics* or the last surviving bamboo seed under heaven. I don't understand why the Conservatory of Architecture is considered one of the two greater conservatories, equal to the Conservatory of Wu Liu.

As soon as class is over, Suki and her girls race to the next class at the Conservatory of Music with our instructor, Sensei Madame Yao. Suki approaches her with another of my cakes of soap. As she starts to tell Sensei Madame Yao that I have a present for her, someone else skates up.

Doi. She swipes the cake of soap out of Suki's hands.

"Sage and venerable Sensei Madame Yao," says Doi. "I played

a bad trick on our new friend from Shin. I sold her these cakes of soap when she arrived and told her that it's Pearlian tradition to give them to our senseis at the start of term." We're all too surprised to speak.

Why is she helping me? We're rivals.

Suddenly, I realize she's not helping me. She's only doing this because she hates Suki even more than she hates me. Doi is just using me to get back at Suki.

Sensei Madame Yao's entire body begins to heave with anger. It is apparent that beneath her robe, she is muscled like a bull. She fumes at Doi from under bangs so severe and perfect that they look like they were cut following the edge of a bowl. "All that you students care about is wu liu, but do you think that because this is only music, you can turn my classroom into a riot? You students . . ." She assumes a half-crouching position. ". . . make me . . ." She looks as if she were about to start a speed race. ". . . so angry!"

She explodes out of her half crouch and skates furiously toward the gong at the far end of the classroom. At the last instant, she stamps and executes a perfect two-footed flying kick with her skates pointed at the gong. She crashes into it, sending it toppling over, and the hall thunders with a metallic *bwong!*

Sensei Madame Yao picks herself up from the pile. She points at Doi and says, "Go to the corner and stand on your hands. Stay there until I tell you."

Doi tucks her length of waterfall hair down tightly into the back of her robe. Without a glance at any of us, she places her hands on the hard pearl and flips into a handstand.

Sensei Madame Yao straightens her back, clears her throat, and begins to sing a lecture to us in the exaggerated style of Meijing opera. The song is an instruction about how to sing clearly and how great Chiologists can hear blockage in a voice and thus can tell if what is coming from someone's mouth is unwilling, and thus they can read human hearts and are greater than warriors of wu liu.

The lecture is somewhat interesting, but I'm watching Doi the whole time. After a quarter hour, her arms are trembling badly; the sweat is sprinkling from her brow to the pearl below.

Sensei Madame Yao finally finishes, and Suki and her entourage clap as hard as if they were trying to knock their hands off their wrists. Sensei looks at them and gives them a short nod and grunt.

I think she's going to let Doi stand upright now, but no.

She brings out an orb formed of two halves carved of the pearl covered by a membrane of pearlsilk. She sings into the orb, clamps the two halves together, and pulls out the membrane from between the halves.

By this time, Doi's arms are trembling as hard as if she were having a seizure. Her mouth is constricted into a circle as she tries to breathe deeply and stretch out her energy.

Sensei Madame Yao holds up the orb. She twists the two halves open. From within, the tinny sound of her singing comes out.

Doi's arm buckles and she almost topples over, but she punches the pearl, forcing her arm straight and pushing herself back up to maintain the position. And still Sensei Madame Yao ignores her, while Suki and her entourage gleam. Hateful, vicious people!

At last, Doi topples down in a heap.

"Be quiet!" yells Suki. "You're interrupting Sensei!"

Doi is on her knees with her legs splayed out to keep her balance, like a fat goose. Her face is so deep with color that it looks bruised. Her smoked spectacles have fallen off. Sensei Madame Yao looks at her and says, "Get up. Go sit."

When at last this miserable class is over, I feel I should talk to Doi, but I'm not sure what to say. I'm not even sure if she was doing this for me.

When she sees me approaching, she scowls and skates away in a swirl of black robe.

She blames me for this.

So now I have made a second enemy without even trying.

And as much as Suki and Doi hate each other, I think they're both starting to hate me more.

CHAPTER
SIX

That afternoon, I skate into one of the strangest buildings I have ever been in.

The outside is covered in words.

The inside is covered in birds.

The Hall of Literary Glory, where we shall have our first class at the Conservatory of Literature, is scrawled all over with the logograms for *Silence!* and *Do Not Let the Birds Out!* in loud, red writing.

Inside, Sensei Madame Phoenix sits behind a desk at the far end of a lofty atrium. The walls have branches sticking out of them on which sit a hundred or more green birds, the kind with the curved beaks that can talk. Most of them are resting quietly, some with their heads turned in sleep.

She keeps crossing her palms in front of her mouth. I guess that's meant to tell us to be quiet. When the whole class has arrived in the hall, she holds up a great paper paddle with the words *Do not overexcite the birds or they will swarm and might not be calmed down in time to perform the newspaper.*

Suki unwraps a cake of soap and begins to whisper, "Honorable Sensei Madame—," but the Sensei shoots her an angry stare and furiously waves another paper paddle on which is written the words *Too Exciting!*

Suki continues, "But, Sensei, you don't—"

Sensei Madame Phoenix skates to Suki and slaps her on the top of the head with the paper paddle. We smother our giggles as a rustle passes through the birds.

Sensei Madame Phoenix gestures for us to take our seats at the desks arrayed in the hall. She hangs a great scroll from one of the branches sprouting from the wall. It gives us our assignment. We have to memorize an entire chapter from the *Classic of Yellow Beans* and then write it from memory. Since the chapter that Sensei Madame Phoenix chose for us is a table of figures recording grain tax collections from the Shinian imperial silos inventory records, half the class is soon nodding off to sleep.

Throughout the class, I think of poor Cricket going through the same thing with the cakes of soap that I forced him to take this morning. Ah, August Personage of Jade, please let the boys here in Pearl be less cruel than the girls!

After an hour has passed, the students are awakened by a horrible sound. The birds are screaming like a cyclone of howling ghosts. Sensei Madame Phoenix is skating in circles around the room with her arms in the air, and the birds are spiraling in the hall above us. "Iwi to me! It's brushtime!" she cries. She skates straight out through the two sets of front doors, followed by Iwi, the leader of the flock, followed by a green, honking, screeching swarm.

I guess that we're dismissed from literature class. I don't know what we're supposed to do with the chapter we copied. I guess it was just to keep us busy for the hour.

As we follow Sensei outside, I can't help but look for Doi. All I see is her back as she rushes out the doorway of the hall.

In the sky outside, the birds are weaving and looping. Below them, Sensei Madame Phoenix is skating in odd patterns across the campus, weaving with her hands in the air as if she were writing with them on the sky above her. Many students are watching the birds, as if reading something in their flight path.

One bird in the lead files behind Sensei Madame Phoenix, and the rest of the flock follows. It responds sensitively to every one of her turns as she skates across the campus and even follows the nuances of her gestures with dips and rolls. It's as if the lead bird were the tip of a great invisible brush held in Sensei Madame Phoenix's hand and the other birds were a tail of ink trailing behind on the—Heavenly August Personage of Jade! That's exactly what it is! Sensei Madame Phoenix is skating out a path for the birds to follow and writing logograms with them on the sky!

I have to look carefully to make out the words being formed by the birds. It's a little hard to read because it's written in that style of calligraphy that looks like blades of grass caressing each other.

I look around at the students skating by and see the girl with the mole on her chin.

"Hey, you. Girl." She skates over, as eager as a puppy. "Are they writing something?"

"Oh, it's just a sensational headline to try to get you to buy their newspaper. It always ends with 'Buy *Pearl Shining Sun News* to get whole story!'"

"Sensei Madame Phoenix works for a newspaper?"

"No one ever got rich being a sensei. She just delivers the headlines. They do it with the birds from Pearl Famous because the whole city can see it from here."

I pick out the logograms one by one.

"Empress. Dowager. Still. Refuses. To. Return. Mayor's. Sons. While. Mayor. Calls. For. Resignation. Of. Chairman. Niu. Buy. Pearl. Shining. Sun. News. To. Get. Whole. Story."

I freeze.

"The Chairman has sooo failed to keep the monkey pleased!" says a girl with a honking voice. "Do you think there's going to be a war?" She sounds delighted.

"Don't say that!" says the girl with the mole.

"So that's why the Empress Dowager sent you here." The crowd parts to reveal Suki skating slowly toward me. "You're not really a skater. You're a spy."

I say, "So it must sting that you lost to someone who is 'not really a skater.'"

"You saw the headline! It sounds like the Empress Dowager is holding those poor skaters, the mayor's only sons, as hostages. That old imperialist snake wants the secret of the pearl."

"That's ridiculous," I say. "The Empress Dowager has invited them to extend their stay because she's a great admirer of wu liu."

"They've been there since last year."

"You don't understand anything about how these things work. That's why she sent my brother and me in exchange. As goodwill ambassadors to thank Pearl for letting her enjoy the company of her guests for longer."

"That's not why she sent you. Everyone, mark my words! This girl is a spy sent by the Empress Dowager to steal the secret of the pearl! And if they find out where it comes from, they'll take it all. Just like they tried to take our bamboo during the Bamboo Invasion."

The students begin to whisper. They're all looking at me.

"They'll take our city apart piece by piece to build their own city of the pearl. They don't know how to make anything themselves. They only know how to steal. They're Shinian, after all." Suki smirks.

I don't have time for this ludicrousness. I have to go find Cricket. I should never have made him bring those soaps to class. I start to skate away, but Suki whispers something at my back.

I should ignore her. But I can't resist.

"Say it to my face," I say.

She skates so near that I can smell the plum blossom–scented thread woven into her hairstyle today.

She says quietly so that only I can hear, "I said that it doesn't have to be true. It just has to look like it's true. That'll be enough. And you know why?" She smiles and whispers slowly, "Because you're not from here."

I turn away and leave, but I'm unnerved.

Because she's right. I'm not from here. And that makes all the difference.

I skate to the point on the Principal Island where rails connect it with the Conservatory of Music, the boys' last class for the day. I wait for Cricket, but it seems as if all the boys are already gone.

"Peasprout," I hear from behind me. Cricket comes out from where he's been hiding behind a fountain in the form of a dolphin. In his hands he holds white crumbles. His robe is powdered with crushed soap.

"I'm sorry," he begins. "Please don't be angry with me. I know they were so expensive. But the boys—"

What a terrible day. Especially after such a glorious yesterday. I move toward him, and he winces as if I were going to yell at him. Am I really that hard on him?

I pull him into a tight embrace. He muffles his sobs in the front of my robe. Curse these Pearlians! This horrible place! Why did we ever come here?

"It's not your fault," I tell him. "Never let them make you believe that." This makes him weep harder. My poor little Cricket.

"Now, enough," I say. "Let's go eat. The line at Eastern Heaven Dining Hall will be longer than the Great Wall of Men by now."

"I can't face them again so soon."

"We can't let them think they can shame us into hiding from them."

"I'm not like you, Peasprout."

What am I going to do? He's cutting up the pearl with his skates.

"You go," he says. "I'll only pull you down. I don't belong here."

"That's not true." I rub his back and say to him softly, as if telling him a fable before bed, "Do you remember the story that Nun Hou told us once about the young Shinian courtesan who was skilled as a dancer?"

"I don't think so."

"You were really small."

He casts his gaze down at the word *small*. I say, carefully, "They called the courtesan Little Pi Bao Gu, even though she was a grown woman. One day, she fled to the island of Pearl. She applied her knowledge of dance by blending kung fu with skating to create the deadliest martial art under heaven."

He lifts his face toward me as this sinks in.

"All of wu liu comes from her," I continue. "All of this that Pearlians claim as theirs was invented by a tiny young woman. Who came from Shin. Like you did."

He blinks to squeeze back the tears.

I take his hand and say, "So you skate with me into that dining hall, and when we do so, you hold your head high. We're not from here. But that doesn't mean we don't belong here. Don't ever let anyone make you believe that. No one belongs here more than we do."

CHAPTER
SEVEN

I'm in a nightmare.

"Small hong-fist double toe jump!"

That nightmare that every student knows.

"Yin-yang health-form triple-stamp double jump!"

The one where you are taking an examination on things that you've never studied.

"Monkey-fist triple-scissor heel backflip!"

And everyone can see your wrong answers.

Except it's not a nightmare. It's wu liu class.

"Thousand Cleaver Goddess Sliding Across a Placid Sea!" shouts Sensei Madame Liao.

As all the girls start doing this move, which I've never even heard of before, I'm realizing that the wu liu moves I learned in Shin only constitute a tiny fraction of what most of the students here already know. And Supreme Sensei Master Jio announced that we'll be doing Lady Ming's Hand-Mirror. My opponent and I will take turns copying each other's moves back and forth in an ever-lengthening string of different moves, until one of us makes a mistake. I'm never going to learn all these moves in time. I bow to Sensei Madame Liao to request permission to visit the toilet.

I leave, go in a stall, and close the door.

It's not just the idea of having to copy moves that I might never have seen before during a Motivation. It's also the pressure that this training is putting on my skate blades. I run a finger along the edges to check for any damage. Luckily, there aren't any nicks. I'm relieved to see the spring formed by the dragon tail curling up and under my heel is undamaged. I was worried with all those jumps. Sixty-three jumps this morning! Blades cost as much as three months' rice. In Shin, we have to make the blades last a year. The rich students here at Pearl Famous never have to worry about such things and learned moves using dozens and dozens of steps each. They didn't have to limit themselves to moves that emphasize gliding and their own center of gravity to propel them forward to conserve steps.

Suki said I won the first Motivation because I was lucky. And in a way, she was right. It didn't involve combat, only racing on rails and leaping. Combat is what really eats up steps. And I could use whatever steps I wanted instead of having to copy moves that I've never seen before but that everyone else already knows how to do.

How can I face this Motivation? I don't know if I can even face the rest of today's class. Maybe if I sit in here long enough, class will end and they'll all leave without me.

Stop it, Peasprout. I straighten up and collect my emotions. So it's going to be difficult. That's nothing new to me. I need to go back and show those Pearlians that Shinians don't give up.

I reach into the box of paper wipes in the stall to wipe my nose. Instead of squares of white paper, there is a stack of something strangely shaped and colorful. I take one out.

Ten thousand years of stomach gas! It's one of those paper dolls of me dressed like an assassin with the words *Peony-Level Bright-star Chen Peasprout, the Stealthiest Skater in Shin!* printed in gold logograms above my head, stamped with the imperial seal. Who put them here? It must have been Suki or one of her friends.

I snatch the papers dolls out of the box, claw them to tatters, and throw them all down the toilet.

As I watch the dolls disappear, I realize just how devious Suki's stunt is. It's not just the insult—it's the implication. Stealthiest Skater in Shin. As stealthy as a spy. Just like Suki accused me of being in front of all the other girls.

I think back to Suki whispering, "It doesn't have to be true. It just has to look like it's true."

I go into the other stalls. Every single one of them is stocked with a thick stack of the paper dolls. She's probably placed them in the girls' bathrooms throughout the whole campus.

When I finally come out of the toilet, all the girls are kneeling on the pearl and looking at me.

"Well, hurry along," says Sensei Madame Liao. "You're the last one."

It seems that while I was in the toilet, she tested the girls individually. In front of everyone.

Doi looks at me, expressionless, but Suki smiles her evil smile, her tongue poking into her cheek.

I face Sensei Madame Liao, ready to see what move I have to try to copy. She says, "Open-palm blossom foot single-toe jump." She performs the move. I've never seen it before, but I'm relieved because it's just a simple half spin with feet together, one skate extended farther than the other, and hands open for balance. She's being easy on me.

"Use your stealthy powers!" says a girl. A giggle passes through the crowd.

The girl who interrupted me was not Suki. Has everyone else already seen the paper dolls?

"Silence!" cries Sensei Madame Liao. "Begin, Chen Peasprout!"

I attempt the blossom double jump, or whatever it is. As soon as I land, everyone bursts into laughter.

I must have failed on my very first move. A move that the other students have probably been doing since they were seven years old. Even worse, I thought I did it right. Are you supposed to land on both skates, not just one? I'm so ignorant of these moves; I don't even know when I'm doing them wrong.

Class ends and the other girls sit, unscrew and snap the blades off their skates, and toss them into the trash bin. They take out new blades from packs of six and fasten them on their skates.

The amount of money that all those perfectly good blades they are throwing away cost could have fed our whole wu liu temple back in Shin for years. A memory of Nun Hou comes to mind, during the bad winter when I was eight, in the kitchen, scraping the grains left in the bowls when she thought no one was looking, after she had told me she wasn't hungry and given me her rice.

It's not just wasteful. It's offensive. If being rich means skating through life so blindly, then I'm glad I grew up poor.

I wait until almost all the girls are gone and the rest aren't looking. I paw through the bin to see if any of the blades will fit on my skates. The sockets connecting the blade to the boot are all differently shaped. I'd have to buy an entire new boot, and not just one but two, to match.

I look up to find that Sensei Madame Liao has been watching me. Heat flushes into my cheeks. So this is what it's come to. Me, the greatest skater in Shin, picking through the trash of these Pearlian students. How stupid I was to think that I could find my way here, let alone achieve top ranking and get the lead in the Drift Season Pageant.

She skates to me and says, "There is much that you never learned."

"I can learn all those moves before the second Motivation."

"That's impossible."

Her words hit me like a stone fist.

She continues, "But you don't need to learn the moves. You only need to learn how to copy what you see when you see it."

"How is that any different?"

"Those birds that Sensei Madame Phoenix uses for her newspapers. They can sing the whole 'Pearlian New Year's Song.' They can repeat all the words in sequence without understanding what the words mean. It's like copying a sequence of logograms upside down, even if you can't understand the words. You just have to learn to make your mind bend enough to hold these new forms."

"How?"

"Chi."

I nod to indicate my understanding, and Sensei Madame Liao skates away.

I have no idea what she means. Command of Chi is essential to wu liu, but how will it help me win the Motivation? Chi? Logograms? Birds memorizing "The Pearlian New Year's Song"— Wait, that's it! She's talking about Memory Palace meditation!

I skate off to the Skybrary at the Conservatory of Literature to research it.

I learned about Memory Palace meditation during my studies, but I never had the chance to read a book like the *Treatise on Chi Practice and the Visual Music of the Memory Palace* that I found in the Skybrary. It must be a very advanced book because I had to execute two third-gate nightingale loops to reach the shelf where it was stored.

The book teaches how to turn information you want to remember into things such as songs, the layout of a house, silhouettes, and other patterns in your mind, in order to train your memory to memorize long sequences of details instantly. I need to practice these meditation techniques every free hour between now and the second Motivation.

That afternoon, I skate to the Courtyard of Supreme Placidness filled with hope. I've brought sheets of paper and a charcoal pencil. I'll write a sequence of random numbers on one side and then, after meditating, see if I can reproduce it on the other side of the paper. Luckily, almost no one ever uses the Courtyard of Supreme Placidness.

I arrive and sit in one of the squares near the center of the eight rows of eight and begin to focus to start my Chi practice. Just as the gong in the clock pagoda begins to toll the hour before evenmeal, someone comes racing in.

Doi.

We both stiffen. She has not so much as looked at me since the horrible class with Sensei Madame Yao.

"What are you doing here?" she demands.

"I'm trying to meditate," I reply. Who is she to be taking that tone?

"Meditate in your dormitory chamber then," she says. "I need to use the squares."

"There are sixty-three other—"

"I need all of them."

"I got here first!"

She turns toward the clock pagoda as the gong finishes sounding the strike for the hour before evenmeal. Her face bunches with urgency and anger. She opens her mouth.

"Please," she says. A softness comes into her face that reminds me that this is the sister of the boy who was kind to Cricket.

I shouldn't have to, but I get up. However, I don't leave entirely; I walk to one side of the square. I want to see why she needs the whole place to herself.

When she understands that I'm not going to leave the square while she does whatever she's going to do, she begins to scowl but then covers it with a smile and a bow. She says. "Forgive me; you don't have to leave, but could I please ask you to stand near the entrance to the square?"

I skate to the entrance. Doi stands with her back to me in the lower left corner of the grid. She stands there gathering her focus with her hands cupped in front of her as if about to receive a thrown ball. Her Chi practice must be very advanced, because she finds her focus also immediately. Maybe I can learn something from her.

She steps to the next square and stands for a moment, then moves to the next square. Sometimes she makes a cross with her skate in the sand of the square before moving on to the next square. She quickly proceeds through the eight columns of eight squares. When she is finished, she goes to the end farthest from the entrance where I stand and looks back for a moment at the pattern. She seems satisfied with what she sees. She kicks the frame, making the sand in the squares shudder and clearing the marks she made in some of the squares.

When she has completed this lucky times and is about to kick the frame again, we hear shouts of excitement from outside the square.

"There's been a letter orb! From Shin!" It's the girl with the honking voice. "It's probably from the hostages! There's going to be sooo much trouble!"

Suki will find some way to use this against me. I can't let Doi see this affecting me, though, because I'd just look guilty. However, Doi seems more upset than I am. Is it because people are blaming her father for putting the mayor's sons in this position by sending them to Shin as goodwill ambassadors? Doi abruptly skates out of the square after Honking Girl.

I try to go back to practicing my Memory Palace meditation, but I'm too distracted to do any real Chi work before evenmeal. I'm about to kick the frame of the boxes to clear the squares of sand when I notice something. The pattern of squares that have a mark in them forms a strange picture. It looks like a box with ears and little feet. I draw it on the back of the paper that I brought to practice number memorization on. It looks like the form of a logogram, but unlike any I've ever seen. What could it mean? As I slip the paper back into my pocket, Doi comes racing back in. She frowns at the sand, then at me. She kicks the frame and clears the pattern from the squares.

This must be something related to preparation for the second Motivation. Some secret technique that she doesn't want her rival to learn. That's why she was so angry to find me here. But it seems like there was some time limit on it. I recall that certain wu liu maneuvers can only be done at a certain hour. Doi was pressed for time, so she performed it in front of me even though she clearly wasn't happy about it.

I have no idea what it means. All I know is that somehow, this holds the secret to how I can make it through the second Motivation. And I'm going to find a way to make Doi teach it to me.

I know the key to convincing Doi is to present myself as an ally against Suki. But to do that, I need to find out why they hate each other so much, so I can decide the best way to insert myself between them. I need to find out what happened between them at Pearl Rehabilitative Colony for Ungrateful Daughters.

CHAPTER
EIGHT

In music class the next day, Sensei Madame Yao is demonstrating how to play a whole orchestra solo by using wu liu kicks to bounce beans off the strings of the instruments. *Ping! Ping! Pah-Ping!* The room fills with the sound of music.

As the class watches her, I skate up next to friendly Mole Girl and ask if she knows anything about Pearl Rehabilitative Colony, making sure I'm out of earshot of both Doi and Suki.

"That's a horrible place!" says Mole Girl. "It's a cram school penal colony that rich parents send their daughters to in order to make them shape up for the entrance exams for Pearl Famous— Ahh! There's a bean in my nose!" She collapses to the ground, holding her nose.

Sensei Madame Yao stops the class and rushes over. As she helps Mole Girl to the Hall of Benevolent Healing, she commands,

"Continue practicing on your own! Any students found slacking off will receive gong duty!"

"If they can't get the bean out, she'll probably suffocate. I heard of a second-year girl who died that way," says Honking Girl, her eyes glimmering.

I hate gossips, but they can be good sources of information.

At midmeal, I sit next to Honking Girl and ask her if she knows anything about the history between Doi and Suki at this Pearl Colony place.

"Of course!" she says, her face lighting up. "I heard that they had to share a tiny cell together for years. Their captors forced them to cut parts off each other to prove their obedience. And the students were starved until they had to kill and eat each other to survive."

That's what I get for asking a gossip.

After midmeal, I go to the Hall of Benevolent Healing to check on Mole Girl. As well as get more information out of her.

"We discharged her after removing the bean," says an old healer with a head as thin and angled as a folded paper figure. "It would have been interesting to learn if the obstruction affected the magnetization of the sinus bone, but Sensei Madame Yao wouldn't let me remove the nose for study. Here. Feel how heavy the bean was." She tries to drop it in my hand, but I pull away quickly. The bean sticks to her palm.

"No, thank you, Healer. Do you know where she is now?"

"I sent her to the Arch of Chi Retuning. Her Chi was terribly disturbed. I wanted to acquire her for further study, but Sensei Madame Yao can be so difficult."

I skate to the Garden of Whispering Arches and find the Arch of Chi Retuning, but Mole Girl isn't there. As I pass under it, I can feel the frequency humming from the arch resetting my Chi. Back home in Serenity Cliff, there was an old tree that the children called the Blame Tree. Whenever children scraped their knees or dropped a sweet in the dirt or had anything unlucky happen to them, they would kick the tree and feel strangely better. Until one day, the tree died. Passing under the arch makes me feel better in the same way.

I notice that the sound is strange here in the garden. Echoes don't work the same. I read in the Pearlian guidebooks that if you clap your hands, it might echo once, twice, or never, or only after the count of eighty-eight beats, or after one year, depending on what sort of arch you're standing under.

That's why I don't hear Hisashi skating here until after I see him. He's on the far side of the false river of pearlsilk ribbons flowing under a whispering arch.

I raise my hand to wave to him, then hesitate. Has he heard about how his sister was humiliated by Sensei Madame Yao because of me? When Hisashi sees me, he smiles and gives a slight bow. Is his manner slightly colder than it was before?

Hisashi smiles again and bends to speak into the whispering arch, nodding to indicate that I should also lean in.

I bend near the base of the arch and hear his whispered message, carried over the arch as if he's speaking next to my ear: "Gee-Hong went to take a nap."

I whisper back into the arch, "Who?"

"No one you need to know about, apparently," says Hisashi with a laugh. I don't know what's so funny, but I'm relieved that he's laughing.

We skate atop the arch, but just as we meet in the middle, a terrible screeching of birds fills the air. We read the words being traced on the sky, standing side by side.

"Mayor's. Sons. Send. Letter. Orb. Claiming. They. Are. Voluntary. Guests. Of. Empress. Dowager. Chiologists. Confirm. They. Hear. Blockage. In. Tone. Indicating. Words. Spoken. Against. Speakers'. Will. Buy. Pearl. Shining. Sun. News. To. Get. Whole. Story."

"I don't care if ten thousand Chiologists hear blockage in the skaters' voices," I cry. "Who knows why they might have spoken those words against their will? The Empress Dowager isn't holding them as hostages. Your father sent Zan Kenji and Zan Aki because they were the two best New Deitsu Opera Company skaters. The Empress Dowager sent Cricket and me here in a cultural exchange between our two countries. We're not spies. No one can possibly believe Suki's allegation."

"Peasprout, there is so much distrust right now," Hisashi says, placing a hand on my shoulder and turning me away from the birds. "My father intended a goodwill gesture." He leads us off the bridge and down through the path of whispering arches. "However, the government of Pearl believes that if New Deitsu doesn't share with Shin the secret of where they get the pearl, the Empress Dowager will eventually invade and take our city apart, piece by piece, to build a pearl city of her own."

"You don't know that!" The sound of my words as we skate under a scalloped-shaped whispering arch vibrates in a sustained echo, as if my voice were being stretched on a torture rack and crying out with a voice of its own. "And, anyway, why can't you share?"

"I'm not sure. There might not be enough to build and maintain two cities," Hisashi says. "That's not my father's fault. But we Nius seem to get blamed a lot for things that aren't our fault."

He must have heard what happened to Doi over my soaps. Heat flushes up my whole head in shame for what his sister suffered for me.

"Your sister must hate me after what happened in Sensei Madame Yao's class." As I speak these words, we skate under another whispering arch that has an underside patterned with little indentations. They must capture very select sounds, as only one word of my sentence is whispered back in echo. "Me, me, me . . ."

He pauses but then says, "No, I'm sure she knows that whatever happened was Suki's fault."

Here's my chance to ask about the hatred between Doi and Suki!

"Yes, Suki clearly has some history with Doi," I say quickly. "What happened between them at Pearl Rehabilitative Colony for Ungrateful Daughters?"

"All the girls have to get their hair cut when they arrive there.

On the first day, Doi helped the nuns cut off Suki's hair. You can imagine how happy Suki was with Doi after that."

"Is that why Suki and the other girls all have bobbed hair?"

"Yes."

"How did Doi avoid it then? Her hair is like a waterfall. It couldn't have grown back so quickly."

I turn to him as we skate under another whispering arch. I see his mouth open and start to form words, then close, open, then close, but I hear nothing. Is this an arch that swallows sound? No. He wants to speak, but he doesn't want to speak. Another secret.

I see that my question has made Hisashi uncomfortable. Maybe Doi and Hisashi get special treatment as the Chairman's children. Whatever it is, he clearly doesn't want to talk about it.

"Well, whatever the explanation, I'm glad," I say. "If for no other reason because of how furious it must have made Suki."

He smiles. I like it that I made him do that. He says, "Peasprout, sometimes appearances— My sister might not seem very— You're not like anyone Doi—or I—have ever met, so if she acts confused . . . or I mean— And how Suki— Oh, I don't know what I'm saying. Just remember that every time something good happens to Doi or you, some part of Suki dies inside."

"Good," I say.

He smiles. How did I ever think that he smiled too much? His warmth is endless, like the sun's.

"But even if Doi and I both beat Suki," I say, "at some point, it's going to be Doi against me. Only one of us can take first ranking and get the lead in the Drift Season Pageant."

"Don't worry about that until you take down Suki. Doi won't."

"Did she tell you that? I thought you avoid each other."

"Doi doesn't talk much. She's different from other people. You must know what it's like not to fit— I mean, it's hard for Doi to know people. Don't let her confident Chi fool you. It's like how so many Pearlian opera performers are really shy when they're not onstage playing a— No, it's not like that; it's like sometimes a boy likes a girl—he's afraid he'll be made fun of by the other boys, and he's confused by his feelings, so he pushes her into a puddle, or he talks and talks whenever she's around about everything except . . ." He catches himself and slows. He looks into the sky as if the words he needed were written there and finishes: ". . . what he's really thinking."

He pauses, and the awkwardness rings in the silence.

Now it's my turn to be confused and silent. I've never sought attention from any boy because I never wanted it. Now that I might have this boy's attention, I realize I wanted it from him. Because he's not just any boy. But now that I have his attention, I don't know what to do with it. All I know is that I understand what it is to be confused.

"*Aiyah*," he says. "I'm sorry. If you, ah, heard all these noises come out of my mouth just now, it's just a trick of the, ah, sound here in the garden. I didn't say anything. Not a word. Is my face red? Please say no."

"That's the nicest thing a boy's ever said to me," I say.

"Is it? Well, I practiced to get all the words just right."

When he smiles, it's like beams of sunlight are shooting out of his dimples.

"I'd like to show you a special place in the garden. The Arch of the Sixteenth Whisper."

He takes my hand in his. Despite the gentleness of his figure and manner, the knuckles on one hand are all rough, as if he'd been training in fist work. The palms are rough and scratchy. I find that I like it.

"It was built by Cloud-Tamer Zwei herself, as one of her first experiments," he says as he leads me to a slender, filigreed arch. "You whisper words into the base of the arch at this end. The sound will rebound back and forth sixteen times before it can be heard at the other end of the arch, sixteen beats later. Only eleven students in the history of Pearl Famous have been fast enough to get to the other side in time to hear their own voices. Want to try it?" Hisashi's eyes are shining. "You can be the twelfth."

I look at the vast arch and the span I have to cross. Does he really think I can do it? Or is he trying to make me attempt something he knows I can't succeed at to make me question my skills? I am his sister's rival, after all. Whatever his intention is, I don't want to risk failing in front of this boy. So I'll just have to make sure I don't fail.

"Let's do it," I say.

"Ready yourself. *San. Ni. Ichi!*"

He whispers something into the base of the arch, and I explode out toward the other end. I lunge forward with each stroke of my skates, as my will reaches for the other end and the arch rises above me, then descends again. I must not miss Hisashi's words.

I arrive at the other end of the arch, slap my hands against it to halt myself, and press my ear into the base just in time to hear Hisashi's voice whisper, "I knew you could do it."

Eight beats later, Hisashi himself arrives. He touches the end of the arch, his fingers brushing a bit of my shoulder, then skates on without a word.

CHAPTER
NINE

We have newspapers like *Pearl Shining Sun News* back in Shin. According to them, I am the Empress Dowager's secret heir in disguise; I was murdered by palace eunuchs and replaced with a boy eunuch who looked like me; and I am actually seven twin sisters, each skilled in a different school of wu liu, pretending to be one skater. They print whatever nonsense will sell copies.

However, even nonsense can be dangerous if believed.

The birds circle in the sky above us in the open court of architecture class and begin to write dangerous nonsense.

"Empress. Dowager. Declares. Mayor's. Sons. Hostages. Demands. Secret. Of. The. Pearl. In. Exchange. As. Mayor. Demands. Chairman. Niu's. Arrest. Buy. Pearl. Shining. Sun. News. To. Get. Whole. Story."

"See," says a voice. We all look away from the birds to see Suki get up from her desk at the back of architecture class. Her spreading cloak drapes about her figure as she rises, like the folding wings of a crow. "I told you." She skates to my desk. "Your Empress Dowager was planning this all along. She took those boys as hostages and then sent her 'Stealthiest Skater' to steal the secret of the pearl."

She flings a paper doll onto my desk. The sunlight flashes off the gold logograms celebrating *Peony-Level Brightstar Chen Peasprout, the Stealthiest Skater in Shin!* Make me drink sand to death. I thought I got rid of all of them.

"Everyone, mark my words!" she announces. "She's not really a skater; she's just a spy who is decent enough to pass for one. Don't turn your back to her. She's probably going to try to kill one of us during Lady Ming's Hand-Mirror!"

At that, Supreme Sensei Master Jio arrives. He doesn't say anything about the newspaper headline. I don't pay attention to his lecture. I've got more important things to worry about than architecture. It's even more important now that I do well at the second Motivation in three days. If I don't, it'll confirm Suki's accusation.

I don't believe for a moment that the Empress Dowager actually declared Zan Kenji and Zan Aki hostages, but doesn't she know how holding on to them might look for her two emissaries here in Pearl? She puts us in an urn filled with scorpions. And then shakes the urn.

If she wants to build a city of the pearl in Shin, why can't she just buy the material from here?

It must have something to do with the nature of the pearl.

I suddenly realize my mistake.

I haven't been paying attention to architecture class. If I want to understand why the Empress Dowager's putting Cricket and me in this position, I need to understand more about the pearl.

And architecture is all about the pearl.

At the same time, Cricket and I can't look too interested in the pearl. That'll seem to confirm Suki's accusation that we're Shinian spies.

The problem is that Supreme Sensei Master Jio never teaches us anything about what the pearl really is in architecture class.

"Sweet embryos, you are little. But how little? Are you excellently little? Please each take one of these." He presents a lacquered tray filled with little cones with a sharp pick at the end. "Place one on the smallest finger of your hand. You will use it to unravel a silkworm cocoon to see who can extract the longest unbroken thread. Twelve years ago, a student produced one that was so long, it would take half an hour to skate its length, ahihahaha!"

When I make the first incision into my cocoon with the pick, I push too deep and it pierces into the flesh of the silkworm inside. Thick fluid leaks all over my cocoon, ruining it. Make me drink sand to death.

After that, Supreme Sensei makes us stretch up an arm, hold by its top tip a brush that's as long as our arms, and write our name on the nail of the long finger of the other hand. I'm holding the brush as still as I can, but the bristles are lurching back and forth with the trembling of my fingers, like they're trying to smear ink all over half my hand. Which is exactly what they do as soon as I try to touch the brush to the nail. Why are we doing these ludicrous exercises?

Finally, we're each made to place a small ring on the back of our hand and count the pores in the skin within the ring. I count twelve pores. I recount them to make sure my eyes are seeing correctly. The second time, I count five. Ten thousand years of stomach gas.

This is useless. It isn't teaching me anything about the secret of the pearl. I wish I could just openly ask Supreme Sensei or a fellow student, but I can't do anything that appears to confirm Suki's accusation that I'm after the secret of the pearl.

My hopes rise when Supreme Sensei announces that there will be two additions to the first-years' architecture course of study. However, they both turn out to be useless.

First, he announces that there will be an optional sculpture competition. The entrants choose a structure on the campus of Pearl Famous to carve in miniature out of a block of ivory wood, which comes from the dried trunks of the giant kelp trees in the sea around Pearl. The students who carve the three best sculptures will help the third-year students create the set for the Drift Season Pageant at the end of the year. I, of course, am not going to participate. Useless.

Second, there's a new thing that happens in architecture class. A horrid new thing. Sessions with Chingu, the oracular monkey.

Supreme Sensei Master Jio takes us to the edge of the great square on the north side of the Principal Island, Divinity's Lap.

We line up facing the water, next to a sculpture of the Enlightened One. An old man is waiting for us there. He's holding a monkey holding a cleaver. Supreme Sensei Master Jio laughs, calls us sweet embryos, recites words that add up to a string of gibberish, and leaves us with the old man and the monkey and the cleaver.

Mole Girl is nearby, and I ask her who the old man is.

"That's Sagacious Monk Goom, who serves as spiritual guide for Pearl Famous."

"Why does he have a monkey?"

"That's his legendarily ill-tempered monkey, Chingu!"

Honking Girl hears us and says, "I heard that Sagacious Monk Goom achieved enough spiritual advancement to receive enlightenment from the gods and become a great sorcerer. He went up to the mountaintop with his beloved yet hideously spoiled pet monkey, Chingu. The bolt of enlightenment missed the monk and hit the monkey instead. The heavenly ether went into her and she was made into a great sorcerer with awesome powers but none of the self-restraint of a human."

I turn away from this silly girl. Does she really think I'm stupid enough ever to believe anything she says again? However, Mole Girl sees my sneer and says, "No, it's true! She's an oracular monkey. If you manage to grab one of her hands, she'll fall into a trance and select three tiles from a set of sixty-lucky, each with a different logogram. The three logograms together hold your fortune."

"That sounds useful," I say.

"Yes," says Mole Girl. "But the problem is the cleaver. Chingu got hold of a cleaver twenty years ago, and no one has been able to get it away from her since. And if you think that there's anything more terrifying under heaven than an irritable monkey with a cleaver, you haven't met Chingu."

"Is that why everyone says 'failed to keep the monkey pleased' when they mean 'made a horrible, horrible mistake'?"

"Yes! If you irritate her, Chingu will try to chop something off of you *and* give you a bad oracle, which always proves to be true."

I suppose no one has been able to bathe her in twenty years, either. She looks as tangled and smeared as something you'd mop the toilet-room floor with. I watch her grab the ornate pearlsilk cap covered with stars and moons from her head, scrub it between her legs, and smell it.

Sagacious Monk Goom makes us form a line leading up to a lip of the pearl overhanging the sea. He skates, as rickety as a house built of ropes and branches, to the second student in line.

"Count the number of drops that splash up from the water," says Sagacious Monk Goom.

"What drops?" the second girl in line asks.

Sagacious Monk Goom pushes the first girl in line into the water.

Chingu immediately begins to chop the pearl beneath her feet with the cleaver. She brings the blade down in both of her little hands with such force that her hind legs splay out in front of her and she lifts entirely off the pearl for an instant, balancing on the cleaver. All the time, she's shrieking as if she's being pulled apart into pieces.

"How many?" says Sagacious Monk Goom.

"How many what?" asks the girl.

"How many drops of water splashed up?"

"I don't know! Seventy?"

Sagacious Monk Goom turns to Chingu. She finishes chopping out the count. Sagacious Monk Goom says, "Chingu says seventy-two! Mmm, very nice, very nice." He smiles at the girl, and she smiles back and then he pushes her into the water. Chingu starts chopping and shrieking again.

"How many?" he says to the next girl.

So it goes all morning, with splashing and chopping and shrieking and Sagacious Monk Goom saying, "Mmm, very nice, very nice." When my turn comes, I focus my Chi and stare at the ring of droplets that splashed up before my eyes as Mole Girl plopped into the sea. I close my eyes and try to picture their image burned in reverse on my retina. I can actually see some of them in the flashes of green and red behind my eyelids, but there is no way that I can accurately count them before they fade. I guess, "Seventy-eight?"

Chingu finishes chopping out the count.

Sagacious Monk Goom cries, "Chingu says seventy-eight!"

I smile in relief. Then Sagacious Monk Goom shoves me into the water.

By the end of the day, we're as unnerved and disoriented as if we had been strapped to the wheels of a chariot and driven seven thousand li from Jinfeng Mountain down to the Purple River.

As I skate back to the dormitory chambers, wet and shivering and trying to center my Chi, the revelation comes to me. I thought all these exercises were useless. However, I learned two strange but critical things about the pearl today:

1. Building with the pearl requires outstanding eyesight.
2. Building with the pearl involves something very, very small.

CHAPTER
TEN

Two days. That's all I have left to prepare until the second Motivation. Learning about the pearl and why the Empress Dowager has put us in this position are important but so is performing well so that I don't look like a mediocre skater sent as a spy.

I haven't made anywhere near the progress that I needed to in my meditation memory practice. I've been training by myself every day before morningmeal in the memory palace exercises at the Courtyard of Supreme Placidness. During wu liu class, my ability to remember these strings of moves with many quick steps has been improving as a result. However, I know it's still far from what I need in order to take first ranking at the second Motivation. I need to do more in these last two days. I need to make Doi teach me her meditation technique.

That evening, half an hour before evenmeal, I go to the Courtyard of Supreme Placidness and find Doi there just as she is finishing her meditation practice. It's clear that she's not happy about my being here.

It's the first time I've seen her alone since the meeting with Hisashi in the Garden of Whispering Arches. I have to try to win Doi over so I can ask her about her meditation technique. Perhaps I can use what Hisashi told me about the history between Suki and Doi at Pearl Rehabilitative Colony.

I bow to Doi. She bows back, but there's no expression on her face. Then again, there never seems to be anything on this girl's face except two eyes, a nose, and a mouth.

"What do you think the nuns at Pearl Rehabilitative Colony for Ungrateful Daughters did with Suki's hair after they cut it off?" I ask, trying for a smile. "Should one of us come in wearing it as a belt during the second Motivation?"

Doi's face doesn't change. "You don't need to come here when I do. It's not going to help you with the second Motivation."

Her words feel like a slap.

"I've seen you meditating, but it won't help you win," she continues. "The second Motivation doesn't really have anything to do with memorization."

She's so rude. How can Doi and Hisashi share the same mother and father?

"So," I say, "if it's nothing to do with the second Motivation, you shouldn't mind me joining you here."

"I'm done here."

"What about tomorrow night?"

"I'd prefer if you'd not come when I'm using the squares."

"There are sixty-fo—sixty-lucky of them. I only need one." I cross my arms. "Why can't I be here? What is it you're doing?"

"It's just a game that my brother and I came up with when we were young."

"Then why won't you tell me?" This girl is impossible. "I'm only talking to you because Hisashi—"

"Hisashi's a fool!" She gets up and skates out of the square.

So I'm on my own for the second Motivation. Nothing new to me.

I skip my architecture, music, and literature classes the last morning before the second Motivation. I spend the extra time studying the *Treatise on Chi Practice and the Visual Music of the Memory Palace* and meditating. During wu liu class that afternoon, Sensei Madame Liao has us form a line and face her. We are to copy her moves, and any girl who makes a mistake is eliminated from the line.

I focus my Chi. I must be relaxed so I can absorb. I must loosen every muscle in my body, even the muscles that I didn't know were clenched, muscles I didn't know existed, muscles in my ears, muscles in my eyes, muscles in—

Suddenly, Sensei Madame Liao has already done two moves and all the girls beside me have done them in imitation.

I have no idea what they did and stand there stupidly.

"Chen Peasprout, you are eliminated!"

I skate to the sideline. I was trying too hard to relax. That only made it impossible to relax. How am I ever going to survive the second Motivation?

After our evening baths, as I am readying for sleep, Doi crosses my path.

"They never taught you back in Shin how to do walking meditation," she says.

"Of course they did," I say as I try to skate past her. What does she want? I need to get a good night's sleep before the second Motivation tomorrow. The last thing I need is to be distracted by another argument with this girl.

"So then you must know that some people are able to stay in a meditative state while skating?"

"That's impossible. You'd come out of the meditative state as soon as you moved."

"Not if you are deep enough in it. You just need something strong enough to send you that deep."

If she's trying to intimidate me with how good everyone else's Chi practice is during the second Motivation, it's not going to work. I skate away from her, open the paper shoji door of my dormitory chamber, and slam it shut behind me.

I sleep a long sleep filled with uneventful dreams.

The morning of the second Motivation, we skate in a group down the path to the rails connecting to the Conservatory of Wu Liu. The path winds past the Pagoda of Filial Sacrifice, where the boys will be doing Vertical Battlefield for their second Motivation while the girls do Lady Ming's Hand-Mirror. When I near it, there is already a crowd of students and senseis gathered there, but the strange thing is that the students include as many girls as boys. Why aren't the girls moving on to our Motivation? They're all looking up at the pagoda.

I gasp as I see what they're pointing at.

There are great gashes in the tiers of the pagoda. It looks like a giant took a sword and slashed it down the side of the pagoda, slicing through the roofs of the eight tiers, all the way down to the bottom one.

I know it couldn't have been a giant sword, but look at the scale of the damage! It sickens my stomach. The sections of roofs next to the gash of each tier are buckled and skewed. Some of the pagoda's inner parts show through. It looks like someone cut open a crab to pry its halves apart and scrape at the living meat inside.

One of the students says, "We've been attacked!"

Attack? Who would want to attack a pagoda? Murmurs rise. Several of the students look at me and whisper to one another.

"I told you," says Suki, triumph cracking her voice. "Now do you believe me? She's not a real skater. She's just decent enough to pass for one. The 'Stealthiest Skater in Shin' is finally starting to do what the Empress Dowager really sent her here to do!"

I'm as shocked by this as anyone. No, it can't be. The Empress Dowager wouldn't order an attack on the academy. She must know what position that would leave Cricket and me in as the only Shinian students here. Some student who wasn't happy with his or her ranking at the last Motivation must have done this. All I know is that I don't know any more about this than anyone else.

Everyone is looking at me.

And Suki is still talking.

More and more students and senseis are arriving for the second Motivation. They're starting to form a circle, and I'm in the center of it. I feel their stares and their whispers and, above all of it, Suki's poisonous lies.

So I do something I have never done.

I turn and flee.

I hop on the rails to the Conservatory of Wu Liu.

When Sensei Madame Liao and the other first-year girls arrive, I don't look up from my Chi-centering exercises.

Sensei Madame Liao says, "The first-year boys' second Motivation shall be delayed. The first-year girls' second Motivation shall proceed as scheduled."

My emotions are still too uncollected for me to absorb this. I focus on the Chi energy filling from my toes. I visualize it carrying the venom of this news, rising out of me, exiting my body.

It's not working. I can't expel the shock. I can feel it lodged in my Chi, and every time I push against it, I only drive myself backward, deeper, down and back and down.

I open my eyes to a world moving so slowly.

The sounds of the girls around me are drawn out, even though some part of my mind tells me that they're talking as quickly as they can, they must be talking about something significant that happened long ago this morning, but to me it's like the sound of birds that I can mimic without understanding.

I skate as if outside my own body to take my place and face my opponent for Lady Ming's Hand-Mirror. Now, I'm watching myself standing in front of this girl, and she is doing a move and I'm copying it and adding a move, and so it goes back and forth, and the moves are laying themselves out in a strip in my mind as a rhythm of musical beats. But the other girl acts before her Chi is centered. Even though the rounds aren't timed, she's quickening the pace to intimidate me, but I keep up, and it's not long before she makes a mistake and the round is over, and I take a point for each move in the string, and my opponent takes nothing.

I watch my body skate to face my next opponent. My being is brightened because I have won the first round, but I know it would be better for my opponent and me to perform our parts slowly, until the number of moves has climbed higher. The longer and more complicated the sequence of moves we successfully complete, the more points each round will be worth when I win it.

I face girl after girl. Each time, when I finish in victory, I look down at my body and see my aura of Chi brighten briefly, but then it dims again, because I only earn average points against each girl. I try to move deliberately, hoping my opponent will follow my lead, but girl after girl panics and drives the pace too fast for herself until suddenly she is splayed on her rear end on the pearl in front of me.

I watch my body work its way through the line of opponents to the two beings who have the most significance for me in this space. Deep in this state, I can see the cords of energy binding my body to them; the one linking to Suki is orange and burning white in the center, but the one to Doi is a color I have no name for, a color that makes me feel like I am blind.

We three stand like pillars in a lake, for we are undefeated in all our rounds, but it is a shallow lake. The other girls keep losing to us before we are able to gather many points in any round.

Finally, I see my body standing before Doi. I use my Chi to try to establish a link with her and hope that she understands that we must skate as if carefully linking a string of beads; we are making a necklace between us, and we should make it slowly, bead for bead, until it is long enough to be worth winning.

We dive into a chamber of sound, air, sight, and instinct that becomes a conversation, punctuated with thoughtful pauses and courtesies and glorious style, as we chain our moves so that they're answers to each other.

Doi leaps and kicks the air in a third-gate grasshopper backflip, to which I spread my arms to gather the air under them to add a luckieth-gate nightingale loop, since the nightingale eats the grasshopper, to which she retorts by leaping and spinning into a jump, then diving down headfirst in a fifth-gate falcon spiral, since the falcon eats the nightingale, all of which I perform and then surpass by springing off the coils under the heels of my faithful skates in a fifth-gate tiger leap. She conquers this by flinging herself into a furious spin on one skate with the other skate pulled behind her in a luckieth-gate triple phoenix spin, since the phoenix eats only bamboo seeds and harms nothing, and it tames all beasts with its grace.

It's exquisite to dance against an opponent of such skill.

Around us, all the other girls gather, as they have long since ended their rounds, and when Doi and I have strung together thirty moves, we give in to the urge to push the rounds faster and faster. When I add in a single-footed orchid flip, Doi slips at this simple child's move and lands with both feet.

I am hauled out of my state as if by a rope from the bottom of the sea. The scale of time in my mind collapses in and comes crashing into the scale of time around me.

I'm here at the Conservatory of Wu Liu. At the second Motivation. I've won the round against Doi. There's no applause. Just murmuring as the other girls glare at me. Because someone or something attacked the Pagoda of Filial Sacrifice just an hour ago. And everyone thinks I'm involved. The shock of the vandal attack and the accusations against me pushed me into a meditative state that helped me copy the moves of my opponents. A skating meditative state, just like Doi told me about.

There's just one more opponent left to beat: Suki. We're given only a moment to rest before the next round. I quickly center my Chi to get back into that state before I take on Suki.

"Don't try to beat Suki." It's Doi.

"Please don't interrupt me, I'm getting back into my meditative—"

"She's better than you. You need to lose to her."

"Don't tell me what I need to do." She's sore that she lost to me.

"Count," she says and skates away.

Count? What does she mean?

Then it's my turn to go against Suki. There's no time to get back into the meditative state.

"What did you use to attack the pagoda?" Suki says. "Did you fire thousand-year-old preserved bladder stones at it?"

Insipid laughter rises from the House of Flowering Blossoms girls who have gathered to watch the final round.

I shouldn't have fled. I shouldn't have panicked.

I say, "Even a thousand-year-old bladder stone wouldn't be as old as that joke is by now. Are you going to do a move, or are you going to just stand there reusing jokes?"

"You'll be reusing your clothes for toilet paper when they throw you in prison."

"Maybe when I get to prison, they'll give me a nice haircut like the nuns gave you."

Suki seethes and begins the round by doing a kingfisher sporting in the Purple River quintuple jump. Everyone gasps, because this is a seventh-gate east-directional move, requiring her to jump and twist her body like a hunting bird to reverse direction lucky times while in the air. However, kingfisher sporting in the Purple River quintuple jump is one of the few moves in all of wu liu originating in the region of, obviously, the Purple River in Shui Shan Province. Where I'm from. It's one of the moves that I mastered to become wu liu champion of all of Shui Shan Province, which qualified me to compete for the title of Peony-Level Brightstar. I've been doing it since I was six years old.

I execute the move flawlessly.

We launch into a furious round, whipping faster and faster. She's using fifth-, sixth-, and seventh-gate moves to intimidate me. I'm not afraid, because they're all centered on difficult jumps, and I'm the best jumper in the class. The dragon tail coil under the heel of each of my skates is absorbing the jumps beautifully, so I feel nothing on the knees, while giving me lift for the next jump.

When we've strung together thirty-one unbroken points, my focus wanders and I start thinking that I need to win this Motivation to prove that I'm not a spy. It'll prove that I was sent here because I truly am the most talented skater in all of Shin. I begin tallying up my score. I've gained thirty-one points from the round against Doi, so Suki has to win thirty-two points herself. . . .

Suki leaps in the air and pivots with one knee lifted before her in a north-directional metal monkey spin, but I was too busy counting my points and can't remember if she did three rotations before landing or lucky, but I don't want them to see me hesitate. I know that Suki is reckless, so I complete the move with lucky rotations.

As soon as I do so, the House of Flowering Blossoms girls erupt in sneering laughter and cheers.

It should've been three rotations. Suki has won thirty-two points, enough to take first ranking.

Too late, I realize my mistake.

Count! That's what Doi meant!

I've given Suki the thirty-two points she needed to win. If I had deliberately failed immediately, rather than matching her move for move and building up the value of the round, Suki would've only gotten one point from me and I would've finished with the top points. I should have intentionally lost the round against Suki to deny her enough points to win. Now, I've thrown away first place.

Doi wasn't trying to intimidate me. She was trying to help me.

I've taken second place in this Motivation. Because of the weight given to this Motivation, that combines with my performance at the first Motivation to drop me to second place overall.

I quickly gather my things and skate away from the other girls who are now crowding around Suki to congratulate her. After all the work I did to make up for the deficiencies in my training. Am I just going to rank lower and lower in every Motivation? Was I just lucky in the first Motivation?

Now, I have to finish first, not just for myself or Shin or the Empress Dowager. I have to finish first because my safety depends on it. I must prove that I deserve to be here, that I'm not just a barely decent skater sent here to spy on Pearl.

As I skate toward the rails leading back to the Principal Island of the academy, something catches in the dragon tail coiled under my right heel. I turn and see that Suki has lodged the front tip of her skate in the coil of my skate. I stop so that her skate doesn't damage my blade.

Before I can say anything, Chiriko and Etsuko race up and shove me forward just as Suki twists the toe of her skate.

The tip of her blade breaks as the dragon tail of my blade snaps off.

"You broke my skate blade!" says Suki. "You're so clumsy."

I test the weight on my skate. Three of the supports connecting the blade to the boot are intact, but the luckieth support connecting the coil at the heel is now connected to nothing but a pocket of empty air that sickens me. It feels like Suki cut off half my foot. My life is in my feet. How am I going to compete at the Motivations? How am I going to prove that I truly was sent here because of my skill as a skater if I don't even have two complete blades?

I look for Sensei Madame Liao. She is at the far end of the training court, with her back to us. She saw nothing. It's my word against all the other girls'.

Chiriko opens a pack of blades and gives one to Suki. Suki replaces her broken blade with a fresh one. She finishes screwing it in. She and the House of Flowering Blossoms girls hop onto the rails and skate away.

Suki makes a half turn on the rail and skates backward while looking at me. As she recedes, she holds the coil of my dragon tail to the side of her head, like a peony tucked behind her ear.

CHAPTER
ELEVEN

"**W**here were you last night?"

"Asleep in my dormitory chamber."

"What do you know about the attack on the Pagoda of Filial Sacrifice?"

"Nothing!"

I thought Sensei Madame Liao was sympathetic, but she interrogates me here in this personal audience chamber as if I were a criminal. The senseis say they're questioning all the students, but, of course, I'm the one they're most interested in.

"Have you had any communications with the Empress Dowager since coming to Pearl?"

"No."

"Have you made any enemies here?"

I don't answer. I don't have to. She looks at me for a long time without speaking.

"Sensei, there's no proof that I had anything to do with this."

"They found this embedded in one of the roofs of the Pagoda of Filial Sacrifice," she says as she unfolds a square of silk.

My dragon tail coil lies there on the cloth, glinting like some assassin's curved throwing blade.

"She put that there," I say.

"Who?"

I open my mouth and stop. I need to be careful here. I'm in no position right now to make any allegations without proof.

"I had nothing to do with any of this, Sensei. I'm innocent."

"Being innocent is not enough," Sensei says quietly. "Do you understand that?"

Yes. Because Cricket and I aren't from here.

When I exit the audience chamber, I almost trip on the ramp leading down from its entrance. I'm not used to having the dragon tail coil gone from under my heel. Not only is my knee going to have to bear all the weight of every jump on that leg, but my balance is thrown off and the jagged remnant of the blade catches on the pearl.

My skate blade is broken. I lost the second Motivation to Suki. Everyone thinks that the Empress Dowager is holding the New Deitsu skaters hostage. And people are starting to believe that I was involved in this strange attack on the Pagoda of Filial Sacrifice.

Suki did this. She found some way to vandalize the pagoda. That's how she was able to "predict" that something was going to happen and set me up.

Outside the audience chamber, the clouds are parted and the sky is clear. On the ground I see the shadow of the logograms forming in the sky.

"Vicious. Attack. Investigated. As. Part. Of. Empress. Dowager. Hostage. Plot. As. Attention. Turns. To. First. Students. From. Shin. Buy. Pearl. Shining. Sun. News. To. Get. Whole. Story."

Make me drink sand to death.

That afternoon, the New Deitsu Pearlworks Company team arrives to repair the pagoda. I had thought that they would come with a great crew of workmen and perhaps animals and equipment and tools and enough materials to repair a great pagoda. Instead, it's a small team of eight. They're dressed more like artists than workmen. They come bearing a palanquin.

What's strange about the palanquin is that it's so small, the size of a box for stage makeup. It couldn't possibly seat a person, not even a child. Yet it's so heavy it requires eight people to bear it on long staffs.

Supreme Sensei Master Jio announces during the morning assembly, "It is the sweet honor of Pearl Famous to welcome Chairman Niu Kazuhiro of the New Deitsu Pearlworks Company."

I look for Hisashi to see his reaction to the arrival of his father, but I don't see him or Doi.

"Please bow to him ten thousand obeisances of gratitude, little embryos!"

I hear a rustling behind me and turn. Doi is skating toward us. Heavenly August Personage of Jade, what is she wearing?

She's changed from her black academy robe into some white costume covered in rows of pearl-like beads, with a skirt that's open in the front but ends in great spreads in the back, like a half circle of wings. It's majestic but much too small for her. It looks as if Doi outgrew it long ago. On her head is a crown of false pearl-silk feathers. She stands at the far edge of the gathering of girls and looks at her skates. What under heaven is she trying to do?

Chairman Niu skates to the dais. He's tall and handsome, like his son. The gold mandalas embroidered on his robe make him look less like a businessman and more like a statesman.

"No need to bow ten thousand obeisances of gratitude, little birds," he says. "You just had morningmeal. Eight thousand eight hundred and eighty-eight bows of obeisance will be more than plenty." The students giggle. He has the same easy charm as Hisashi. I understand why the government asked him to handle political matters with Shin.

"Now, the most important thing to me is that none of you worries about this damage to the Pagoda of Filial Sacrifice. There's nothing more important than your studies. We're investigating whether there was a rogue waterspout that damaged the pagoda or an unmapped earthquake spine, but none of that matters. We'll have the pagoda repaired as quickly as possible so you first-year boys can get on with your Vertical Battlefield Motivation. You'll be hopping all over the tiers of the pagoda like a handful of grass-hoppers tossed onto a hot skillet before you know it!"

He smiles. I see where Hisashi got his dimples.

"Now, I've got a job for you to do. While the New Deitsu team does its work, no one except the three third-year students who have devoted to the Conservatory of Architecture will be permitted to face the worksite. So don't face south until your senseis say you may. Can you do that for me?"

The students murmur and giggle.

"What happens if we face south?" asks Honking Girl.

"You'll be expelled, of course." The Chairman assumes a mock stern expression and wags his finger. "And then imprisoned in a horrible torture chamber that will shrink until it crushes you into a tiny pebble that I can pop in my mouth!"

All the other students laugh as if it were a game.

But I grew up under the rule of the Empress Dowager. I know that when powerful leaders do strange things, it's not something to consider a game. It's something to fear.

"So remember," he says, skating past the rows of students, "don't face south until your senseis say you can. Now, concentrate on your studies so you can bring honor to your esteemed parents."

I watch Doi's face crumple as the Chairman skates right past her in that outrageous outfit, as if she weren't there.

Doi looks at her father's back as he leaves. The muscles in her jaw are set like stone.

The girls begin to disperse to do the day's regimen of Chi-lengthening exercises.

"Nice outfit." Suki comes skating over to Doi, flanked by the girls of the House of Flowering Blossoms. "Too bad your father didn't see you in it. Maybe you'll get another chance when he visits again. In another eight years." The girls titter behind their hands.

Doi doesn't look at them. She skates to the bench where she laid her academy robe. She begins to change out of her costume.

"When was the last time?" continues Suki. "Eight years ago? Twelve? Apparently, he doesn't even know what you look like anymore, since he skated right past you."

What is she talking about? Suki is an eternal waterfall of ludicrous accusations. But it's true that Doi's father ignored her. How could he miss her in that outfit?

Doi peels down to her undershirt.

Suki says casually, "So is it true that your father caused your mother's death?"

Now she's just saying things to Doi because there are people around to hear them. I want to tell Suki to shut her mouth, but I don't want her to turn her waterfall of accusations back on me.

Doi's elbow snags in the sleeve of her costume. She struggles and loses patience with it. She just rips the sleeve and half the bodice down, then tugs the rest of her costume off. Beads go bouncing and rolling everywhere. She pulls on her academy robe and skates away from the rest of the girls.

"Some people just can't handle the truth," says Suki.

While the New Deitsu team works on repairing the pagoda, Sensei Madame Liao trains us at the Conservatory of Wu Liu. She teaches us an unusual hybrid tan-toe routine involving a short wooden practice sword called Wall of Steel. We do it facing north, in formation side to side because it was originally invented to beat back an invading army. It also doesn't require us to make any rotations, so we don't have to face south. However, someone occasionally forgets and almost turns south before someone else screams out a warning and they all erupt in nervous giggles.

I nearly face south myself during a break, but Suki immediately grabs my arm and holds me in place. The House of Flowering Blossoms girls crowd around her.

"See! She's trying to look at the building site!" Suki points at me and hisses, "I know you want to watch the pagoda being rebuilt so you can learn the secrets of our pearl and report it back to the Empress Dowager."

"Like when you invaded us for our bamboo," says Mariko.

"Vandal! Thief!" sneers Suki.

Nothing would give me greater happiness in this life than to kick her into the ocean. However, the last thing I can afford now is to break any rules.

I shake my arm free and turn to face north, mumbling something under my breath. I make sure they can't hear anything except for the word *Suki*.

"What did you say?" Suki demands.

I look down at my skates and mutter again.

"Say it to my face!" she says.

She skates close to me, her face to mine.

I lift my face to hers, look her in the eyes, and say, "I said that the only thing I want to steal is a look at your face when you realize that you're facing south, Suki."

All the other students screech when they see this. Sensei Madame Liao whips her gaze toward us just a heartbeat after Suki spins to face east. I skate away and my heart is full of delight.

However, my joy only lasts a moment because this really is a disaster. Not just Suki's rumor that I'm a Shinian spy. I'm also worried because the pagoda is so damaged that it will likely take days if not weeks to repair. How can I practice if I can't face south that entire time?

And the pagoda was the site of the boys' Motivation. What if they start accusing Cricket?

I hear a cracking noise in the distance. Sensei Madame Liao kneels down and places her ear to the pearl. She rises, turns to us, and announces that the New Deitsu team has finished its work and that we may resume use of all directions.

How can that be? It's only been an hour. We all hop on the rails to skate toward the worksite. We arrive to find the Pagoda of Filial Sacrifice fully restored. Sensei Madame Liao skates to the entrance and speaks with Chairman Niu. He goes inside the pagoda.

Sensei Madame Liao ushers the students toward Eastern Heaven Dining Hall for midmeal.

"Chen Peasprout." I freeze at the sound of Sensei Madame Liao calling my name.

"You need to answer some questions."

"What else do you want to ask me?"

"Not I. Chairman Niu would like to speak with you."

CHAPTER
TWELVE

Sensei Madame Liao directs me into the Pagoda of Filial Sacrifice. She does not enter. She slides the door closed behind me.

The space inside is round and sealed, like an ossuary. The Chairman stands at the back of the chamber and watches me enter. He sips his tea anemone. He's powerfully built but holds his body oddly. He's tipping forward like he's being dragged down by some great weight. Is he ill?

He doesn't speak, holding me in his unblinking gaze. The charming Chairman from this morning is gone. There's nothing that looks like it could belong to Hisashi's father in this man. The occasional tap of the long nail of his littlest finger against the porcelain is the only sound in the chamber.

At last, the Chairman smiles and flashes his dimples. "Little bird. I'd like to ask you to please turn in place. Slowly. Can you do that for me?"

I can't think of a reason to disobey, so I reluctantly begin to turn.

"Stop," he says. "Please."

I stop two-thirds through the rotation.

"Look straight ahead," he says. "Please."

Why is he doing this? From the corner of my eye, I see him take the blunt knife used to score the tea anemones to release their flavor. My Chi flashes.

"Open your mouth," he says. "Please."

This is beginning to frighten me, but surely he wouldn't hurt me with Sensei Madame Liao waiting right outside the door. He skates to me and places the handle of the knife in my mouth.

"Bite down, please."

I clench my teeth on the knife. He adjusts it. Then the Chairman balances his cup of tea anemones on the flat surface of the blade. He returns to the back of the room where he can see me but I can only catch a glimpse of him.

Now I understand. He'll use this method to detect any lies. He wants to see my reaction to his questions, and if anything he says makes me turn my head to him even the slightest, he'll know, because the cup will fall.

"I find it easier to get the truth this way, rather than rely on spoken answers," the Chairman says. Then he begins speaking question after question in a steady voice.

"Where were you last night, little bird?"

I need to stay calm. I can't react, or the knife will shake and spill the cup of tea.

"Did you bring anything from Shin to Pearl Famous?"

He has no right to be doing this. I want to cry out and deny what he's suggesting.

"Have you communicated with anyone in Shin since you arrived?"

I don't want him to read anything I do as guilt.

"Do you love the Empress Dowager?"

He's not a sensei. He's not a government official.

"Do you love your country?"

He's just a businessman.

"Do you love Pearl, little bird?"

How is this an effective way to tell if I am lying? Just because I react to one of his questions doesn't mean I'm guilty. It could mean that I'm angry or insulted. Both of which I am right now.

All of a sudden, I see why he's doing this. It's not to tell if I'm guilty. It's to frighten me into confessing that I'm guilty. I refuse to be afraid of him. I refuse to give him anything.

I can see at the edge of my vision that he's read nothing from my reaction. The Chairman comes to me and takes the cup and the knife from my teeth. He stands over me. I stare straight ahead at his shoulder, where the complicated mandalas embroidered in pearlsilk match perfectly across the seam where shoulder meets sleeve.

He lifts his hand. With the long nail on his small finger, the Chairman digs the toggle open on the breast pocket of his robe. He reaches in and pulls out something. He straightens his posture.

He holds out the object in his palm.

It's a cord with some sort of trinket. Something small and black.

"A token for you, little bird."

He lets it slide off his hand. When it hits the floor, it's so heavy that it doesn't bounce or slide. It simply stays where it lands.

He skates toward the door.

"You did not do well, little bird," the Chairman says as he passes me. "I would ask you to do better the next time, but there will not be a next time. Do you understand?"

Without waiting for my answer, he leaves. It's one thing to have someone like Suki as an enemy. Suki practices a school of treachery I understand. It's all heat. The Chairman's strange, quiet attacks are different. They are chilling.

I bend to pick up the pendant.

I try to lift it by the cord with a finger. Then I grip with my whole fist and heave it up. It weighs as much as a great jug of water.

The trinket suspended from the cord looks like a little black house with a sloped roof.

The number *2,020* is carved on the back.

I look closer and see a little indentation in the house. A minuscule door.

But it's been sealed shut.

As if something is trapped inside.

CHAPTER
THIRTEEN

I have to find Cricket. If the Chairman put him through the same interrogation, Cricket's nerves would be smashed into ten thousand pieces. And the Chairman would say that Cricket's reaction was evidence of his guilt and use that to force whatever false confession he wanted out of Cricket.

Students are finishing up midmeal and coming out of Eastern Heaven Dining Hall. When I see Cricket skate out, I hook my arm through his and drag him away from the others. I take him to a maintenance rail built into the side of the cliff over the sea behind Eastern Heaven Dining Hall. No one comes out here, and the sound of the sea prevents us from being overheard.

"Cricket, what happened this morning after the boys' Motivation was postponed? Did the Chairman speak to you?"

"No, just Sensei Master Bao. He asked all the boys one by one if they knew anything about the damage to the pagoda. Did you see it, Peasprout? What could have done that? It couldn't be fire, because the damage went down from the top tier to the bottom in a neat line. How did they repair it in just an hour?"

"Don't let anyone hear you asking any of those questions! Don't look too interested in architecture or the pearl."

"Why not?"

"Because Suki's trying to set us up! Or at least me. Suki committed the attack to try to make me look like I'm a spy. She's come up with some ridiculous story that I've destroyed the pagoda so I can watch the pearl being rebuilt and learn its secrets."

"But, Peasprout, wouldn't Suki have had to commit an actual crime to do that?"

"That wouldn't stop Suki! That's why she's dangerous! That's why—"

I cut myself short. Why didn't I see this before?

The vandal attack has a secret gift in it.

Suki's trying to set me up as a criminal.

But Suki had to commit an actual crime to do it.

Thus, if I can prove that Suki is responsible, I wouldn't just clear my name. *I would take down Suki.* My bitterest rival for first ranking would be thrown in prison, or at least expelled.

I'm going to catch her in her own trap. My safety and Cricket's safety depend on it.

After my evening bath, I sit on my futon in my dormitory chamber and consider how to ensnare Suki. The first step is to figure out how Suki wreaked that terrible damage. Knowing what destroyed the pearl will help me know what sort of evidence to gather.

As I think, the Chairman's trinket catches my gaze. I'm certain he gave it to me as a warning. It's intricately carved, but it doesn't look anything like the pearl. It's small, black, and heavier than anything under heaven.

I try to bite it, but as soon as I put it in my mouth, I feel like it's trying to suck my whole tongue into it from within my own mouth. I quickly spit it out.

I know that Hisashi doesn't have any special knowledge just because he's the Chairman's son. Especially if it's true that, for whatever reason, the Chairman hasn't seen his children in years, even though they live in the same city. And I really don't think Hisashi knows anything about the pearl. Still, I should show him the trinket.

The next day, I look for him everywhere on campus. It's hard to find him because it's difficult to see anyone now. The season has changed, completely and unmistakably, like the switching of the stage between operas. The Season of Spouts has ended, and the Season of Spirits has begun. In this season, a mist rises from the pearl so that the city is filled with shrouding, billowing clouds.

I don't bother to look for him in Eastern Heaven Dining Hall. I've never seen him eat there, probably because everything they serve has meat or other animal parts in it. He's never come to tea anemone hour, either. It occurs to me that he might like sitting in the gondolas to eat his meals, like the first time I met him. After mid-meal, I skate toward the entrance to the academy. It's hard to see because the mist in the Season of Spirits collects everywhere into thick forms that float above the pearl and gather around us. It's one of the two seasons when everyone doesn't have to wear smoked spectacles against the gleam of the pearl. I'm almost at the gondolas before I can see that they're empty.

Cricket said that Hisashi almost never goes to classes. Attendance isn't mandatory, but how will he perform well at his Motivations, Recitals, and Composition projects? Even if he wants to devote to architecture, they post the rankings in every discipline publicly. Who wants to finish last?

That afternoon, I leave wu liu class as quickly as possible to skate to the site of the boys' wu liu class. As I cross the Conservatory of Wu Liu, the pearl is doing something that it never did during the Season of Spouts. It makes noises as I skate across it, little sighs and whistles, like steam escaping from the pores of the world.

When I get to the boys' training court, I peer at the crowd of boys coming out. However, at that moment, the thick mists part and sunlight pierces through. It stabs into my eyes because I didn't bring my smoked spectacles and because the sun is intense, since it's summer in the world. My eyes are watering trying to see the boys in this light, but I definitely don't see Hisashi. I should be irritated, but the beauty of the scene before me quells that.

With the golden beams and slats of light slicing through the tumbling mists and sweeping across the academy, Pearl Famous looks like the capital of heaven.

Finally, three days after the Chairman's interrogation, I skate through a great tumbling cloud, like a cauliflower lanced with rays of sun that looks as if it's illuminated from within, to find Hisashi on the other side of it, skating in the other direction. I skate over to him.

"Where did you get that?" he says when I show him the trinket. "It's so heavy." I grow alarmed when I see he's alarmed.

"Your fath—the Chairman gave it to me. What is it?"

"I don't know."

"Do you think Suki used something like this to attack the pagoda?"

"No, but this is bad. I remember now that I heard about an employee of New Deitsu who was given one of these," Hisashi says slowly. "He was never seen again. I thought maybe it was some kind of poison."

"Poison? I put it in my mouth!"

"No! You should go get checked by Doctor Dio."

"Who?"

"The healer at the Hall of Benevolent Healing."

Oh, her. I don't want her to try to remove my nose for study, like she tried with Mole Girl.

"No, thank you. I don't feel any different. It don't think it's poison. When I put it in my mouth, it felt strange, so I skated under the Arch of Chi Retuning just in case. I feel fine."

"Still. *Aiyah*, why did you put it in your mouth?"

"Because I wanted to find out more about it!"

"That's a good reason to put something in your mouth?"

"Yes, a wonderful reason. Doesn't the Arch of Chi Retuning cure everything?"

"I don't know. Why don't you put it in your mouth and find out?"

All throughout midmeal at Eastern Heaven Dining Hall, I feel better knowing that I'll have Hisashi to talk to about the vandal attacks and the mysteries surrounding the pearl. I know he'll help me in any way that he can.

If only there were some way that he could help Cricket as well. He didn't do too well in the boys' second Motivation. Vertical Battlefield is all about jumping skill, and Cricket is a weak jumper. Our parents didn't choose an apt name for him. He finished twenty-seventh.

I decide to check on him during White Hour, the hour after midmeal when no classes are scheduled. It's officially intended for rest, but students with discipline and ambition and a future in wu liu take the extra hour to train so that rivals don't pull ahead of them.

I skate to the boys' practice court at the Conservatory of Wu Liu, but he isn't there. Ten thousand years of stomach gas. He needs the extra training more than anyone. Where can he be?

I skate across the Principal Island looking for him. On a little islet just northeast of the Principal Island sits the round structure that is the Temple of Heroes of Superlative Character. A group of students is gathered at its entrance. The figure in the center looks like Cricket. But why would Cricket be surrounded by other boys? Are they making fun of him? I skate faster.

As I near, I see that, in fact, it is Cricket, but the boys aren't taunting him. They're listening carefully as he lectures.

"The walls inside are lined with a ramp that spirals around the figures in the center," he says, pointing to the half-carved miniature sculpture of the temple in his hands. "The ramp makes the structure more pliant in earthquakes, but if anything damages the ramp, the whole structure will come toppling down around it."

"Cricket, what do you think you're doing?" I yell out. All the boys turn to look at me. Cricket shrinks like a snail that has been dusted with salt.

"Peasprout, please," he whispers.

The other boys leave us, but I almost want them to stay and hear this.

"Why aren't you training?" I demand.

"I was working with my friends on the competition," he whispers.

"What competition?"

"The architecture sculpture competition."

Fool! I clench my teeth.

"You need to be using every White Hour to improve your miserable wu liu skills! Not wasting your time making toys! And what did I tell you about not looking too interested in architecture? Do you know what they're saying about us while you're playing with *this*?"

I grab his hand clutching the ridiculous little sculpture of the temple and lift it to his face.

He whispers, "No one else is carving the Temple of Heroes of Superlative Character. It's too difficult. You have to carve the statues inside with a tiny metal wire. I'm going to win the competition."

"Cricket, do you want them to blame us for the attack on the Pagoda of Filial Sacrifice?"

"But we didn't—"

"It doesn't matter! We have to work twice as hard and do twice as well and look twice as innocent as everyone else now. Because we're not from here!"

"I couldn't have done that damage to the pagoda. I couldn't even get up to the third tier. Anyone who saw me jump at Vertical Battlefield knows that."

He makes a fair point. Maybe that's why Suki has been focusing on accusing me. Still, I'm not going to let him neglect what he came here to do.

"Cricket, you remember what the Empress Dowager does to returning emissaries who fail to accomplish their duties?"

"Yes."

"You want to be sent to a labor camp?"

"Don't talk about that, Peasprout."

I don't want to frighten him, but we have very real dangers on many sides of us. We're not safe here in Pearl, but we're not safe back home in Shin, either. He must understand how important it is that we do well at Pearl Famous.

"Then why aren't you taking your wu liu seriously?"

The only reply I get is silence, like an empty field with nothing but the sound of crickets. Except the one Cricket I'm talking to.

"She never should have sent me here," he mumbles. "I'm just not good at wu liu."

"Yes, you are. You've sacrificed more for wu liu than anyone here."

"I'm better at architecture."

"Only three students in each class will be invited to devote to Architecture. These rich kids have been tutored in architecture their whole lives. You're going to neglect your wu liu training because you think you'll be in the top three in architecture? When were you ever in the top three at anything?"

Cricket plunges his chin into his breast.

"Cricket," I say. "You know why I do this. We can't look too interested in architecture. Don't be irrational."

"Yes, Peabird," he squeaks.

"It's up to me to keep you safe now. Father and Mother would want that, wherever they are. I want the best for you. You have the ability to attain it. I have faith in you, Cricket." My own eyes begin to fill. "Even when you don't."

He doesn't say anything. I put my arm around him, and he throws his arms around me. And I know that he's still my little Cricket and always will be.

I coach him on his wu liu practice during the rest of White Hour. I mime the moves, since I want to preserve my blades and my right knee now that I don't have the dragon tail coil on that skate anymore to cushion my landings or help me leap.

After White Hour, I head toward the Conservatory of Music. There's a scroll posted in front of the rails leading there. It says that Sensei Madame Yao suffered a gong injury and that we're each to spend the hour in private practice by ourselves.

As I watch Suki skate into the practice room, I have an idea. I skate back to my dormitory chamber and get the Chairman's little trinket. He must be trying to send me a message. Suki taunted me during the second Motivation about lobbing bombs at the pagoda. Maybe the oddly heavy trinket is some sort of tiny bomb. Maybe the Chairman gave it to me because he thought that if I were the vandal and used one of these trinkets to attack the pagoda, giving one to me would scare a guilty reaction out of me. Maybe I can do the same thing to Suki. If Suki really did attack the pagoda with a trinket like this, nothing would be sweeter than baiting the trap with it.

I'm going to put it outside the practice room that Suki goes into. If she's guilty, she'll want to hide it as soon as she sees it. I'll conceal myself in the sound-insulating hedges of the pearl sculpted to look like *loropetalum* bushes. When I see Suki open the shoji and pocket the trinket, I'll summon a sensei to search her.

However, I'm slowed down by the weight of the trinket hanging around my neck and my damaged skate blade. When I get to the Conservatory of Music, everyone has already chosen a practice room. How am I going to find which one she's in? The shoji doors are solid pearl without windows. I skate down the rows of rooms arrayed in rings around the central performing stage.

I go past all the rooms lucky times, but there's no way to tell. I've already wasted half the practice hour. I don't care about ranking highly in music, since it has no impact on my wu liu ranking, but Sensei Madame Yao is sadistic and I don't want to give her any reason to humiliate me in front of Suki. I decide that I'll put the trinket outside her dormitory chamber tonight instead.

There's only one practice room available, with a ten-stringed zither, which is an instrument I need more work on. As I close the shoji behind me and prepare to kneel down on the pillow to the instrument, I notice that there's a little cradle on the floor, and in the cradle is a real pearlflute! They are so prized in Shin, not even the Empress Dowager has one.

The guidebooks said that the pearlflute has the sweetest sound of any wind instrument, like silver and rain made into music. It must never be played while contemplating worldly matters, because the pearlflute is said to make music that's not of this world, and doing so will cause the Chi in one's body to be confused. It must never be played out of doors for fear of calling all birds within hearing to descend on you, since all birds want to sing with the pearlflute, like all people want to live in Pearl.

I can't resist picking it up. This can't be a communal practice instrument. It's too valuable. The pearlflute is marbled with swirls of cream on cream. The colors tease at flashing lavender and rose as I turn it. I press it to my lips and blow.

The sound is so much lovelier than the books said. It's powerful but precise. Not like the volcano drum, which flattens everything in a radius around it. It's as if this sound seeks out every person within a half li and trills a private concert just behind each person's ear. As the note dies down, I realize too late that everyone in every practice room must have just heard me blow the pearlflute.

I quickly set it down right as the shoji door slides open with such force that it bounces back in its frame.

"Who blew my pearlflute!" *Aiyah*, it's Suki! Stupid me. She stands in the doorway, twirling a little pearlsilk parasol over one shoulder and wearing ludicrous high-heeled skates. Her face swarms with vicious satisfaction.

"Excuse me, this room is taken," I say with more calm than I feel.

"You blew my pearlflute! I heard you."

"It must have been someone else playing their pearlflute."

"Only three students at Pearl Famous have a pearlflute, and the only other first-year is a boy!"

"You must be mistaken."

"You can't blow someone else's wind instrument without consent! Especially a pearlflute! Now you've really done it, Shinian snake."

I push past her and skate out. To my surprise, she doesn't follow. The clouds in the Season of Spirits help cover me as I speed down the row of practice rooms.

A great noise arises within the walls. It's the sound of little metal balls clattering down mazes. I turn back and see Suki with

126

the emergency cord in her hand, surrounded by her court of girls from the House of Flowering Blossoms, all of them clutching parasols and wearing high-heeled skates.

I look at them standing there, shoulder to shoulder, almost humming with power. Power over me. Power that I gave to them.

At the sound of the alarm, everyone comes out of their practice rooms to see what the matter is. The gaping students crowd the path.

"Let me through!" I say, pressing past, but I'm slowed down by the trinket hanging around my neck. Suddenly, Suki's hand is yanking my hair.

"She blew my pearlflute! You all heard it?"

Students murmur that they did as they gather closer around us.

"Disgusting! Don't put it to your lips again, Your Grace!" cries Etsuko.

"She eats bleached bladder stones!" screeches Noriko.

Suki twists her fist in my hair so that I'm forced to face her.

"Now you've truly failed to keep the monkey pleased. Everyone, you're all witnesses! She defiled my pearlflute!" Suki says. "Further evidence that she is a spy sent to steal or destroy everything!"

"Leave her!" says a deep voice. Everyone turns. Doi stands there, fingers pointed and arm pulled back in the ibis spring-bow position.

"*Wah*! So protective!" sneers Suki. "Is she your girlfriend?"

Doi flings herself toward Suki, but I cross my arms and block her.

"Fighting outside of wu liu class will get you in trouble!" I cry out.

"Listen to your little girlfriend, Doi," says Suki.

Doi shoves me out of the way. She leaps and splits her legs out in a double flying halberd butterfly at Suki's head but I quickly chop her feet down with my palms like cleavers so that they miss their mark.

"Stop!" I shout. I can't let Doi get punished for my sake again.

I hear the sound of metal slicing toward us and kick my skate back by instinct. I block Suki's skate right before it slices into Doi's bare shin.

"Stop! Both of you!"

Suki and Doi hurl toward each other, trapping me in the middle. I use the blades of my skates to block Suki's blades flying at Doi's head and limbs and use my fist and elbows to knock the trajectory of Doi's punches away from Suki.

Doi punching from the left; Suki spinning from the right. Doi lunging from the front; Suki leaping from the back. I'm fighting both of them and it's like writing the same words with both hands at once. My reasons for fighting the two of them are so different but also the same. I'm fighting Suki to protect Doi. I'm fighting Doi to protect Doi. And I'm using only defensive moves to protect myself.

Suki pushes away from Doi and me. She leaps into a triple mantis spin and flies at me with her skate blade pointed straight at my chest. I try to come out of the backward double-elbow block that I'm using to hold Doi back with but I'm too late to block Suki. The steel of her blade strikes me straight in the chest.

I gasp for breath and look down, expecting to see red.

There is no wound. With shaking hands, I pull out the cord around my neck from the front of my robe. She hit the trinket. It saved me.

Doi tries to lunge around me at Suki, but I turn and check her body with mine. Doi and I are face-to-face as she huffs at me, "Do you understand the situation you're in, you fool? You can't afford to be caught fighting!" She kicks her skate under my right skate, where the dragon tail coil used to be, and the impact unbalances me and sends me sliding outside their reach.

There's a burst of motion and the sound of skate blades slicing against each other and a cry and then Doi and Suki are standing apart, panting. Suki's sleeve is slashed, and where the fabric has split, a long scratch starts to seep with blood. Everyone gasps.

Then Suki is on Doi, and there's the metal clash of blade blocking blade as they charge each other and retreat and parry in open, vicious combat. I clamber to my feet, but I can't enter the battle without getting injured myself. I've never seen people aiming flying lotus spins at each other's throats with unpadded blades. It's thrilling and sickening to think that these moves can kill. Their equal skill is the only thing keeping blades from contacting skin further.

Suki uses her parasol to parry and double her reach and springs it open to serve as a shield. She lunges forward and thrusts its point toward Doi's eye. Doi grabs a lucky-stringed *erhu* from the rack next to them to block. The point of the parasol pierces into the instrument with a thrum. Suki throws them aside, grabs a spoon fiddle, and raises it to smash on Doi's head.

Suddenly, the air rings with a deafening *bwong!*

Everyone freezes and turns to look toward the sound. At the far end of the hall, Sensei Madame Yao is rising from the wreckage of a gong, which she managed to actually crack this time.

"What is going on here?"

Sensei Madame Yao skates toward Doi and Suki with one arm in a sling. Her eyes smolder with fury. "So this is what the legendary Sensei Madame Liao teaches you, to fight in music class like vicious cannibals? Come with me! You are both disqualified from the third Motivation!"

CHAPTER
LUCKYTEEN

There is a feeling when you land on your skate incorrectly and you already know before the flare of pain that you've made a terrible mistake. That's what going to classes is like in the weeks after the other senseis confirmed Sensei Madame Yao's punishment.

There are only fo—I mean lucky Motivations left this year. Doi and Suki are both going to forfeit a sixth of their grades. Because of me.

Why didn't Doi just ignore Suki's taunts? I appreciate her protecting me but not at this price. And now, because Doi protected me—her rival—she's given me the chance to overtake her in rankings. I know I should be glad that my path to gaining first ranking is clear, but instead I want to vomit.

Doi and Suki have been coming to wu liu class less and less.

Why should they risk injury training when they'll receive zero points at the next Motivation no matter what?

At least the fight seems to have postponed Suki's plan to punish me for blowing her pearlflute. She hasn't said anything about it to the senseis. However, I know that she can't have forgotten. She's just waiting for the moment when I expose a weak spot so she can shove the spear in as deeply as possible.

That's why I have to find a way to prove that she was responsible for the attack on the pagoda—to take her down.

Whenever I think of what Doi must be feeling toward me, I know I need to thank her for what she did for me. Every time I try to approach her in the weeks after the fight, she skates away. But I have to thank her. Even if she doesn't want to hear it, I need to say it.

Finally, one morning before wu liu class, I knock on her shoji door, as everyone is already headed to the Conservatory of Wu Liu.

"Go away," she says from within. Her voice is so low and so strained, I can barely hear her through the shoji.

"Doi, I just—"

"I don't want to hear it."

"May I enter?"

"No."

"I want you to know that I am so, so grateful—"

"Save it."

"I'm trying to—"

"I said I don't want to hear it."

How do you embrace a wall?

"Oooh, you two have so much to talk about!" says Honking Girl as she skates past me.

"Go," says Doi from behind the shoji. "Before Meizi starts gossiping about us plotting something."

"Who?"

"That girl. Why do you still not know anyone's name here except for the top-ranking girls?"

"I know plenty of names."

"Name them."

"Suki. And Etsuko. And Mitsuko. And Chiriko. And Mariko."

She says nothing, as if in victory.

"And Hisashi," I continue.

Again, her maddening silence. Ten thousand years of stomach gas. She would rather be burned to death than be wrong.

"And Cricket," I blurt like a fool. She makes me angry and say stupid things.

"And Hong-Wei and Masa!" I say. "Those second-year boys."

"You mean Hong-Gee and Matsu."

"That's what I said."

"No."

"So now you know better than I do what I just said?"

Why does she have to win every argument?

"I came to Pearl to become a legend," I continue. "Not to learn names of random people who no one knows anything about."

What an irritating conversation. I came here to say thank you, and instead she's intent on disagreeing with everything I say.

She says, "That knee is never going to last on that broken blade if the third Motivation requires any significant jumping. You're going to lose and get injured."

"Thank you. You always know the perfect thing to say."

"You should get better at Chi healing. You're pretty weak at it."

"You should mind your own business."

"And stop doing those ending flourishes on your moves," she says. "No one here's done those for fifty years."

Why am I having this senseless argument with this impossible girl through a piece of paper? I turn from her shoji.

"Peasprout, remember the first Motivation?" Doi calls out. "Suki cheated and put something in the powder pit that turned into pebbles when it got wet. If she comes at you about the pearl-flute, mention that to shut her up. She won't want to get expelled."

After some effort, I manage to stuff my annoyance down enough to say "Thank you."

Doi's warning comes back to me that evening, in Eastern Heaven Dining Hall. There is a serious chance that I could lose and be injured, or else I'll have to allow my left skate to bear the load of all the landings, which could break the coil on that blade.

As soon as Supreme Sensei Master Jio is finished saying "Ahihahaha!" I already know that his next words will contain my doom.

"Sweet, little embryos, the first-year girls' third Motivation will be . . . Vertical Battlefield!"

The same as the boys' second Motivation. The Motivation that is composed almost entirely of jumping. Conducted on the roofs of the Pagoda of Filial Sacrifice. An eight-story structure.

The next morning when we begin training for Vertical Battlefield, I notice all the other girls have switched to skate boots with reinforced impact absorbers. The other students have so many different combinations of blades and boots, for jumping, for precision, for performances, for formal ceremonies, for dancing, and even for drinking tea anemones.

I have only these two boots and these one and a half blades.

Some part of me wants to just forfeit this Motivation. Save my knee for the other Motivations that hopefully won't be as hard on it. It would also make me feel less guilty for making Doi get disqualified.

What am I saying? My top two rivals are eliminated from this Motivation and I want to throw away my only chance to pull ahead of them? Nobody said that becoming a legend of wu liu was going to be easy. If I wanted easy, I could have stayed in Serenity Cliff.

I'm just going to have to find some way to strengthen my knee.

Sensei Madame Liao has begun to lead us in brief Chi practices before and after every wu liu class to warm up and cool down. After the warm-up Chi practice, I raise my hand.

"Venerable and mighty Sensei," I ask, "are there techniques of Chi practice that strengthen joints?"

"All Chi practice can be focused to bring healing energy to a particular point on the body. But it requires a great amount of Chi."

I raise my hand again. "How much would it require?"

"A lot," Sensei Madame Liao says slowly. "It takes years of meditation practice to summon that magnitude of Chi energy. But it is possible to receive Chi energy sent from another person."

I'd heard about this back in Shin, but since it never worked for me, I figured it must be just superstition. I sneak a look to see if anyone is laughing at my questions.

Sensei Madame Liao continues, "It doesn't work for those with only weak relationships, though."

Why is she looking at me?

"The closer the relationship between the sender and the receiver," she says, "the stronger and faster the transfer of energy and the farther it can travel. It is called Chi entanglement."

Why would I want to have my Chi entangled with somebody else's? I don't want to rely on anybody that much.

"If the relationship is close enough, two people who are Chi entangled can send Chi instantaneously, regardless of distance, and can understand when the sending is interrupted."

I shoot my hand up a third time. "And if you don't have such relationships?"

"It's especially powerful between siblings. Especially twins."

Nonsense; I tried it once with Cricket. He tried to send Chi energy to me and I felt nothing. I tried to send it to him and he said it gave him a sinus headache.

"Although," she finishes, "the relationship might not help if either the sender or the receiver is somehow . . . blocked."

That wasn't much help. I guess I'll just have to work on building muscle strength so my right knee can take the impact of the jumps.

Sensei Madame Liao teaches us moves that will help us leap most efficiently between the tiers of the Pagoda of Filial Sacrifice, meaning that they give us a lot of vertical lift but with little wasted horizontal displacement. Everybody gasps when she demonstrates a riven crane split jump, but then we realize that it wasn't done with a one-legged backward flip. It is a mock riven crane split jump and it is done with a backward flip and a half twist, which makes you land facing the opposite direction of how you started and therefore cancels out the jolt of the landing impact on the knee. Although it is far less beautiful than the authentic riven crane split jump.

I'm glad that there are moves that can spare my knee, but I still avoid doing the jump since it uses the placement of the liver for its center of gravity and thus can only be done on the right leg. I skate to a corner and pretend to be getting ready to do jumps instead of actually doing them like everyone else.

Chiriko and Etsuko are watching me. They and the other House of Flowering Blossoms girls have been doing their best to make up for Suki's absence by taunting me whenever Sensei Madame Liao can't see or hear. Chiriko and Etsuko look at each other, do a mock riven crane split jump in unison, and look at me. I can't show any weakness. I look back at them and do a mock riven crane split jump in return. I land hard on my damaged right blade.

They unscrew and snap off their skate blades, which are perfectly undamaged, and toss them in the trash bin. They smirk at me, their eyes spiteful under their bangs. They screw on new blades and do two mock riven crane split jumps in rapid succession, the coils of the blades under their heels absorbing the impact. I do two of the jumps in rapid succession and land on my right skate with a double punch of force into my knee.

The girls again snap off their perfectly good blades, throw them in the trash, and put on new ones. They do three of the jumps in rapid succession and land balanced on their right skates, their left skates lifted high.

I swing my knee into the air and fling myself into three of the jumps in rapid succession, one, two, *snap!* My broken blade lands wrong on the third jump and a pain shoots through my knee like a shaft of steel.

Everyone turns to look at me as Chiriko and Etsuko skate away, smiling with satisfaction.

My knee is twisted. I can feel the heat coming off it and see it already starting to swell with fluid. It's going to be bad. Stupid me, why can I never resist taking their bait?

Sensei Madame Liao has me sit out the rest of the class. After the other students leave, she comes to me.

"When we were little, my younger sister and I had a game. I would think of an object. Starting in one corner, my sister would place her finger on a square of a chessboard in front of her. If she felt me sending a pulse of Chi energy to her at that moment, she would place a marker on that square. If not, she would leave it blank. The patterns of the marked and unmarked squares would form a picture."

I understand the meaning of Sensei Madame Liao's story, but there's no way that Cricket can send me pulses of Chi energy to help heal my knee. I want to tell her that Cricket doesn't have the capabilities of other boys. That he's allergic to his own saliva. That he's afraid of moths. But I don't.

Sensei Madame Liao says, "Do not be so quick to judge deficiencies. Sometimes, they are just advantages that are interpreted incorrectly, like trying to read a logogram turned upside down. Your ignorance of wu liu moves that involve more than six steps, for example."

"I've learned thirty-eight of those moves now, and my memory palace Chi practice is greatly improved."

"I'm not criticizing you." Sensei Madame Liao rests her hand gently on my shoulder. "There is a strength hidden inside your ability to glide on one step. You could cross five li in five steps. No one else here can do that."

She makes it sound like I'm an innovator. It's true that to preserve my skates, I learned to stretch each step like a Meijing opera singer can hold a note. I invented a technique to sling my center of gravity so that I whip forward in loops on one skate for a very long time. But I wasn't trying to innovate. I was just trying to save money.

"How's that going to help me in the third Motivation?"

"It's not. But one day, the third Motivation will be over. And you will still have your skills."

"It's not a skill; it's just a crutch. I don't want to need a crutch."

She looks at me as if she's about to say something she wants me never to forget.

"At the time of the Great Leap of Shin," she says, "the population of Pearl was five-sixths female, since so many men died in various wars against Shin over the years. This seemed a deficiency."

My Chi seizes up at this. Any time a Pearlian brings up the Great Leap, it's not to say nice things about Shinians.

"Before she fled to the island of Pearl to seek refuge, Little Pi Bao Gu was a courtesan in Shin, where her owners abused and scorned her for her childlike size. This also seemed a deficiency."

So she appreciates that Little Pi Bao Gu came from Shin. What does that have to do with the deficiencies in my wu liu training?

"However," she continues, "as a dancer, Little Pi Bao Gu learned that there are many things that require smallness, litheness, and balance more than brute strength. Martial arts and skating are two of them. So she combined these two things."

I know. She took the "wu" from *wushu* to indicate that it was a martial art and the "liu" from *liubing* to indicate that it was descended from ice-skating.

Sensei Madame Liao says, "She invented a martial art that took advantage of how female bodies are different from male bodies so that the island of Pearl could turn five-sixths of the population into warriors rather than just rely on the small remaining male population. With that, she created the force that stopped Shin from invading Pearl."

Where is all this leading?

She goes on. "And since then, everyone in Pearl honors Little Pi Bao Gu, the failed courtesan and refugee, as much for the lesson she taught them as for creating wu liu. Do you know what that lesson was?"

"What?"

"Heroes come in all shapes and sizes."

As I unroll my bed that night and lie down to sleep, my heart is still touched by Sensei Madame Liao's beautiful words.

I need to think of my deficiencies differently. And Cricket's. Perhaps our deficiencies are truly just advantages that need to be read the right way. Perhaps there is a way he can learn to send me Chi healing. We should try that game that Sensei Madame Liao and her sister played with the chessboard when they—

I sit upright in my bed.

I need to find the sketch that I drew of the pattern that Doi made in the boxes at the Courtyard of Supreme Placidness.

What if she wasn't just meditating? What if she was receiving pulses of Chi energy from somebody to make a picture?

I find the drawing and unroll it. I look at the black and white squares forming a picture of a box with ears and little feet.

I realize that it's not a picture. It's a logogram. I just couldn't understand it because I was reading it upside down.

I turn it right-side up. My Chi goes cold.

It's blocky but legible as *zhi*.

The ancient word for *hostage*.

Does Doi know something about the Empress Dowager's plan? Is she connected to the Empress Dowager somehow?

Whom was she receiving pulses of Chi energy from?

Could she have been talking with Zan Kenji and Zan Aki, since they skate with New Deitsu Opera Company and their fathers know each other?

Or maybe *hostage* wasn't referring to the mayor's sons at all.

Maybe it was referring to me.

CHAPTER
FIFTEEN

The only thing that I am certain of is that Doi was not responsible for the attack on the Pagoda of Filial Sacrifice. Suki's continued insistence that she told everyone this was going to happen makes it clear that the attack was part of her grand plan to use every weapon she can to get me expelled or arrested.

I'm just grateful that there's no way that she could plausibly accuse Cricket of having the skills to cause the kind of damage we saw done to the pagoda. I should warn him never to talk to Suki, though.

The next morning, I look for Cricket after the morning assembly on the Principal Island of the academy. I don't see him among the first-year boys headed to their literature class.

I find him backed up against a pillar covered in carvings of curling eels. A girl is standing in front of him, talking to him.

It's Suki.

I pump my skates to reach them and swallow down the spikes of pain in my knee.

"Get away from him, you witch!"

She turns to me and smiles. "Cricket and I were just having a very interesting conversation. It seems that you weren't the two best skaters in Shin."

"How dare you?" I say. "I was the Peony-Level Brightstar and wu liu champion for all of Shui Shan Province five times before—"

"You might have somehow managed to win some village contests. But this one's never won anything. So tell me, why would the Empress Dowager send him to represent Shin?"

She's going after Cricket. He is my soft spot that she's been looking for.

"And he's done so well in the first two Motivations," Suki continues. Cricket seems to crumble as he finally realizes his mistake. "Twenty-seventh in the last Motivation. Tied for last in the one before it. Two poor performances could be coincidence, but three is evidence. As soon as the third Motivation is done, I'm going back to *Pearl Shining Sun* with his miserable result. And with this."

She reaches into her sleeve and pulls out her pearlflute, which she slaps against her palm like a weapon.

"It's exactly like I said. You're not really skaters. You're just spies with enough basic skills to pass for skaters."

What did Doi tell me to use against Suki if she came after me about—

That's right! The thing that Suki put in the powder pit at the first Motivation that turned into pebbles when the other girls got their socks wet.

I smile at her and say calmly, "Why do I make you so uncomfortable, Suki?"

"You wish."

"You look very uncomfortable, like you've got a pebble in your sock." I skate closer to her. "Don't worry, all you have to do is turn it upside down, and whatever it is will be *expelled*."

Suki's face goes from sourness to confusion to rage.

"You don't have any evidence!"

"One way to find out, right?"

"You wouldn't risk me going to the newspaper."

"Try me, Suki."

She seethes and sputters, but all that she can finally say is "Infuriate me to death!"

I grab Cricket, and we skate away quickly. Once again, Doi has saved me from Suki.

Cricket has to do better at the third Motivation. Our safety depends on it now. My stomach clenches when I remember that the boys will be doing Links of Eternity, a pairs combat exercise where each boy must keep hold of at least one of his partner's hands while performing moves.

Back home in Shin, Cricket only learned girls' moves. He learned mostly jumps, spins, and evasions, not punches, chops, and tackles.

The first and second Motivations only involved racing and jumping, but now he's going to be doing combat against boys employing boys' moves. There's no way he's going to survive, much less place well. He can't ask the senseis for special tutoring. And what boy would be generous enough to spend time to teach a potential rival?

Hisashi's kind face comes into my mind. I can't expect him to choose to pair with Cricket. Hisashi's ranked fifth. But I have to try to persuade him and explain why it's so important that Cricket do well. I make up my mind to tell Hisashi about the ivory yin salts.

He's never easy to find. It's clear that he doesn't like crowds. I look for him where there are no gatherings of students. He's not at the Courtyard of Supreme Placidness. Maybe he knows that Doi meditates there, so he avoids it. He's not at the edges of the Principal Island. There are only Shinian servant girls washing the shore with buckets and brushes where the sea laps at the pearl.

After making a quarter circuit of the campus, I find Hisashi riding the rails between the Conservatory of Architecture and the Conservatory of Music, where they slope down so far that they must actually sink below the waterline at high tide. He's wielding a two-handed staff, dipping it into the sea in graceful, precise pinwheels, and coming up with ribbons of a sea vegetable.

Before I skate close enough to say anything, he looks over his shoulder and smiles. As if he knew he would see me here, and as if nothing could please him more.

He takes off his smoked spectacles and hops around to face me while skating backward. Doing this on winding rails over the open sea should seem like boastful skating, but there's nothing boastful in his manner.

"I was just thinking about you," he continues. But when he sees the expression on my face, his smile disappears. "You have something serious to discuss. Let's go someplace quieter so I can give you all my attention."

I follow him along the rail leading to the Conservatory of Music. A tower rises out of the sea on the northern side. The tower is skirted with a balcony formed of sculptures of the Great Benevolent Jade Council of Divine Tortoises. He does a deft little double-heel syncopation and pops off the rail and onto the balcony with a confident one-footed skid that's all boy. A boy's move I've never seen before and that Cricket hasn't, either.

I copy his move but misjudge my release of Chi a bit and end up colliding into him. He steadies me with a hand around my hip. I start to think that I liked that part, but then I see that there's a pot of stew simmering over a fire.

"You left this open fire here?" I ask.

"I only had wakame left to collect." I assume that *wakame* is the Edaian word for that long sea vegetable.

"Unattended?"

"What do you mean? The pearl doesn't burn," Hisashi says. "You knew that, didn't you?"

I open my mouth to say that of course I knew, but I close it, feeling stupid. Of course the pearl can't burn if it's always near water and spray. Every structure here seems to have a waterfall flowing down its side, or else it's planted in the middle of a pool or rising from the sea itself. Will I never figure out anything here? Here, in this place, I'm ignorant of something that every child probably knows.

Hisashi looks into my face. He says carefully, "I've always wanted to visit Shin. I think I'd want to see the Great Wan Hua Temple in the Codpeak Mountains first."

I know he's trying to make me feel less lost here. But thinking about that temple made of dried chrysanthemum petals only makes me feel how far away I am from Shin.

He continues softly, "I'd feel lonely being so far from home if I didn't have friends in the Codpeak Mountains waiting for me."

He's kind. Maybe I can convince him to help Cricket after all.

Before I can speak, he says, "I really do want to hear what you have to say but if I don't add the wakame now, the fashion soup porridge will be ruined."

He stirs in the sea vegetable that he calls wakame. He ladles the porridge into the bowl and presents it to me. "I only brought one bowl."

When I taste it, I almost cry. Other than the wakame, it's like the savory morningmeal rice porridge that we have back in Shui Shan, woodsy mountain flavors of coarse-grained rice, fleshy black mushroom, fragrant wood ear, mustard tubers, sweet potato, eight-horned star anise, and sesame oil. It could use some salt, but otherwise, it's the first food I've had in months that hasn't been torture to eat.

"I've thought about rice every day since leaving Shin."

"We don't eat much rice in Pearl."

"I noticed," I say between exquisite bites. "Why?"

"After the Great Leap of Shin, the tsunami left most of the fields too salted to grow rice in. We planted cotton instead and traded it with Eda for millet and sweet potatoes to keep from starving. After a time, people stopped missing rice."

"Is that why everyone here loves Edaian things so much?"

"In part."

"But Shin and Eda are enemies. And Pearl belongs to Shin."

"Not anymore. And Eda helped us after the Great Leap."

Two hundred years later and they're still blaming us for the Great Leap. Are things really so tense between Pearl and Shin? Why didn't we hear back in Shin about how bad things are with Pearl? What situation has the Empress Dowager sent us into?

I bite into something in the porridge that I don't recognize. Some savory vegetable or root that's both fibrous and crisp to the bite. It's delicious. I pick a slice up with my eating sticks.

"What's this?"

"Bamboo shoot."

"Real bamboo?" It feels like eating something out of legend. "I never saw bamboo in Shin."

"Of course not. That's why your country invaded Pearl. Shin used up all its own bamboo and wanted ours."

"Do you mind if we don't talk about the Bamboo Invasion? Or anything about politics?" I've lost my appetite. "I just came here to study wu liu."

"You're right. That's what my father was hoping for. Cultural exchange. He's under so much pressure. No wonder he didn't stop to see us. He's really busy. I'm not upset at all." He smiles.

I came here to ask him to help Cricket, but there are so many other things I want to ask him, too. About Doi in that bird costume and her reaction after their father left without seeing her and whether it's true that their father hasn't visited them in years and Suki's ridiculous claim about their father causing the death of their mother.

I don't ask any of them, because I don't want to upset him. I need him to be open to my request for help.

I quietly finish the porridge and thank him. He fills the bowl with the remainder in the pot for himself.

"I'd like to tell you a story," I say. "Did you know that in Shui Shan Province, wu liu is a sport for girls? It's not like Pearl, where there are separate forms for girls and boys. Any boy who wants to learn it learns girls' moves. Which require a girl's body.

"Do you know what ivory yin salts are? They suppress the development of yang in the body. Once you begin using the salts, they keep your body lithe and your voice high. But you stop growing, and everything stays the exact same size as when you first started taking the salts.

"Everyone in my village knows the story of one boy who started taking the salts when he was just six years old. No one had ever allowed a child to begin taking them so young because it interferes with the development of the heart and lungs.

"He did it because his parents had to disappear to escape a harsh law passed by the Empress Dowager and left him to be raised at a wu liu school. He thought that if he worked hard, he would be able to attend a great academy of wu liu, join an opera company, become a legendary performer, and get rich and famous enough to find his parents.

"However, over the years, he got older, but he barely grew. The boys around him began to turn into young men. He also learned that he would never be as good at wu liu as he had hoped. So he finally started to understand the price he had paid to follow a hope that turned out to be just a tendril of a shadow of a dream."

I watch this story settle into his heart. Hisashi says, with shining eyes, "That boy should have been here."

"That boy is here!" I give him time for the shock to sink in. "And Cricket needs all the help he can get to do well at the third Motivation. So much depends on it now, with all these accusations in the air about us not really being wu liu skaters. Cricket sees some rich, handsome boy who never goes to class take fifth ranking with no effort, when he himself needs so desperately to do well, when he has sacrificed more for this than any of us will sacrifice for anything in this life. I beg you to help him do well; I beg you to teach him the boys' moves that he needs to learn!"

We stare at each other in silence.

"You think I'm handsome?"

I gape at his breathtaking arrogance. He smiles.

"I'm sorry, I shouldn't have tried to make a joke. Believe me. Your words have pierced me as they should. If I don't show it, it's just because my heart is more raw right now than I'm used to showing. I promise I'll help Cricket in his wu liu in any way that I can. Now, I need to leave you because my heart is breaking and I don't know you well enough yet to let you see that, but thank you. May we meet here in the New Year."

"May we meet here in Pearl," I say, a bit stunned.

Hisashi bows, climbs onto the rail, and skates back toward the Principal Island. When he's out of view, I take to the rail as well and skate in the opposite direction, to the sound of waves kneading below my skates and of blood beating within my ears.

CHAPTER
SIXTEEN

As soon as I see Supreme Sensei Master Jio rush into our wu liu class on the morning of the last day before the third Motivation, I know something is wrong because it's the first time that I've seen him without a smile on his face.

He summons Sensei Madame Liao from our training and reaches into his sleeve. When she sees what he produces, she dismisses the class.

As he turns away, I see in his hand a letter orb.

That afternoon, we arrive at the Conservatory of Literature to find a scroll that says class has been canceled.

In the sky, the drifts of mist seem to be caught in an unusual air current. Then we hear the squawking.

"New. Deitsu. Dancers. Send. Letter. Orb. Claiming. That. Empress. Dowager. Threatens. To. Bind. Their. Feet. If. She. Does. Not. Receive. The. Secret. Of. The. Pearl. Chiologists. Agree. That.

There. Is. No. Blockage. In. Tone. And. Dancers. Were. Not. Speaking. Against. Their. Will. Buy. Pearl. Shining. Sun. News. To. Get. Whole. Story."

This has to be a lie. The Empress Dowager would never bind the boys' feet. She'd have to break the bones in their feet and fold them in half to bind them. They'd never skate again. They'd barely be able to walk. And Zan Kenji and Zan Aki are boys. Only girls ever have their feet bound in Shin because they consider it a sign of feminine delicacy. This is all just a slur against Shin by *Pearl Shining Sun*. The Empress Dowager's never done anything that unreasonable.

Except for the Bamboo Invasion. And the Tianshang Birthday Party Incident. And the Baby Catbear Bonfire. But those were different because now Cricket and I are here, and she would never do something that would endanger us.

All the girls are looking at me. Suki begins stamping her skate on the pearl. The other girls take up the beat. They stamp in time, all of them staring at me, not caring if they're cutting up the pearl, harder and harder, until the sound feels like blows. I hop on the rails leading away from the Conservatory of Literature.

I have to find out what the Empress Dowager is actually doing to the New Deitsu skaters because it's putting Cricket and me in a terrible position. Doi must know something. Why else would she be receiving Chi pulses from someone about a "hostage"? She must know Kenji and Aki through New Deitsu. As soon as the third Motivation is over, I need to focus on this.

However, right now, it's most important that Cricket and I do well at the third Motivation to prove that we really were sent here because of our wu liu abilities.

I skate to find Cricket so we can do one more Chi healing session before the third Motivation tomorrow. To my surprise, the Chi healing sessions with Cricket have been helping my knee. However, I can't get the balance of Chi flow back and forth between us right. Cricket sends me Chi energy for me to direct to my knee, but it drains him terribly. Then I have to spend twice as much time sending him Chi healing, drawing energy from every part of my body other than my injured knee, and that leaves me exhausted.

He needs all the Chi energy he can get. Hisashi spends every White Hour teaching Cricket essential boys' moves, and another two hours after evenmeal. As much as I am grateful for this, my heart throbs with soreness when I see how utterly depleted Cricket is at the end of every day.

The morning of the third Motivation, my knee is still throbbing with excess heat, but the swelling has gone down to the point where I can't see it anymore. Sensei Madame Liao states that Doi and Suki have been instructed to stay in their rooms during the Motivation as part of their punishment for fighting. At least I don't have to worry about Suki trying to distract me. Thank you, Sensei Madame Liao.

When the Motivation starts, we swarm up the eight tiers of the Pagoda of Filial Sacrifice like a cloud of black locusts. Most of the girls try to claim a space on the highest tiers they can, but that is a strategic mistake. To eliminate an opponent, we have to knock her down to the ground level. It's better to get a girl down on the first tier and force her off from there than from the top level.

I stay on the first tier and hope to avoid combat. When a girl comes down to my tier, I fight her, but I am free to use long glides on my left skate along the circular rim of the roof of the tier, conserving my right knee and my skate blades.

Most of the girls get swept up in the excitement of the Motivation and start unnecessarily using third- through sixth-gate level jumps just to intimidate each other. The moves are flashy and risky, and before long, there are only two other girls left in the round beside me: Chiriko and Etsuko.

They each start to hop down from their tiers toward me. If I stay here, they're going to trap me from the left and the right. I hop up onto the second tier. To my surprise, the roof of the tier flexes as I land on it! Of course! The thin tiers are just ornamental, and they don't bear any weight. Perhaps I should have paid more attention in architecture class.

I hop to the eighth tier and race to the center of the circular space atop the roof and begin to spin. As Chiriko and Etsuko jump up to the top tier, I unleash a sweeping leap in a circle across the roof. The impact blows Chiriko clear off the roof so that she lands on the ground near the entrance of the pagoda near Sensei Madame Liao and the other girls. Etsuko goes flying off the back side, but she manages to grab the first tier and haul herself up. I leap down there, alternating between left and right skates.

As soon as I land, Etsuko spins and takes an illegal swipe with her blade straight at my throat. I flip back and catch her skate with the jagged broken end of my right blade. I use the force of my flip to whip her down onto the ground. She hits so hard that she bounces just as Sensei Madame Liao and the other girls come racing around.

However, I was so surprised by Etsuko's illegal attack that I can't stop my own fall, and I tumble through the air. It doesn't matter if I touch the ground now, since I am the last one, but the force is too strong in too small a space. I don't want to crush my knee or make my left blade take all the impact, and I don't have time to right myself, so I land on my two hands.

Pain screams through my left wrist, but I hold my position because everyone is looking. I push off my fingertips, land on my feet, and string two seventh-gate spins together into a beautiful ending flourish in the shape of a calligraphic figure. I bow to Sensei Madame Liao.

Afterward, as the other girls begin to disperse, Sensei Madame Liao asks me quietly, "Your knee?"

"It holds."

"Give me your wrist."

I wince as she holds it.

"Not broken. But you won't be able to do any combat with that arm until it heals."

She pauses and says, "Not bad."

I don't know why, but these little words fill my heart with warmth.

She continues, "But enough with those ending flourishes. You look like my mother."

Ten thousand years of stomach gas. Doi was right. Again. But still, I took first. That puts me back in first place in overall rankings. I know that would never have happened if Doi hadn't gotten herself and Suki disqualified from this Motivation.

I need to go thank her. I begin to skate back toward the dormitory. Then I think of Cricket alone among all those boys at their Motivation. Was Hisashi's extra coaching enough to help Cricket from failing terribly? Whom did Cricket convince to partner with him?

A great cheer rises from the direction of the Radial of Mighty Tranquility. The boys must still be doing their third Motivation. The girls never cheer for each other like that. I skate toward the noise, but I stop. I really need to go thank Doi now. Another cheer comes roaring from the boys' Motivation. I can't resist.

I arrive at the great, circular arena on stilts over the water. The crowd chants, "Twelve! Thirteen!" Hisashi is in the center of the court. He and his pairs partner are working as a team to fend off two powerful attackers.

The two boys they're fighting must be older boys brought in to administer the Motivation because they seem like giants next to Hisashi and his partner. I can't tell if they're second- or third-years from the trim on the front seam and cuffs of the robes because they've stripped down to the waist. Waves of corded muscle flutter and dance under their skin at every movement. I recognize them! They're the two kind boys who ate with me my first day at Pearl Famous, Hong-Gee and Matsu.

Hisashi holds his partner's hand, swings him at the older boys, and shouts out a move. Hisashi's partner performs it, landing another toe kick on their opponents! The older boys move with so much flowing power, it's like watching a pair of lunging tigers. However, Hisashi and his little partner flutter aside with moves that are boys' moves but executed with as much nuance and efficiency as girls' moves. The older boys are no more able to catch them than tigers can catch moths. The crowd counts out each contact they make in their unbroken string of landed strikes on the older boys.

After they've strung together sixteen strikes, one of the older boys finally manages to land a backhanded chop on Hisashi and his partner. Their hands separate and they go flying into the audience, taking down half the circle in twin tsunamis. They stop just before sliding off the edge of the arena into the sea below.

The crowd applauds as Hisashi and his partner stand and clap and bow at their opponents. The two older boys, still clutching hands, bow their powerful frames low to Hisashi and Cricket, and then each extends a free arm out to them. They clasp forearm to forearm in that gallant and glamorous grip that pilots of battle-kites do with their comrades. Everyone is smiling and applauding, and— Heavenly August Personage of Jade, it's Cricket! Cricket with Hisashi! Cricket scoring against those boys! My little Cricket.

I skate to them. I never minded Hisashi's lack of the traditional physical traits desirable in boys his age. Now I'm grateful for it, because he's showing Cricket that a boy who doesn't have a rumbling voice and a muscled form can still be a champion of wu liu. He's showing Cricket that heroes come in all shapes and sizes.

I babble at Hisashi and I'm saying something about "My

gratitude—" and "What you did for Cricket—" and "The beauty of your wu liu—" and he's turning so red that he looks more girl-ish than ever, but I don't care, because I'm telling him he's "the bravest, truest boy I've ever met—" and at this moment, I worship this boy, this "generous and humble and brave—" boy, not for the courage of his wu liu, but for helping Cricket see that those gifts are still alive in himself and just waiting to be born.

I stop, because my eyes begin to mist, and Cricket's eyes begin to mist, and I don't know if Hisashi's eyes begin to mist, because I'm too emotional to look him in the face.

I simply say, "Thank you for what you've done for my brother."

"Did you do well in the third Motivation?" he asks.

"Yes." I start to tell him the details, but I'm suddenly ashamed, because I would not have done as well as I did if Doi and Suki hadn't been eliminated.

"I need to go see how your sister is doing," I say.

As I ride the rail leading from the Conservatory of Wu Liu, it hurts me to think of Doi believing for one moment more that she's unappreciated. I've decided that I'm going to be her friend. Even if she refuses to be mine. That's her business.

There is also a part of me that realizes that if I gain her trust, she might tell me whom she was talking to about a "hostage" and what she might know about what the Empress Dowager is actually doing with Kenji and Aki.

As I skate down the dormitory hall, I hear Hisashi cry out behind me, "Wait! She won't want to see you. She's probably not even in her chamber."

"She has to be. Sensei Madame Liao ordered it."

Hisashi pauses and says gently, "She's my sister. Let me talk to her first."

Hisashi and I skate to Doi's door. It feels like we're approaching a tiger to make it take a pill it doesn't want to swallow.

Hisashi knocks softly. There's no answer. "Doi," he says as he slides the shoji open a crack. His voice is kind, like the sort of brother every girl could admire. He slips in and closes the shoji behind him. I can't see their silhouettes or hear their voices.

Mere moments later, the shoji opens. Hisashi hurries out and closes it. His face has gone pale.

He puts his hand in mine and leads me away from Doi's dormitory chamber.

I ask him what Doi said. He doesn't reply. He's protecting me. He doesn't want me to know what she said about me.

He takes me to the Hall of the Eight Precious Virtues, the highest structure on the academy campus. We fling ourselves up each of the hall's ten tiers of roofs. He directs my gaze to the city of Pearl across the water. It spreads in cream terraces from the waterfront up the side of the mountain so completely that no green is visible.

"Peasprout, you were kind enough to tell me Cricket's story," Hisashi says finally. "So I'd like to tell you Doi's story. When my sister was ten years old, she became the youngest person ever to win first ranking at the Season of Glimmers Pageant of Lanterns Wu Liu Invitational because of her routine, 'The Dragon and the Phoenix.' She played the phoenix. A train of skating *taiko* drummers with black lacquered drums formed a twisting, thundering dragon chasing after her."

Immediately, I think of Doi in her bird costume.

"The moves she invented for the phoenix became legendary. Little wing flutters and furtive glances behind her. Crossing her feet and taking little steps on the points of her toes. Pulling her arms and one leg back up behind her in a spin, like a spiraling blossom. Baby phoenix Doi.

"Just a few years ago, that whole city out there cheered for Doi. Except for one person. Do you understand?"

No wonder the costume was tight on her. It'd been years since she'd worn it. She wanted her father to see her in it. Why wouldn't he stop to see her?

I don't know what their family history is, but I know how it feels to be unappreciated. I know what it is not to be seen for what you are.

I say slowly, "The Empress Dowager's hair has never been cut. Once a year, it's woven strand by strand into the tapestries that adorn her throne. The throne is composed of living tortoises that are trained to stack themselves together for her to sit on. She only sits on it once a year to name the Peony-Level Brightstar. All that for me. But now, here, in this place, people laugh even at my soap. So yes. I understand."

CHAPTER
SEVENTEEN

"**I** need to say something to you," says someone behind me.

I haven't heard her hoarse voice in weeks.

After missing the third Motivation, Doi dropped to twelfth place. Every time I tried to talk to her, she would skate away. And this is the sister of the boy who helped Cricket bring his ranking up to eleventh place after the third Motivation, because of the special weight given to pairs scoring in boys' moves. It's true that I wanted to try to get the truth out of her about why she was talking to someone about a "hostage." But I also did want to thank her.

"Doi! I've been trying and trying to talk to you and tell you how profoundly sorry and grateful and humbled and—"

"Shut up, please. No one makes my choices for me. I only want to say something about the luckieth Motivation."

"Yes, I know your performance will be legendary," I cut in.

"As soon as Supreme Sensei Master Jio said we would be doing Iron Fan Dance, I knew that you would excel because the fans are like knives when folded up, but they can be snapped open and thrown, like flying metal saws with the handles weighted on one side so that they arc back to the thrower, and I saw how you handled Suki with the opening and closing of her parasol, and I knew that—"

"Shut up, please. I just wanted to tell you that I've decided what my Multipliers will be and—"

"And the Multipliers are so important," I agree. "Our entire score is going to be based on how many hits each of us blocks and how many we score on our opponents before being disarmed or falling, and they apply one negative Multiplier for every piece of armor, so the less we wear, the more we risk, but the more we score and the higher—"

"Peasprout, shut up! What I'm going to do during the luckieth Motivation will make up for what happened with the third Motivation if I do it correctly, but I'm—"

I stiffen, but I do the right thing and say with dignity, "I will not resent you at all if you take first place. You have my blessing. But just in this Motivation."

"Will you shut up and listen to me! I'm going to pay a price for what I plan to do. I want you to know that I know what I'm buying with it. And that it has nothing to do with you." She bows and says, "May we meet here in the New Year."

"May we meet here in Pearl," I reply.

As I watch her skate away from me, so hard, so determined, I'm certain that a price that others would call too costly, too desperate, she would call necessary.

What could Doi be planning for the luckieth Motivation? Iron Fan Dance will be the most dangerous Motivation that we've done so far, especially because it's the Season of Spirits. The thick cloud cover that haunts the ground will hide the flight of the deadly fans. We'll have to learn to use the clouds as a central element of combat, so our sense of hearing will be critical in predicting and defending against attacks.

Boys don't do Iron Fan Dance because only girls are lithe and nimble enough to do it. Boys would be cut into ribbons.

At least my knee continues to hold up due to the Chi healing sessions with Cricket, although the exchange leaves us both so drained. As for my injured wrist, there's no way to deny that it's bad. Just the pressure of doing the fastens on my skate boots every morning makes it throb with pain. It's not going to be better by the luckieth Motivation.

I try an additional session of Chi healing on my wrist with Cricket. He almost passes out from exhaustion in the middle of it.

"Cricket, what's wrong?" He looks like a shriveled husk.

"I just need to rest a moment."

"We have to stop. You need to save your strength for the next Motivation."

"It's all right. We're just doing Emperor's Second. It's just a race and not even for first place."

"You're going to be doing ten laps inside the Palace of the Eighteen Outstanding Pieties. Have you seen how big it is in there? And then you're going to fight a mass battle at the finish line."

"Everyone will be fighting to push someone over the finish line and then leap for second place. I'll just stay off to the side and sneak . . . sneak over . . . when it's . . ." He closes his eyes, and his head begins to hang in utter depletion.

My poor little Cricket. I can't put him through any more of these sessions to heal my wrist. I'll just have to work around it.

Thus, it is with great joy that I listen to Sensei Madame Liao explain that the most critical skill in Iron Fan Dance is defensive strategy.

"You think you've used defensive moves in the first three Motivations," she says. "Your understanding of defensive strategy is trash! Defense is more than wearing armor and employing tortoise-school moves and using your skates to block."

When she mentions this, Suki and the House of Flowering Blossoms girls start tittering and smirking at me.

I can't afford to use my skates to block. They could get chipped and ruined. Also, the weight of any armor on my arm causes pain in my wrist. It's even more painful when I receive a blow on my armor. I can't afford to get struck on that arm with or without armor. I'm going to have to rely on dodging maneuvers for the Motivation.

"Some of the most powerful moves in all of wu liu are defensive," continues Sensei Madame Liao. "The Dian Mai are a class of moves used to neutralize an attacker through disruption of Chi. I demonstrate for you the five-point bone-shatterer hollow fist. Come here." She points to Mole Girl, who skates forward slowly.

Sensei Madame Liao makes a loose fist, faces Mole Girl, and says, "If I strike the five essential meridian points on her body with a hollow, not closed, fist, I could immobilize my attacker until I could seek help to bring her to justice. Come. Attack me."

The poor girl looks at Sensei Madame Liao, then at all of us in a silent cry for help. *Sorry, Mole Girl. You're on your own with this one.* With a face full of misery, she cries, "Yah!" and raises her arm to do some sort of simple chop. Before she's even begun to bring her arm down, Sensei Madame Liao executes four swift but soft strikes on Mole Girl.

"If," Sensei Madame Liao lectures us, "I were to strike the fifth essential meridian point, every bone in her body would shatter if she takes six steps. Thus, she would be locked in an invisible, wall-less prison. For, as ancient Pearlian wisdom teaches us, 'the steps of an honorable person lead through walls; the steps of a dishonorable person become a prison.'"

Mole Girl freezes.

"It's all right," says Sensei Madame Liao. "The meridian points don't lock if the fifth one isn't activated right away." Mole Girl slowly returns to our ranks and appears ready to faint.

I raise my hand and ask, "Venerable and mighty Sensei. What if you had completed the five strikes? How would you remove the Dian Mai?"

"Only the most powerful instruments of Chi retuning can re-move the Dian Mai. However, use of Dian Mai moves is strictly forbidden to students and punishable by expulsion. I raise them as an example only to make you appreciate how worthless and completely without qualities your understanding of defensive strategy is."

Suki follows me after class and says, "Are you worried about how to remove the five-point bone-shatterer hollow fist Dian Mai when they imprison you for attacking Pearl Famous?"

"Suki, why are you so obsessed with me? Get a hobby."

In the final week leading up to the luckieth Motivation, I concentrate on my defensive wu liu practice. The pain in my wrist decreases with twice daily Chi practice, but my ability to bear armor with that arm is still compromised. I start to think about the Dian Mai. Could whatever ominous thing Doi is planning for the luckieth Motivation involve Dian Mai somehow? Could she be planning to take down Suki in front of the whole academy in some spectacular way, even if she gets expelled for it?

Maybe she's planning on not using any torso armor to goad Suki into dropping her torso armor, too, so that she can hit her in the five essential meridian points and perform the five-point bone-shatterer hollow fist on her? I don't think she's that rash, but what do I know about her except that everything she does hits me as a surprise.

Then I realize what this would mean for me.

If Doi uses the Dian Mai on Suki during Iron Fan Dance, that would take out both of my opponents again. Doi would be expelled or arrested. And even if Suki weren't sliced to ribbons while immobilized and they could retune her Chi somehow, she would be knocked out of the Motivation. There would be no way that she could recover and overtake me.

If Doi uses the Dian Mai on Suki, my path to first ranking for the whole year and the lead in the Drift Season Pageant is cleared.

What am I saying? I can't believe I'm considering this. I want to win. But there's no honor in winning like this. I consider what Hisashi would think of me using his sister this way and I'm ashamed. He makes me want to improve my character. He would want me to do something to try to stop Doi.

I put the thoughts of trying to capitalize on the rivalry between Doi and Suki out of my mind and concentrate on my defensive practice in the final days before the luckieth Motivation.

The night before the luckieth Motivation, my emotions are uncollected. As I lie on my bed, I suddenly realize how I can help Doi.

Students can volunteer to serve as attackers to gain extra points during Iron Fan Dance. Most girls don't want to because the additional points aren't worth the risk of injury. But it's too late to sign up. I'll have to be prepared to jump in and interrupt the Motivation if Doi starts to perform the Dian Mai. I don't know if I could be punished for interfering with her performance. Also, perhaps if she sees me trying to help her, I can win her trust and get her to tell me why she was talking to someone about a "hostage."

I don't know if Doi is my friend or my enemy, but tomorrow, I might have to fight my friend or my enemy for her own good.

I don't realize I'm asleep until I'm wrenched out of it by the sound of shrieking from the hallway. I wrap my robe around myself and fling open the shoji door. The clatter of metal balls within the walls begins vibrating through the air over cries and the sound of shojis slamming open.

Girls are streaming out of their dormitory chambers in the dark, racing down the hall with their futon-side lanterns swinging, making shadows pitch and yaw like reaching ghosts.

"What happened?" I ask a girl skating past.

"The Palace of the Eighteen Outstanding Pieties!"

"What about it?"

"There's been another attack!"

When we approach the Palace of the Eighteen Outstanding Pieties, I see plumes of vapor billowing out of the top. We skate into the palace. Sensei Master Bao, Sensei Madame Liao, and other senseis are in furious discussion.

I follow their gaze to the roof.

There's a hole torn in it, large enough to sail a ship through. Its edges aren't jagged and ripped. They're smooth, like rock formations sculpted by drips of water over uncountable ages. The edges steam with tendrils of vapor that rise up into the dark sky through the hole.

Below, rows of rough, featureless mannequins of straw wrapped in white-plastered cloth have already been stationed around the racetrack laid out on the skating court for the boys' luckieth Motivation in the morning. They stand like a ghostly, silent army.

Parts of several mannequins lie crushed around the track.

Straw has burst out on the pearl in front of their faceless plaster heads, sprayed in the patterns of fans.

A great wedge from the ruined ceiling as large as a carriage has fallen with such impact that its point is buried deep in the track, right at the starting line.

CHAPTER
EIGHTEEN

How did Suki do it? Even if those trinkets are explosives and she could get her hands on large amounts of them, why didn't we hear anything? And explosives wouldn't make a hole whose edges look like they've been licked apart, not ripped.

Two vandal attacks now. And the Empress Dowager's threat to bind the hostages' feet if she doesn't get the secret of the pearl. And *Pearl Shining Sun* waiting for enough evidence from Suki to write my name and Cricket's across the sky for everyone to read.

I don't know how she attacked the palace, but her purpose was clearly to upset me right before the luckieth Motivation, to get her revenge. And she's succeeded.

"She could have killed someone!" screeches Suki. "She's threatening to kill us if we don't give the Empress Dowager the—"

"You're the one trying to kill us," I yell back.

"Silence!" says Sensei Madame Liao.

We're sent back to our dormitory chambers to try to sleep until morning comes, but I lie awake all night.

In the morning, Supreme Sensei Master Jio announces that the boys' Motivation must be postponed. However, the girls' Iron Fan Dance luckieth Motivation will go forward this morning as planned.

For me, the whole Motivation proceeds in clouds. Clouds roam across the Radial of Mighty Tranquility while each girl competes against her attackers. Clouds roam through my mind as my concentration on the Motivation competes against my thoughts about the attack on the palace.

Suki does well. She takes on ten attackers wearing nothing but a pair of forearm gauntlet shields, a torso plate, a sleeveless pearlsilk top, a pleated skirt, and pearlsilk underclothes, of course.

Sensei Madame Liao announces, "Disciple Chen Peasprout will be skating to Multipliers of ten attackers, wearing seven articles including two pieces of armor."

I choose the same number of attackers as Suki did and wear the same armor except I don't have a gauntlet on my left arm because of my injured wrist. So my Multipliers are higher than hers, but so is my risk. I skate onto the court.

I look at the practice mannequins standing on the perimeter to act as shields against stray fans. I think of the head of that mannequin burst open, the soft bodies crushed under the wedge of the ceiling on the starting line of the boys'—

An iron fan comes flying through the air at my unarmored arm.

I dodge just in time. *Be here now, Peasprout.* I focus my Chi. Then I do a forward flip and sling one of my fans back at the row of girls in front of me.

My opponents don't rely on just their armor to block my fans; they also use their skate blades to block. I'm relying on dodging and reversing direction and twisting with mostly hummingbird-school moves, because I don't have much armor and I can't afford to use my skates to block.

I quickly discover that my deficiency is actually a great advantage. The fact that I have less armor doesn't just mean that I have a higher Multiplier, it means that I can dodge and use defensive maneuvers much better than the other girls can. It also means that I am not as weighed down and thus can glide on my skates to preserve my knee and blades.

Finally, as the court rings again and again with the sound of my opponents' skate blades blocking my fans, I'm noticing more and more of them stumbling as they skate. My fans are nicking their blades! However, they aren't permitted to stop the Motivation to change their skate blades. They've never had to preserve their blades before like I've had to and thus they are no match for someone who can make her blades last.

I finish, triumphant and panting for breath. I end up placing slightly higher than Suki.

When Doi's turn to skate comes, the dread hurts my stomach like monthly cramps. I know that Doi's about to do something unforgettable and terrible. And that I might be the only one who can stop her.

When she skates out, the cloud cover is so dense that I can barely see her. There's only a pale figure. At first, I think that she's one of the practice mannequins.

Sensei Madame Liao announces, "Disciple Niu Doi will skate to Multipliers of ten attackers, wearing two articles including zero pieces of armor."

The whole crowd of girls gasps. As the clouds slightly part, I see Doi in the middle of the court. She's only wearing the thin, white underclothes that we all wear under our robes. No armor.

No, Doi, don't do this!

A few of the senseis are whispering and complaining to Sensei Madame Liao, but she's unmoved. She takes out a scroll, scans it for a clause, and stabs her finger at it. The other senseis cluck, but Sensei Madame Liao says firmly, "That is final!"

She turns back to Doi and nods.

The clarion sounds for the combat to begin. My stomach twists again when I see that Suki and her House of Flowering Blossoms girls have volunteered to be among Doi's ten attackers.

However, even as they sneer at Doi, they're uncertain how to proceed. Iron Fan Dance is no child's game. Iron Fan Dance can injure, even kill. Doi can't afford to be hit by even one fan. As much as the girls hate Doi, they hesitate. No one has ever fought ten fully armored girls while being completely unarmored. As the girls look to Suki for guidance, we hear the whistle of two fans cutting through the air. The ten attackers leap, then duck, to avoid being shortened a foot from both ends by Doi's flying fans. Tired of waiting, Doi has started the battle on her own terms.

The skating court stirs into action. It starts as a game of shrouding. Doi uses the end of her fan to stir the clouds floating about into little balls that she whips at the faces of her attackers. However, it doesn't provoke them into throwing their fans at her in earnest. They're still afraid of being punished if Doi ends up leaving the Radial of Mighty Tranquility in twenty pieces. They only throw their fans in coordinated sets of three or more and clamp down together in a huddle as her fans fly at them in tortoise-school formations, which gain Doi no points.

Doi has no choice but to spend all her time dodging. They refuse to use any throws that can be blocked or that can leave them open to her scoring a hit on them, even if that means they have no chance to gain points from her. They don't care about that. They only want to prevent her from earning any points until she lashes out in frustration and does something rash or injures herself.

When Doi sees that her tactics aren't working, she begins doing one real riven crane split jump after another, aiming directly for the attackers' throats to try to force them into engaging her in earnest. The girls around me gasp, not only because of Doi's savagery, but also because everyone knows that the real riven crane split jump can only be done 608 times in one's lifetime before the knee bearing the force of the landing is destroyed forever. She's wildly wasting jumps over and over again, as if we have as many riven crane split jumps in us as words.

Suki and the other attackers still don't engage her properly and continue throwing fans only in conservative, unblockable formations. The irritation is clear on Doi's face. She still hasn't scored any points. What good is a towering Multiplier if you don't score any points to multiply?

Finally, Doi throws her fan at the attackers. While the fan whips through the air, slicing the billowing clouds like egg custard, she races toward the girls. They brace for her blows in a ten-faceted tortoise wall, but she doesn't strike them. She skates straight at two of her opponents. As she nears them, she does a strange twisting single-toe flip that I've never seen before. She flies up over two of the girls, bunching their lengths of hair together with one hand as she rises. As she pulls their hair taut, her flying fan returns on its arc and slices through the girls' hair.

Everyone screams. I don't know if this is an illegal move, but for the House of Flowering Blossom girls, just touching another girl's hair without permission, much less amputating it, would be a vicious and open declaration of war.

The combat comes alive. Suddenly, the girls are flying at Doi from ten sides, skates, closed fans, and spinning open fans churning like a storm of knives around her. We all scream with excitement as we watch Doi block and dodge and pull and throw and parry and weave, all while stretching the clouds into ribbons and balls that she whips into the faces of her opponents.

The attackers realize that Doi has blocked every one of their strikes and that, during their attack, they have just given her at least eighty points to be multiplied. Suki nods to them to assume a new formation. They skate away and form a ring around Doi.

The girls open their fans, but they don't throw them. Instead, they all leap up and bring their fans down hard on the pearl. The rush of air goes racing across the pearl, blowing the cloud cover away, tightening in a circle that collides at Doi. The gust shoots straight up her figure, lifting her top pearlsilk garment into the air. Suki leaps to snatch it and flings it over the mannequins ringing the Radial of Mighty Tranquility into the sea. Hateful, vindictive girls! If they can't beat Doi, they want to humiliate her.

It's like I'm watching that horrible dream where for no reason, I'm at school naked in front of everyone, except it's really happening to Doi, and it's not a dream; it's happening before my eyes, and it's happening because she missed the third Motivation, and she missed the third Motivation because she protected me against Suki, and she protected me against Suki because I blew Suki's pearlflute and lied about it. I want to curl into a ball. I'm unable to watch, unable to turn away.

The ten girls' fans have swept away all the clouds from the arena. Doi's standing there, covering her exposed torso with one arm.

The attackers launch their fans at her. The girls throw them at an angle so that the fans don't arc back. Instead, they travel at twice the speed in a straight line for the girls across the ring to catch and then throw back. The attackers launch salvo after salvo of these throws at Doi. She fields them valiantly, but one of her fans is knocked out of her hand, and it flies off to impale itself in one of the mannequins ringing the court. She's now fighting with one fan while desperately trying to cover herself with her other arm. I can't help but fold my own arms across my chest in horror and sympathy.

Then Doi stops resisting. With a stony expression, she takes her one fan in both hands, and from that moment onward, she doesn't bother covering herself up. She's completely vulnerable, but her wu liu form is confident. She claps one open palm on top of the other, with the spread fan pressed between them. She spins sixteen and a half rotations and releases the fan straight at Suki.

Suki is prepared for it and is already coming out of her own sixteenth and a half rotation when she receives the blade. They're engaging in the thousand-tiered pagoda to heaven challenge.

Suki receives the spinning fan but doesn't stop it. She meets it at the exact speed and arc and, instead of disrupting that force, continues it, whipping it back at Doi but adding the accumulated Chi of her own sixteen and a half rotations, which Doi returns and sends flying back at Suki even faster. The other girls step back to give Suki full room to maneuver.

The fan flies faster and faster, each combatant hoping that the other will make a mistake and miss the return. By the seventh circuit, the fan is spinning with such speed and traveling with such velocity that the air is ringing with the high hum of singing metal.

After the completion of the tenth circuit, the metal is flying so quickly that I can barely see it. As Doi receives it, instead of catching it with her hands, she kicks it into the air, causing it to roll on its axis as it travels back toward Suki. Each roll causes it to wobble in its flight path. The spinning fan weaves in and out between the girls as if they're an obstacle course, cutting the straps that bind their face, breast, and gauntlet armor in place.

As the blade finally buries itself in a mannequin, pieces of armor fall to the pearl in a great clatter. The attackers are unmasked and unarmored, down to their pearlsilk underclothes. The senseis haven't tallied the points and Multipliers yet, but they don't have to.

We all know that that girl, standing there heaving with exhaustion, has not just finished first at this Motivation.

That girl, uncovered but unharmed, has just done something legendary.

That girl, stripped but unashamed, has just made academy history.

CHAPTER
NINETEEN

After the luckieth Motivation, Doi's ranked first, I'm second, and Suki's sixth. The first-year boys' Motivation will be delayed a day longer than last time. I guess that this is because the damage to the Palace of the Eighteen Outstanding Pieties was much worse than what happened to the Pagoda of Filial Sacrifice.

I wish it were delayed even longer, because I know that when the New Deitsu team comes, Chairman Niu will want to see me.

Suki continues whispering to the other students at every opportunity about the attack on the palace. "You see! The Empress Dowager won't stop until she has the secret of the pearl, no matter how many hostages' feet she binds or how many structures her spy destroys!"

However, it appears that she still hasn't taken her claims to *Pearl Shining Sun* yet because I don't see my name or Cricket's written in birds. Maybe she knows that she doesn't have enough evidence.

Maybe she believes that I have evidence about her cheating at the first Motivation. Or maybe it's simply that it's usually too cloudy during the Season of Spirits for Sensei Madame Phoenix and her birds to do the *Pearl Shining Sun* headlines.

Or worse, perhaps it's because Suki's too busy with her new favorite target. Doi can't seem to go anywhere without Suki and the House of Flowering Blossoms girls spewing comments after her.

"Some girls will do anything to get attention!"

"Did your father finally realize you exist?"

During literature class, Suki recites her essay about Princess Eyun Dei-Bwun. She tells us that during her reign, Princess Eyun Dei-Bwun, commonly known as the Mad Seductress of Pearl, wreaked havoc on Pearl's system of measures by constantly revising the standard unit of measurement to match the length between her hips and the hem of her dresses, which became shorter and shorter throughout her reign, until her sister had her drowned in a well for her depravity. Since the assignment was to write an essay about famous speeches by military leaders on the eve of battle, it's clear that Suki's just using this to humiliate Doi again.

During architecture class, Sagacious Monk Goom calls Doi to the front of the class to take her turn at another weird counting exercise with Chingu, the oracular monkey. As Doi skates up the aisle, Suki leans out to yank at her length of waterfall hair. Before her fingers brush a single strand, Doi has spun around and is frozen in position with her skate blade at Suki's throat.

"She's attacking me outside of wu liu practice again!" squeals

Suki, and the House of Flowering Blossoms girls all shriek like starved hatchlings.

The squealing sets off Chingu, who starts jumping from desk to desk, screeching and chopping at them with her cleaver. We cower underneath the desks as this spoiled, deranged monkey hacks at them. I don't need to be an oracular monkey to predict that the price for getting close enough to Chingu to receive an oracle is a hand, or at least a few fingers.

Doi never says anything in response to the abuse. I don't say anything, either, because I'm too ashamed to say anything. And I'm only more ashamed that I don't say anything.

There is so much rage in her. And such willingness to do things that everyone else would call too reckless, too extreme. I still don't know whom she's talking to at the Courtyard of Supreme Placidness about "hostages." All I know is that I don't know how to talk to her, because I'm a little afraid of her.

As announced, the New Deitsu team is soon here. Supreme Sensei Master Jio tells us that we're not to face south while they repair the Palace of the Eighteen Outstanding Pieties. The boys and girls are put together in a joint wu liu practice session on the Conservatory of Wu Liu. Since no one can do a complete spin or flip without facing south at some point, we're simply given the task of speed racing. Sensei Madame Liao and Sensei Master Bao have us form ten queues and skate as quickly as we can northward, and then skate back southward to return to where we started. It's a boring but dangerous exercise because it's easy to collide with another student in these tight lanes of speed skaters going in opposite directions.

Cricket accidentally hooks his arm with the arm of another student going in the opposite direction. They twirl each other around like dancing partners before taking out two more skaters with them in a terrible crash. Ten thousand years of stomach gas. All of them are made to sit out the rest of the session. Fortunately, Cricket and the skater he hooked aren't punished for momentarily facing south because they were twirling too fast to see anything.

Not long after, we hear a great popping sound. Sensei Madame Liao puts her ear to the pearl below our skates. She announces that we may resume use of all lucky directions. I turn south, but the palace is far off on the Principal Island and obscured from view by the clouds. We hop on the rails and skate back toward the Principal Island. Out of the clouds comes Cricket, skating directly into me. He's beaming.

"I heard it, Peasprout!"

"Heard what?"

"After I got taken out of the training session, I skated in the direction of the worksite."

"You didn't look at it, did you? We can't afford to break any rules!"

"No, I promise! I skated backward and stayed on the south side of the Conservatory of Wu Liu. The palace was across the water, and I kept my back to it. I heard a great sizzling sound. And then I heard water washing over something. And then there was a great popping sound."

"I heard it, too. Don't go near it again. Wait here."

I leave Cricket and the other students and senseis. I skate toward the Palace of the Eighteen Outstanding Pieties. Clouds obscure it, but when the wind changes direction, they part.

The palace is completely restored. The sloping roof is covered in tiles like a dragon's scales, as if nothing happened.

Someone grabs my arm. I feel the long nail of the Chairman's little finger digging into my sleeve.

I cry out, but there aren't any senseis or students around. He hauls me toward where the New Deitsu team is gathered.

We enter the palace. Within it is a structure I have never seen before. A small, simple pavilion with a sloped roof and a door. He pushes me inside it. I have to duck to avoid striking my head on the lintel.

He remains outside.

"So the Empress Dowager sent you here to learn about the pearl, little bird?" he says. All his false smiles and charm are gone, and I no longer see any resemblance to Hisashi. "By attacking the structures and seeing how we rebuild them?"

"I didn't have anything to do—"

"Since you want to learn about the pearl so badly, I will share a fact with you. You have noticed all the water that flows over and throughout every structure here? What do you think it is for?"

From the way he asks, I know that it's not to keep the pearl from burning.

He continues, "Seawater keeps the pearl from shrinking. There is a law in Pearl that gives New Deitsu Pearlworks Company authority to punish criminals who threaten the secret of the pearl. The criminal is sealed inside a structure. Then we cut off its supply of seawater. The structure shrinks around the criminal day by day until he's slowly crushed to death."

I'd thought that Pearlians were so different, so evolved. They can be just as brutal here as the Empress Dowager.

"All that's left at the end is a miniature black structure, small enough to wear as a pendant. We have a chamber full of these trinkets at New Deitsu," the Chairman continues. "If you are endangering the secret of the pearl, you could be number 2,021."

The trinket. On the pendant. That I put in my mouth. That's why it weighed so much. It was the body of a prisoner trapped inside a shrunken structure shaped like a tiny pavilion.

Like the pavilion I'm standing in now.

I try to push my way out, but the Chairman and his team block me.

They're going to seal me inside it.

But they can't legally do that! I take a deep breath to calm my Chi. They don't have enough proof. That's why he hasn't thrown me in prison yet.

He's just trying to intimidate me.

The Chairman starts pounding on the roof of the pavilion above me to scare me, like a boy taunting an animal in a cage.

He's pouting! Because he can't figure out a way to beat me!

How can I get him off my trail?

By finding the true criminal who caused the attacks.

But how do I do that?

I try to focus my Chi, but it's hard with his palm beating on the roof and the pavilion ringing around me like a war drum, as if he were a spoiled, deranged—

That's it! I know how to find out who the criminal is!

"Stop it!" I cry. "I'm going to prove to you that I'm innocent."

The beating sounds stop. The Chairman ducks his head down to peer at me. "How?"

"I know the identity of the true criminal. I just need to gather the evidence."

I begin to press my way past him. He tries to push me back into the pavilion.

"Let me go so I can get you your evidence. Or do you want to wait until another attack happens?"

"You're not going anywhere, you disrespectful, corrupt, lying girl!"

"Yes, I am. Because you don't have a choice. And you know it."

The Chairman steps back. His eye is twitching.

"See," he says. "This is why I hate children. You'd better hope that another attack doesn't happen before you get your evidence."

I skate away as quickly as I can and don't look back until the palace is out of sight. I stop and catch my breath.

Why didn't I see it before? It should have been so obvious how I can prove that I'm innocent and find out who the true criminal is.

I have to consult Chingu, the oracular monkey.

CHAPTER
TWENTY

At the Skybrary at the Conservatory of Literature, on a platform high above the central atrium, on the fifth tier of shelves that required me to do fifth-gate grasshopper double jumps while bouncing between columns to reach them, I find the *Master Record of the Academy Rules and Statutes of Perfectly Upright Character*.

I note with relief that statute 547 states that if someone accuses someone else of causing damage to the property of the academy, the accuser must bring proof. That's why Suki and the Chairman haven't been able to do anything to Cricket and me, yet. They only have inferences and allegations.

I consult the index, then flip to foundational principle of values number thirty-nine, which states that Chingu, the oracular monkey and earthly vessel of heavenly enlightenment, is never incorrect. Her oracles are always presumed true, though the interpretation may be inaccurate. Thus, if Chingu makes an oracle identifying a criminal, it's presumed to be valid proof to satisfy statute 547 unless the criminal can show that the interpretation was flawed.

So that's how it's going to happen. It's strange to see in this book in my hands an oracle of how I'm going to take Suki down. I snap the book shut with satisfaction.

After White Hour, before class at the Conservatory of Music, Suki and the House of Flowering Blossoms girls skate to me. They've adorned their academy robes with hundreds of luminescent, feathery, gold scales that wave and shimmer as they move. They look as if they're being eaten alive by a school of goldfish. Sensei Madame Yao has not arrived yet, so the girls see their chance to squeeze in some abuse. Since Doi's not in class today, I'm the target.

"So," begins Suki, "have you decided which structure you're going to attack next, Stealthiest Skater in Shin?"

"Oh, Suki, is that you under all that gold?" I ask. "I thought someone was being attacked by a gingko tree."

"*Wah*, so she's an expert on fashion now! In prison, you'll be able to wear the latest fashions made out of discarded turnip sacks."

"You should know," I say, "that I intend to consult Chingu, the oracular monkey, and ask her who is attacking the structures of Pearl Famous. Enjoy your last few days at the academy, Suki. You had some talent, but you had more hatefulness."

"Is that supposed to scare me? Make me die of laughing!" She giggles behind her hand, sending waves fluttering through the gold scales on her robe.

Sensei Madame Yao arrives, and so the insults end there. It would have felt good to deliver a last slice.

That afternoon, I visit Sagacious Monk Goom and Chingu. They live in a little temple on pillars rising directly out of the water off the southeast edge of the Principal Island.

I knock the suspended pole against the bell hanging outside of the front door to the temple. I immediately hear the sound of shrieking from within.

Sagacious Monk Goom opens the door. "Very nice. Very nice."

Inside, Chingu is seated on top of a sort of great box, large enough to seat two people inside, made of ornate pearl lacquer carved with maps of stars. She's screeching as if she's being boiled alive, hacking at the box with her cleaver, and baring her fangs at us.

"Venerable holy Sagacious Monk Goom," I say, bowing. "Ten thousand obeisances of gratitude for the honor of granting me an audience with you."

"Nice."

"I have never been received by so holy a man."

"Very nice."

"The students of Pearl Famous Academy of Skate and Sword are so fortunate to have so evolved a being, who almost received the bolt of enlightenment himself, serving as our spiritual counselor. How did we deserve such good fortune?"

"You're my punishment for messing it up."

I don't know what to say to this.

"Do you have any money I can borrow?" he asks.

"Ah, venerable holy Sagacious Monk Goom," I say. "I wish to consult Chingu, the oracular monkey."

"Mmm. I see. Are you sure you don't have any money I can borrow?"

"Alas, venerable holy Sagacious Monk Goom, I do not," I say.

He lets out a great sigh. "You students never do. What do you know about consulting Chingu, the oracular monkey?"

"The asker enters the box with Chingu and takes her hand. She falls into a trance, the asker asks the question, she chooses three tiles from a set of sixty-lucky, and the logograms on the tiles form the fortune. The asker's personal meditation on the meaning of the three logograms yields revelation and the oracle."

"Ah, but you'll need my assistance, won't you? What's your question for Chingu?" I don't know why he wants to hear my question, but I know scheming when I see it.

I bow and say, "Ten thousand obeisances of gratitude. But I understand that questions that one asks Chingu are very personal, spiritual matters. And that every student has the right to consult Chingu privately."

His face goes sour. "Sounds like we like to read the academy rules, don't we? But all oracles benefit from interpretation. I can interpret it for you. For a small fee."

"I roll in waves of gratitude for your generosity, but I will struggle with the mysteries of the oracle alone."

I imagine that if you blow on a bear's nose, it'd look like how Sagacious Monk Goom looks.

"Suit yourself," he says. "Yet Chingu doesn't answer questions so easily. Sometimes Chingu is very nice. And sometimes she's only nice."

When we look over at her, she hisses at us like a viper.

"You see. Today, she's only nice." Chingu's protests rise to such viciousness that she chokes and coughs out something into her hand, which she smells and eats.

"Chingu needs a nice treat before she can answer questions," says Sagacious Monk Goom.

"What kind of treat?" I ask.

"Red sorghum wine."

He's a fraud and a cheat, but he's standing between me and Chingu. "I make obeisances in all directions for the honor of your audience, venerable holy Sagacious Monk Goom. I will return with red sorghum wine for y—for Chingu, the oracular monkey."

"Mmm. Very nice."

"May we meet here in the New Year."

"May we meet here in Pearl."

I skate backward and exit the temple.

If I want to get some wine, I'll have to break academy rules and escape into the city. There, I'll have to find someone willing to break the law and sell wine to a luckyteen-year-old girl.

The last thing I need now is to be caught breaking rules and laws. But that nasty little monkey has the evidence I need to prove that Suki has been setting me up. Rules and laws are great, but rules and laws are what made my parents disappear. So if wine is what it takes to get the proof I need out of Chingu, I'm not going to let rules and laws stop me.

CHAPTER
TWENTY-ONE

Two hundred and fifty Sukis. That's how I see the academy now that I'm planning to sneak off the campus into the city. Any of the hundreds of students could see me climbing onto the gondola rails leading back to the city and violating the academy rules. Any of them could report my suspicious behavior that seems to confirm Suki's accusations and *Pearl Shining Sun*'s headlines. It's like Suki's just grown 498 extra eyes.

I could try to sneak out after dark, when the academy is asleep. The second- and third-years take turns patrolling the campus at night, but I could learn the patterns they travel during their watch. However, all the markets in the city are closed at night.

The week after my visit to Sagacious Monk Goom and Chingu, the answer is presented to me, because something extraordinary happens to day and night: they switch places. It's the first day of the Season of Glimmers. During this season, the seas around the city of Pearl glow at night due to the luminescent plants and octopuses that migrate here during this season. The glowing sea life even works its way against the current, up the canals and aqueducts, turning the waterways into rivers of light. Pearlians harvest and use them as decorations during the Season of Glimmers to turn Pearl into a city fashioned of stars.

The whole academy goes nocturnal for the Season of Glimmers. Classes, Motivations, and meals all take place at night. We sleep during the daylight hours.

However, this reversal is just an academy tradition. The rest of the city of Pearl maintains its regular schedule of business. Thus, during the day, the academy sleeps but the markets remain open. I can sneak into the city during the day, as soon as I finish the next Motivation, since almost everyone at the academy is occupied for half a day with the conducting of each Motivation.

The Season of Glimmers brings me a way to get the wine for Chingu, but it also brings the Festival of Lanterns that will take place on the night before the fifth Motivation. This year's festival will mark its two hundredth anniversary, so the whole city of Pearl will celebrate it with fanfare. Despite all the worries on my mind, I'm excited. We have lantern festivals in Shin, but they're nothing like this.

From the eager whispers of my classmates, I learn that the entire academy will be decorated with lanterns made out of luminous octopuses. During the festival, everyone rows in boats into the glowing sea. They net octopuses and place a funnel into the beak of each one. They tie its arms into a bow to make a little basket, which rests under the cone of the funnel. Into this basket, they place a burning coal. The hot air rises through the funnel into the mouth of the octopus, filling it so it floats up. Beautiful shifting patterns of color swarm over the creature's skin as it ascends.

I'm excited to have a chance to wear my flower dress at the festival. When I was young, before our parents disappeared, our mother took in other people's washing for a year to save enough to buy the material for it. I know it's not very high-grade material and that, in all likelihood, the rich students here only use this kind of material to polish their skate blades. However, it has folded cloth blossoms sewn all over it. It's the best piece of clothing I've ever owned, and I want to wear it for Hisashi so that he can see that I'm not just a great wu liu warrior. I'm also a girl.

However, I can't let such thoughts distract me. I have a plan to get into the city, but once I get there, I still have to find someone willing to sell wine to a luckyteen-year-old girl.

I doubt that any of the other students would know anything about the practices in the markets. Even if they've grown up in the city, they probably don't do the market shopping. Parents or servants do that for them. And here at Pearl Famous, everyone has everything that they eat and drink provided for them in Eastern Heaven Dining Hall, so they would never have to shop for—

Hisashi. He never eats in the dining hall because everything has animal parts in it.

He must have secretly been going into the markets in the city all year long! He got that wakame from the sea, but not the star anise or the sweet potatoes. Hisashi would know where in the markets someone might sell me red sorghum wine.

Hisashi will help me get the wine to give to Chingu to receive the oracle to prove my enemy and clear my name and make Cricket and me, at long last, safe.

I don't see Hisashi for over a week after the luckieth Motivation. I finally run into him crossing the Bridge of Serene Harmony. I almost skate past him because his uniform isn't decorated with luminous octopus slices like everyone else's. Further, the lantern he carries isn't an octopus lantern but one of the regular frosted pearl-plate lanterns.

"Good midnight, Peasprout."

"Good midnight, Hisashi. Are you excited about the Season of Glimmers Festival of Lanterns? I never imagined I'd be here for its two hundredth anniversary."

The smile on his face dims.

"What have I said?" I ask him.

"I'm not going to the Festival of Lanterns." He looks at me directly. "Those luminous octopus lanterns? Their bells swarm with light and wild colors like that because the octopuses are still alive when they're being filled with hot air. Eventually, the coal under each one grows so hot, it ignites the digestive gases in the animal, causing it to burst like fireworks. Entire schools are harvested and killed to supply the Pearlian market during the Season of Glimmers."

I'd assumed that he didn't eat meat because he loved animals, but it hadn't occurred to me that that would extend to the octopuses because I hadn't thought of them as animals. How tenderhearted he is to love even things that are so different from us. I knew what the lanterns were made of. I just hadn't stopped to consider the cruelty and suffering in it.

"You think the seas are beautiful now?" He sweeps an arm toward the water. "Nine years ago, before they started celebrating the Festival of Lanterns, the waters around Pearl were a sea of light. The octopuses will probably all be gone in another nine years."

"What do you mean 'nine years ago'?" I ask. "I thought this was the two hundredth anniversary."

"Ah, I thought you knew. It's only the ninth year of the festival. The company that sponsors the holiday didn't see acceptable profits in the first eight years. They thought that this year, if they called it the two hundredth anniversary and hired poets to write some invented history, people would like it more. And everyone does seem very excited. It's like the whole city is the set of a historical opera."

I get that unpleasant feeling in my chest of waking from a dream. This beautiful festival is built on suffering and lies.

"This must all seem so strange to you," he says.

"I'm not going to attend the Festival of Lanterns, either," I blurt.

"I'm sorry, I shouldn't have told you about this being the ninth year."

"Yes, you should have. And that's not the only reason. Many animals will die for no reason. It's a cruel, thoughtless tradition created for money." My heart sinks as I realize that I won't get the chance to wear my dress for him. But I can't unknow what he told me.

"Thank you." Hisashi brings his knuckles to his lips and composes himself. At last, he merely says, "Let's make our own better tradition. Meet me on the night of the festival, and we'll celebrate together."

Before I can escape into the city, I'll have to participate in the fifth Motivation. I have to get wine for Chingu to get evidence to prove I'm innocent, but I also can't let my performance suffer or Suki will pounce.

However, the fifth Motivation is unlike anything I've prepared for. I don't know why they delayed announcing it so long this time, but the anticipation has made everyone expect something very special. Even as Supreme Sensei announced it, I knew what it meant that our fifth Motivation would be "Little Pi Bao Gu and Cloud-Tamer Zwei."

We are going to do aerial combat.

"All know the story of Little Pi Bao Gu, the creator of wu liu," says Sensei Madame Liao in her proclamation voice during our next wu liu class. "Yet her achievement would be useless were it not for the contributions of Cloud-Tamer Zwei. A woman famed for her ugliness who hid from ridicule by living on the sea in floating houses that she built herself.

"After the Great Leap of Shin destroyed the first city of Pearl, there wasn't enough stone or wood to rebuild. Cloud-Tamer Zwei instead used a building resource she discovered in the waters around the island during her years at sea . . . the pearl.

"Thus, Little Pi Bao Gu created a new and deadly martial art, but Cloud-Tamer Zwei created the city that it could be performed on. So it was that a failed courtesan and an old maid together created an undefeatable army of women and girls who defended Pearl against invasion from the greatest empire under heaven. Working together, as partners. So shall you work in pairs for the fifth Motivation."

At the word *pairs*, a storm of titters arises. I assume that all the girls are plotting and considering and weighing and gossiping about whom they should each partner with so they can start training as soon as possible.

"In aerial combat, the partner above shall fight in the air using moves that are descended directly from the combat strategies of eagles and are therefore tens of tens of tens of thousands of years old. The partner below shall catch her and kick her back up into the air, skate to skate, and keep her airborne."

Kicking a partner up skate to skate? How are my skate blades possibly going to survive that? By the end of the fifth Motivation, they're going to be so saw-toothed that the only thing I'll be able to use them for is combing my hair. However, I can hardly afford not to do my best at this Motivation. Suki would use my drop in ranking to support her allegations to *Pearl Shining Sun* or something. I'm never going to skate into one of her traps again.

"You must choose your partners by the time of the fifth Motivation," says Sensei Madame Liao gravely. "Choose wisely."

The girls all hum with excitement. I soon realize that as they're talking, they're all stealing glances at the same three girls—the only three girls not talking to anyone else in the class. Suki, Doi, and me.

Suki's face looks like the masks they use in puppet performances of *The Hideous Warthog Demon of the Western Swamp*. The two people who she hates the most under heaven, the two people who cost her the third Motivation, are the two people who would be the most advantageous partners if she wants to prevail at our most difficult Motivation yet. The two people who would prefer to drink sand to death for ten thousand years than partner with her.

"Infuriate me to death!"

I look to Doi. She looks back at me. We would be unbeatable together. And maybe partnering together would gain me her trust. Then I could find out whom she was talking to about "hostages" and what she knows about the Empress Dowager's actual plans.

"Not so fast!" says Suki as she skates between us. She's afraid that we're going to pair up and form an unbeatable team.

She turns to Doi. "You know what Peasprout said about you? Peasprout said that the Chairman told her that she's the kind of daughter he always wanted."

"You lying, vicious—" I start to say.

"Don't encourage her," says Doi. "It's like leaving table scraps out for badgers."

"*Wah*, so bold!" cries Suki. "Then why did your father skate right past you like a ghost but invite Peasprout to meet privately with him every time he came to Pearl Famous?"

How did she know that? She must have been spying on me!

"And why," she continues, "did he give her that precious pendant that she was wearing around her neck?"

"It isn't a pendant!" I say.

I look to Doi, but her face is unreadable.

"Then what is it?" says Suki.

I don't know how to answer.

"And you," she continues to me. "I'm going to tell you . . ." She slows and begins to smile, pleased with herself. "I'm just going to tell you what you already know about her. Do you know what you know about Niu Doi?"

I don't give her the courtesy of a response. I won't let her drive a wedge between Doi and me.

Suki smiles sweetly and begins to skate away. She turns to say over her shoulder, "Nothing."

I stop and let her word sink in. When I turn to look at Doi's reaction, she is already gone.

CHAPTER
TWENTY-TWO

I hate relying on anyone else for anything because I hate being disappointed. But I find myself forced to rely on so many other people. I'm going to have to convince Hisashi to help me find someone in the city market willing to sell me wine. I'm going to have to choose a partner at the fifth Motivation. Only two weeks left before the Fifth Motivation and my chance to escape into the city, and I haven't made any progress on either of these tasks.

As if this weren't bad enough, a week later, Sensei Madame Phoenix comes up with the worst class assignment. She announces, "You are to form small groups and write a one-act opera based on a historical event by the end of the class hour."

A group project.

I came to Pearl to become a legend, not to work in a group with other students like donkeys leashed to a cart. However, Sensei Madame Phoenix refuses to let me work alone.

I say to her, "Sensei Madame Phoenix, I would like to do the project on my—"

The sleeping birds let out a squawk, and Sensei Madame Phoenix bats me on the head with the *Too Exciting!* paper paddle.

I whisper, "I can produce a much more beautiful script by myself about Little Pi Bao Gu and Cloud-Tamer Zwei."

"So you think you are entitled to special treatment," she replies, "just because you are the 'special emissary' of the Empress Dowager." I don't like how she says "special emissary" and I remember that she's the one delivering the *Pearl Shining Sun* headlines, so I back off.

Meanwhile, all the other students have formed into pairs, signed their names on the scroll listing the members of each group, and pushed their desks together. They're staring at me, ready to begin the exercise.

"Find a group and be swift," whispers Sensei Madame Phoenix.

Two girls with meek faces sit together at the back of the room. I've seen them before in class, I think. They never speak. They just look at each other as if they're exchanging words encoded in Chi pulses.

Their eyes widen as I skate over.

"May I join your group?"

They look at each other, turn expressionless little mouse faces back to me, and say nothing.

A thought strikes me. What if they're a couple, like those second-year boys, Hong-Gee and Matsu?

"Are you two together? I don't want to interrupt."

They exchange looks, peer at me with bright blinking eyes, and say nothing.

"I mean, are you together, as in . . . are you in love with each other?"

That didn't come out as gracefully as I hoped. The girls regard me as if I were one of those vile crusted creatures that suck onto the bottom of a ship or whale. I sense them subtly shift their weight to adopt defensive combat positions.

"Chen Peasprout, do you have a group yet?" whispers Sensei Madame Phoenix.

"Yes!"

"Group partner names?"

"Ah . . . these girls," I say, pointing to them. How can I be expected to learn every student's name here?

"Can we just get through this class?" I say to them. "I don't want this any more than you do."

I skate to my desk to retrieve my brush, ink, and scroll. When I return, the girls have already unsheathed a length of scroll and written on the title line, *The Great Leap of Shin*.

"No, no, we're going to write about Cloud-Tamer Zwei and Little Pi Bao Gu."

The girls look at each other and proceed to write.

"I'm not going to write about such a shameful episode," I say. The Great Leap destroyed both Pearl and Shin. Why under heaven would they choose to write about that?

The girls don't lift their attention from the scroll.

"Sensei said we have to work as a group!"

They continue taking turns to add lines of dialogue.

Fine, if they want to be stubborn, I'll show them stubborn. I go back to my desk and begin writing my script about Cloud-Tamer Zwei and Little Pi Bao Gu. I'll finish my script before they finish theirs and submit it as our group project. I'm not going to let them embarrass me with some mediocre effort.

While I'm writing the thrilling scene where Little Pi Bao Gu courageously leads the women and girls of Pearl to block the Shin-ian soldiers from coming ashore, a tear trickles down. As I wipe it from my cheek, a hand slaps sharply on my desk.

"I told you to work in a group!" whispers Sensei Madame Phoenix. The birds awake and begin screaming as if we'd just dropped a pile of snakes on the floor. Sensei claws the scroll from my desk, tosses it in the air, and slices it in two with a chop of her hand. Ten thousand years of stomach gas!

The two girls look at me, then at each other, and then turn their heads back to their scroll.

I skate over to see what they've written. Their prose is unbearable, their characterization tortured. Worst of all, these girls describe both the eunuch and the boy as heroes!

"Why are you referring to them as heroes?"

They look at each other. One of them says, "The boy refused to kill the eunuch when he had the opportunity."

So they can speak, after all.

"That doesn't make him a hero! The boy spared the eunuch who proceeded with the Great Leap of Shin, and the earthquake created a tsunami that destroyed your city! Pearl should hate the boy!"

"We know you hate the boy in Shin."

"Of course we do! And the eunuch, too! The Great Leap caused the lakes and rivers of Shin to flood, and the earth cracked open and released poisonous gases. The Great Leap killed hundreds of millions of people in Shin! Everyone should hate both the boy and the eunuch!"

"They were heroes because the——"

"They were criminals! The eunuch was executed by Shin for his errors in calculation and the boy was executed in Pearl as a traitor!"

As the last drops of the water clock count down the final portion of the hour, I take my brush and blot out the word *hero* everywhere that it appears in the script and replace it with *criminal*.

The girls stare at each other with ghastly expressions, then turn and squeak, "Sensei!"

Sensei Madame Phoenix skates to us, furiously waving her *Too Exciting!* paddle, and says, "What is it now, Chen Peasprout?"

"This is supposed to be a group project. I get to make a contribution, too."

Sensei looks at the water clock and says, "Finish now."

I add lines at the end of the script for the Chorus of Heavenly Sages to denounce Mu Haichen and Lim Tian-Tai as filthy criminals with low characters. I submit the scroll to Sensei.

The two girls seethe. Let them. They'll thank me when we get our grade.

In the last days before the fifth Motivation, this irritating experience in literature class makes me realize that whether I like it or not, sometimes I'm going to be forced by circumstances to rely on others. And the longer I wait to choose whom to rely on, the worse my options will be. I only have two days left to decide whether to ask Doi to partner with me at the fifth Motivation. Most girls paired up as soon as Sensei Madame Liao announced that we could choose our own partners.

Doi is clearly the best skater for me to choose. But what do I really know about her?

Why did she defend me over the soaps? Why did she fight Suki? Why won't she talk with her brother? Is there any truth to what Suki said about their father causing their mother's death?

Doi didn't use a Dian Mai technique on Suki at the luckieth Motivation like I feared she might. However, what she ended up doing was almost as reckless, so I don't know what else she might do. Maybe the Chi pulse exercise in the Courtyard of Supreme Placidness where she was talking about hostages didn't have anything to do with the New Deitsu skaters. What if it had to do with a Dian Mai?

A Dian Mai could be used to hold a hostage, since it turns your own body into a prison. What if she's planning to use a Dian Mai to imprison Suki as a hostage to make her miss the Motivation? Or use a Dian Mai on Suki during aerial combat? What could be a more spectacular way for Doi to take down Suki than to lock Suki's body while she's in midair so that she drops out of the sky like a stone for the whole academy to see? Suki could get killed. However, Doi is so extreme, she probably wouldn't care if it gets her expelled or imprisoned. And her partner along with her.

All this time, I'd been trying to get closer to Doi. Not just because she could further my ranking or tell me about the hostages and what she knows about the Empress Dowager's plans, but also because she was kind to me. But Suki was right. I really know nothing about Doi. If I'm going to make a decision about partnering with her, I have to know more about her than nothing. I need to find out once and for all whom she is communicating with through Chi pulses about hostages.

The night before the fifth Motivation, an hour before evenmeal, I'm here, hiding on the tiles atop the wall forming the far side of the Courtyard of Supreme Placidness. This is the side from which I'll be able to read the logograms that Doi is forming in the boxes of sand. She made me stand at the other side near the entrance the first time so that the logograms would be upside down to me and I wouldn't realize that they were words. If I can see the whole message, maybe I can find out what she's planning and whom she's gotten mixed up with.

She skates in just as the clock pagoda begins to strike the hour before evenmeal. She assumes the first square. She closes her eyes and cups her hand in front of her. Her Chi practice is outstanding because almost immediately, she has established the connection. She begins to walk across the sixty-lucky squares of sand, marking some and passing over others. The squares begin to form logograms, and the logograms begin to form sentences.

"Plan. Failed. Situation. Grown. Dangerous. Don't. Tell. Anyone. About."

She stops. She opens her eyes as if jolted awake. I know the look on her face. It's how I feel when Cricket gets a coughing fit while we are Chi connected and the link is abruptly severed. Whomever she is talking to has been interrupted. Whomever she—

"Hisashi? Are you still there? Hisashi?"

CHAPTER
TWENTY-THREE

So she's been talking with Hisashi through Chi pulses.
Sensei Madame Liao did say that twins have the strongest Chi entanglement. But why won't Doi talk to him in person? Is it because they don't want to be seen together? Why not?

Doi and Hisashi go to the same school and talk to each other every night through Chi pulses but refuse to be seen together. Their father lives in the same city as they do but hasn't seen them in years and walks right past his daughter when he visits the academy.

What is going on in this family?

The more I discover about Doi, the less I know. As much as I want to win in the fifth Motivation tomorrow, I don't know if I can partner with her. How can I trust her?

There are things that I don't understand about Hisashi, but I know in my heart that I can trust him because of his kindness to

Cricket. Which is why I shouldn't keep putting off asking him for help. Who knows when Suki will attack next? I need him to help me find where to buy red sorghum wine for Chingu to clear my name. I plan to talk to Hisashi tonight, at our private celebration in place of attending the Festival of Lanterns.

I leave my dormitory chamber to meet Hisashi with my Chi in an uncollected state. It's not just because of the Motivation. All the other girls I come across are dressed in fine pearlsilks for the festival. The fashions are so strange. They all wear black or silver high-collared, sleeveless *qipaos* with embroidery that's the same color as the fabric.

Out on the central path of the Principal Island, I pass Suki and the House of Flowering Blossoms girls. When they see my dress, they all burst into laughter.

"What is she wearing, a burlap tent?" says Suki. "And look at those flowers; they look like crumpled toilet paper."

I refuse to look down at my dress with eyes colored by their hate. My mother worked a whole year to buy this cloth. This might be the last thing from her that I ever receive.

However, when I arrive at the entrance of the Temple of Heroes of Superlative Character, I'm glad that it's so dark. I'm ashamed of my dress, and I'm ashamed that I'm ashamed.

I see the light of Hisashi's dim little futon-side lantern approaching from the distance, and I quickly wipe my tears.

"You look beautiful, Peasprout," he says. "Pink chrysanthemum is Doi's favorite flower. Mine, too. How did you know?"

He means it. He's not being kind. Good. I don't want him to be kind. I want him to like how I look.

"I have a gift for you," he says.

"Ah, and I have nothing for you."

"You already gave me a gift by being here tonight. But you have to do what I say if you want the gift."

We pass under the main archway into the round temple. I've never been inside it. There are braziers and candles lit throughout. It's like stepping inside a great drum lined with fireflies. I hate the idea of Cricket having to leap off these steep walls at tomorrow's Motivation. Maybe all the wasted time he's spent carving the little sculpture of the temple will help him understand its structure so he can take advantage of it.

In the center, towering stories above us, stands the massive sculpted likeness of a man with his hand resting on the shoulder of a boy. At their feet is a plaque engraved with the words *The Heroic Mu Haichen and Lim Tian-Tai.*

My heart sinks. "You mean this temple is for them?"

I look closer at the statues looming before us. They are in fact likenesses of the eunuch and the boy.

"Why is there a temple honoring criminals?" I ask.

"Criminals. What did they teach you about the Great Leap back in Shin?"

"During the Zhang Dynasty, the vermillion emperor of Shin

213

had his eunuch Mu Haichen organize two hundred million men to act as a human explosive. They jumped in unison on the central spine of the earth to trigger the impending great earthquake."

"Did they teach you why he did that?"

"The eunuch wanted to schedule precisely when the earthquake would strike. The populace of Shin could be warned to be outside so they wouldn't be killed when the structures came falling down."

"And what did they teach you about the boy Lim Tian-Tai?"

"He was sent by his father, the leader of the city of Pearl, to stop the eunuch Mu Haichen because the tsunami that would surely follow the earthquake would destroy their entire island. The boy didn't kill the eunuch when he had the chance, and the Great Leap destroyed both Shin and Pearl."

"Ah, I see. You view it differently in Shin. That hadn't occurred to me. Here in Pearl, we honor them as heroes. They couldn't bear to kill each other because they came to see the nobleness in each other's cause. They allowed the Great Leap to proceed."

"But the tsunami destroyed your city!"

"Yes, but it also washed away the old wood and stone structures here. The city would never have been rebuilt so quickly out of the newly discovered pearl. That's why they're both cheered by everyone in Pearl as heroes. It's a city built on the softness of their hearts."

I feel ill. Sensei Madame Phoenix will probably fail our group project for defiling the names of heroes. She already hates me. I don't really care about how I rank in literature, but when I think of how Sensei will humiliate me in front of everyone, and how furious those two girls will be with me, and how overjoyed Suki will be, and how there will probably be some *Pearl Shining Sun* headline accusing me of attacking the graves of heroes or something, I almost want to cry.

Hisashi looks at me with tenderness and says, "I see the sorrow in your face. I'm touched that you're so moved by their story. But don't grieve too much. If Mu Haichen and Lim Tian-Tai had not done what they did, there would be no city of Pearl here under our feet and you and I would never have met." He smiles. "Now, see how the great ramp along the walls spirals up and ends at the arch at the top?"

"Yes."

"We have to skate up it as fast as we can and go shooting out through the arch."

"Why? It's open sea out there."

"It's part of the gift. Do you trust me?"

"If you get my dress wet, I'm going to sue you."

"Your dress won't get wet. When we go out the top, stay close to me."

He twists a ring from his longest finger. It's a band topped with a small, carved animal, perhaps a dog or a *qilin*, but it has no legs and some complicated tail. He untwists the carving from the band and presses the little creature into my hand. He covers my hand with his.

We skate up the spiraling ramp, holding the carving in our clasped hands. The temple seems to spin in place beside us as we skate around, the statutes of Mu Haichen and Lim Tian-Tai turning as if on a potter's wheel. The stars show through the arch, and we go speeding out of it and fly toward the open sea.

Below us, rivers of light marble the dark water and flotillas of boats gather with students and senseis atop them holding up octopus lanterns.

As we hurtle toward the water, our cloaks whipping and snapping behind us, Hisashi yells, "Throw it!"

The little carved ring hits the water below us and swells into the form of a boat with an audible *crack*.

We fall into the boat and send a crown of drops spraying out around us.

The head of a dragon adorns one end of the boat, the head of a phoenix, the other. I run my hand over the sides. It seems to be made out of the pearl, but it has a softer, more porous texture, like a sea sponge.

It expands when wet. And shrinks when dry. Like the trinket.

"You got my dress wet!" I say.

"I'm sorry! It doesn't spray that much when it's just myself."

"I told you it would!"

"I know! I know! Because you're a shining, thousand-story-tall goddess and I'm a cannibal barbarian slave!"

"You have to pay a price for getting my dress wet."

"What do you want?"

"You have to answer any question I ask you truthfully."

"All right."

"Forever."

"So expensive!"

"You don't get to set the price of the vase after you've broken it."

"Start with easy questions."

"First question. Can we do that again?"

"No. We have to wait for the boat to dry before it becomes small again."

"Second question. Where did you get this?"

"I carved it."

"Is this some form of the pearl?"

"Yes."

"But where did you get the material?"

"Ah . . . somewhere I wasn't supposed to be."

He smiles, but it's clear he's uncomfortable. The children of the Chairman of New Deitsu Pearlworks Company must have access to things others don't, even if they don't talk to their father.

I change the subject, as I'm trying to pay more attention to the feelings of others. "I've never seen a boat with two heads. Does it mean something?"

"Yes." That's all he says. He smiles so sadly that I wish I hadn't asked. Do the two heads have something to do with him and his sister? I want so desperately to ask him why he and Doi have been communicating using Chi pulses instead of talking to each other directly. However, the expression on his face at this moment looks so defenseless that I don't have the heart to ask him anything confronting.

Out across the water, the rest of Pearl Famous is beginning the festival celebrations. I don't feel guilty for enjoying the music that washes over the water toward us. However, I refuse to look at the octopus lanterns as they're sent up and burned alive. I hear the sound of them bursting and sizzling as they hit the water, returning the animals to their home as ashes. They didn't die because they had to feed another animal. They died to entertain people. They died for nothing. And over it all, applause. Ignorant, cruel applause.

Hisashi sees me resisting the urge to look each time the blossoms of color light up the sky and our faces. He cups his hands over my hand and says, "Thank you."

I look in his face and almost tell him that there's nothing he needs to thank me for, that I don't want to look at the lights, that no matter how beautiful they are, they're ugly. That no matter how beautiful they are, they can't be as beautiful as what I'm looking at now.

I would gag if I heard someone say that, but when it's you who wants to say it, it's completely different. Still, I find enough discipline to keep my emotions collected.

Hisashi lays out a meal for us. It's sushi made from wonderfully firm braised tofu that has a delightful, chewy skin on it, strings of crisp green pepper and onion, kernels of crispy rice scraped from the side of a stone hot pot, and pickles rolled in sea vegetable as thin as paper and as faintly fragrant of the sea as any fine fish, all of it lightly drizzled with a thin but rich sauce of curry, miso, and cashew cream. He serves it in beautiful lacquered bento boxes. It could use some salt, since it seems to be salted with what I think is just boiled seawater, like all the food here, but I have no complaints.

It seems that having the distraction of eating allows Hisashi to speak more freely.

"The two heads on the boat are a dragon and a phoenix," he says. "Do you know what dragon and phoenix twins are?"

"Doesn't that mean boy and girl twins?"

"Yes. Very lucky symbol. Usually. Not so lucky when the two of them are entwined in the womb so they can't be born naturally. And their father has to decide whether to save the children or the mother. Our father chose us."

My heart aches like a sore muscle.

"I don't blame our father for sending us away all these years. Everyone thinks he's coldhearted. But he's not. He just loved our mother so much that he could never forgive us for causing her death. I can't, either."

Tears well in my eyes. Tears for Hisashi, for Doi, for their mother. Even for the Chairman.

"But it's going to be all right. My sister and I have a plan. To show our father how much we love him. We're going to unbreak our family."

Is that what Doi is talking to Hisashi about through Chi pulses? Do they not want to be seen together so that people won't know they're working on some plan?

I can feel the struggle in his Chi. Whatever their plan is, however much they believe in it, he's frightened of what he has to do. I want to say something to comfort him. Something that lets him know that I feel how he feels.

"I understand this boat," I say slowly. "Two heads. Pulling it in two directions. It doesn't know which way to go. It's uncertain which way is forward. But then, who of us is ever certain which way is forward?"

The fact that I want him to appreciate me for saying it doesn't mean that it's not also completely sincere.

His dimpled smile is like a radiant banner unfurling.

"Do you like your gift?" he says.

"What, you mean this boat? This is my gift?"

"Don't you like it?"

"I can't accept this. It's too big a gift."

"It gets small again when it dries."

"That's not what I mean."

"I know. I shouldn't joke. It's not too big a gift. You've done more than you know. For me. And my sister."

I don't want to pry, but I think he wants to tell me about it.

"Hisashi, what is the plan that you and your sister are working on?"

He stiffens and says nothing.

"Why don't the two of you talk to each other in person?"

"Peasprout . . . there are things concerning our family that I can't tell you about. And if I could tell you, I wouldn't want to."

"Why?"

"Because I'd be afraid that you wouldn't allow me to do this again."

"What? Take me on a dragon-phoenix boat?"

"No. This."

He draws near. His scent is like soft plains sweetgrass. He smiles and it feels like the dimples in his cheeks are making little mirror indentations into my heart.

He's a remarkable boy, but he has secrets. Something tells me that I've yet to see the true Hisashi. I don't know him yet. And I'm not going to kiss a boy I don't know.

When I hesitate, he hesitates. The smile fades but returns.

"I've wondered if reincarnation always has to be vertical," Hisashi says, pulling back. "Why does the next life you come back in have to take place *after* the life you just left? What if reincarnation is sometimes horizontal? And we sometimes come back and live a life that happens *at the same time* as another life we lived? Any living creature that you are cruel to could be someone you love. Or yourself."

"I've never thought about that before."

"And what if we come back to our own time and we meet ourselves and we feel the perfect harmony? Maybe that's what we call love." He gazes down at his hands and thumbs the rough calluses on his knuckles.

"But what if you come back as another boy?"

The dimples press into his checks again. "Who said love must always be easy?"

I can see that he wants to lean toward me again, but I still can't. He relents. He doesn't resent me for my hesitation. And it makes him even more beautiful to me. He's the one person here I can trust.

"Hisashi, I need your help."

"Anything."

"Where can I buy red sorghum wine in the city?"

"Why do you need red sorghum wine?"

"For Chingu. I need to ask who the criminal behind the attacks is."

He tenses when he hears this. "You shouldn't get involved in this, Peasprout."

"I'm already involved. This is the only way that I can prove that Suki's behind this, not Cricket and me."

"You don't know that it's Suki."

"Are you defending her now?" I say. I don't believe what I'm hearing.

"No! Just don't give Suki any more reason to come after you. She's got her attention on Doi these days. Doi can handle her."

"Meaning that I can't."

"No! Just stay out of Suki's way. You can't risk getting caught breaking rules now."

"Well, I have to. Because your father's coming at me. I don't understand why you won't help me. I thought . . . I mean—"

I'm angry, but I don't want to start crying in front of him. I focus my Chi.

"Please listen," I say when I've collected my emotions. "You don't know what Cricket and I have been through. You don't know why we don't know where our parents are. You don't need to know that now. But there is something I need you to know: I am the smartest, most capable person I know."

He laughs. "You're the smartest, most capable person I know, too."

"No, you don't understand! At all."

He looks at me with gentle eyes and says, "Help me to understand."

I swallow down my emotion and say, "Knowing that I'm the smartest, most capable person I know is the most frightening feeling possible. Because it means that if I can't keep Cricket safe, no one can. It means that if I can't save myself, no one can. It means that I'm *on my own*. Can you understand that?"

He says nothing. He takes my hand.

"So that's why I need to get into the city and buy red sorghum wine. Will you help me?"

He squeezes my hand and says, "I'm sorry, Peasprout. I can't."

And so the moment ends.

"I should go check on Cricket," I say.

He doesn't try to change my mind with more talk. He churns the tail-oar of the dragon-phoenix boat. I wipe my cheeks with the sleeve of my ridiculous dress. We reach the shore of the islet of the Temple of Heroes of Superlative Character. We pull the craft up onto the pearl shore. It quickly drains of seawater and is soon small enough to hold in two hands. However, the hole formed by the dragon's claws is still too swollen to run the band through, so I tuck it under my arm. I leave Hisashi there without saying good-bye.

At the festival, I see Cricket included in a game with other first-year boys that involves hopping from boat to boat while imitating the movements of animals in wu liu moves. He leaps and lands on the edge of a boat on only one skate blade. I almost cry out his name. He fights to keep his balance. Any of those boys could push him into the water. But they don't. As he loses the fight to maintain balance, his skate jerks up and my heart lurches as he does a triple-toe dragonfly spin from the edge of the boat and lands on the opposite edge. The other boys laugh and start chanting, "Flyboy! Flyboy! Flyboy!" I didn't read this term in *The Imperial Anthology of the Humorous, the Satirical, and the Serenely Amusing*, so they must not be laughing at him.

Then they're applauding him. Cricket bows and steps down into the center of the boat to cut the applause short. He's always so modest. The boys continue to clap, though, and give him friendly rubs on the back.

Every day, he skates further and further from me and my protection. But I'm the only one who can keep him safe. As soon as I am done with the fifth Motivation tomorrow, I'll find my own way into the city and get that wine for Chingu. No more wasting time relying on other people. Other people always disappoint me. Always. So what if I'm on my own? I'm used to it by now.

I should go back to the dormitory chambers to rest. However, I can't let this evening end quite yet. I know that it was neither the best nor the worst evening of my life. That's ridiculous. No boy should be able to make it that. Still, I return to the Temple of Heroes of Superlative Character just to be in this evening a little longer.

When I arrive in the temple, I find that the candles and braziers have been put out. I thought they'd just light them and leave them, since the pearl doesn't burn.

Something moves within the temple. Something's in here with me. Above me. Up in the archway at the top, there's something black and billowing, like great wings. It turns with a snap and is gone out of the arch.

It has to be Suki. She's going to commit a third attack! While I'm absent from the festival with no alibis.

At last, my chance to catch her in the act.

I skate up the spiraling ramp as quickly as I can. Sounds like bursting vents of steam emerge from above. There are great snaps as something breaks within the temple. I skate up faster. Before I reach the top, I see that the pearl in the ramp above me has been grotesquely eaten. It looks like flesh that has been turned to liquid and has healed over in smooth pink scars. The rifts spread, sizzling, squealing, putting up tendrils of vapor, and sending rents racing down toward me.

I scrape to a stop and reverse direction. I skate down as hard as I can, but the steaming drips of matter have burned through the ramp and dropped onto the level below, blocking my descent.

I remember Cricket holding his little sculpture and telling a circle of boys that if the spiral is damaged, the whole structure will come toppling down.

I leap into the center of the temple onto the statue of the eunuch Mu Haichen, atop the shoulder nearest to the boy Lim Tian-Tai.

A great bulb of viscous matter slides down the spiral path.

Dollops of it eat through the ramp, dripping down in thick wads. When it reaches the bottom, it spreads.

Within moments, the floor is covered in yawning holes, curling up vapor. Through the rifts below me, I see black churning sea.

The statue of Mu Haichen gives a groan as it begins to lean against the statue of Lim Tian-Tai, like an old man on his son.

I throw the dragon-phoenix boat down into one of the gaps in the floor. As it hits the water below, it expands out to full size. I get ready to leap onto it but the heads at either end begin to twist and arc, and the boat starts to cave in on itself. It's pulled under with the chunks of floor that are slipping down into the water.

I ride the statue of Mu Haichen into the sea as the entire temple comes down around me and I'm in the lightless water and my eyes and mouth are filled with the terrible sting of salt.

CHAPTER
TWENTY-LUCKY

I find a path underneath the foundation of the temple and swim back to shore using powerful kicks in the Minghai striped dolphin position. I don't tell people this very often because I'm a humble person, but I was swimming champion for all of Shui Shan Province five times before the age of nine. I only gave up swimming so that I could work toward becoming a legend of wu liu, so I'm never in any real danger in water, even while wearing skates. I'm able to make myself lighter through my excellent breath control, which is why I'm such an outstanding jumper.

As I'm swimming through the water, my heart fills with hope because this time, I saw Suki committing the attack. I didn't see her face, but I saw the back of her academy robe.

I pop my head out of the water. Alarms ring out from across the campus. Students and senseis have rowed over from the Festival of Lanterns. The breeze cuts swaths into the billows lingering over the cavity where the temple once stood. There's nothing left. Just a smoldering pit churning with seawater.

Suki's words reach me as soon as I drag myself out of the water. "You see! She's going to stop at nothing until she gets the secret of the pearl for the Empress Dowager! Imprison that filthy, murderous—"

"It was Suki!" I cry. "I saw her! She brought the temple down. She used some sort of fire jelly to melt it!"

Everyone is silent. Suki is smirking.

"I nearly drowned right now! Because of her! Aren't you going to do anything?"

Sensei Madame Liao says to me, with her brow bunched into a cleft, "Peasprout. Suki was in my boat during the entire festival."

"So she must have gotten one of her House of Flowering Blossoms girls to do it for her. Did she ask to be in your boat? She wanted you as a witness. She set you up!"

"I asked her to join me in my boat," says Sensei Madame Liao.

My mouth drops open. Did she want to keep an eye on Suki? Should I feel betrayed?

Suki shouts, "Did anyone notice that she wasn't at the Festival of Lanterns? And then she happens to be the only one at the site of the attack? Throw her in prison now!"

My Chi shudders. I've skated right into her trap.

"Enough. We will deal with this after the girls' fifth Motivation tomorrow," says Sensei Madame Liao. "The boys' fifth Motivation is postponed, obviously."

She orders the third-year students to usher us all to our dormitories.

I sleep little.

It's even more urgent now that I consult Chingu after this third incident and with me at the site of the crime by myself with no witnesses.

I have to prove my innocence before the Chairman comes back. He'll be here with the New Deitsu team tomorrow, just like the other times. Maybe sooner, since I promised to get him the evidence I needed to clear my name before another attack happened. He didn't have enough evidence before to have a legal right to imprison me in that pavilion. If three incidents are enough evidence for *Pearl Shining Sun* to defame me, will it be enough for him?

I need to go while everyone is occupied with the girls' fifth Motivation. But I have to finish participating in it myself first to keep up my ranking. I can escape into the city while it's night, wait there until the markets open as soon as it's light, and get back while the academy is still sleeping during the day.

So I'm going into the city, and I'm getting that wine, and I'm going to use Chingu's oracle to prove to everyone that Suki is the criminal.

After I knock her out of the sky at the fifth Motivation.

We're awakened at the usual time, and we meet at Divinity's Lap.

Sensei Madame Liao leads the first-year girls to the Palace of the Eighteen Outstanding Pieties. She ascends to the roof of the palace with a single-footed dolphin heel-kick. We copy the move and follow her atop the structure.

When we're assembled, she barks, "Willful, unfilial daughters of Pearl and Shin. I can see from how you stand in your skates that you are all still selfish and depraved and that none of you is prepared for aerial combat.

"Because it will take place in the night sky, you are to tie these rings of luminescent seagrass around your wrists, ankles, hips, and shoulders so that I can see your movements and score you accordingly, and so we can find your bodies should you fall into the dark sea.

"Every pair of girls will fight every other pair simultaneously in an open field of combat on the roof of the palace and in the sky above. If both partners in the pair touch the pearl at the same time, that pair is eliminated. You will be scored based on how long you last. Those of you who have already selected your partners, form a line. Those of you who haven't, you have until the count of one hundred to choose your own partners or you will be randomly assigned one.

"Now, one. Two. . . ."

I look for Doi. She's standing at the edge of the palace roof, looking on at everybody. I still don't know if I can trust her, but I've decided she's my best chance to win the Motivation. I see Mole Girl, and she waves at me. I pretend not to see.

"Eight. Nine. . . ."

Suki's pairing up each of the other House of Flowering Blossoms girls with some girl who has terrible ranking. She's doing it to eliminate as many of her competitors as possible by pairing them with weak partners.

"Twenty. Twenty-one. . . ."

Suki skates to me and says, "If you and I pair up, we'll win. If we win, you'll be in first place."

"What makes you think I would even—"

"If you don't partner with me, I'm going to *Pearl Shining Sun* as soon as this Motivation is over and telling them everything I know about the three attacks. As well as some new 'secret weapon' evidence I found."

"Then I'll tell them all about how you cheated at the—"

"No one's going to believe a word you say after last night. You waited too long to play that tile and you know it."

"Luckity-seven. Luckity-eight. . . ."

I look at Doi, who's looking back at me. What if she has some wild plan for this Motivation like she did at Iron Fan Dance? Can I trust her? I think so. But then, I thought I could trust her brother.

"Sixty-nine. Seventy . . ."

Etsuko stares at us from the sideline, waiting to see if Suki succeeds in convincing me. I guess she's Suki's backup choice. Why do these girls put up with such treatment?

"Eighty-two. Eighty-three. . . ."

Only a couple other girls haven't found partners yet. They're ranked so low that I've never bothered remembering their faces. I'm going to get paired with one of them if I don't choose.

"Ninety. Ninety-one. . . ."

Doi still stares at me. Does she have as many doubts about me as I have about her?

Finally, I say to Suki, "Make me die of laughing! I'd sooner pair with Chingu."

"Ninety-eight. Ninety-nine. . . ."

Suki sneers and grabs Etsuko's hand.

Something tugs my hand. I turn to see Doi holding it.

"One hundred!"

Doi nods at me. "Let's knock them on their butts."

We start our first battles with Doi as the foundation below, hoisting me into the air. Doi launches me up again and again above the roof of the Palace of the Eighteen Outstanding Pieties in great arcs so that I can fight my opponent in the air. It's an astonishing sight to see girl after girl being shot into the air around me like living cannonballs. Meanwhile, Doi spars with her opponent on the ground as she weaves between other girls before racing to meet me at the other end of the arc in time to catch me and launch me back up. Her skate kicks my skate up hard enough to pass sufficient Chi to keep me airborne, but not so much that I can't control my flight toward my opponent.

I force any thoughts out of my mind about how my skates will be ruined. I'll worry about that later. When I feel that Doi's beginning to get tired from supporting me below, we switch positions. Then, I'm the one bumping her up into the air while sending sweeping kicks at my opponent here below.

Pair after pair of girls is eliminated around us and the chaos thins until at last, the field of battle is cleared and there is silence. Doi and I take a moment to catch our breaths. We look across the spine of the palace roof to the only other pair left standing: Suki and Etsuko.

Doi and I look at each other and silently consider which of us wants to take on Suki more.

Doi says "She's yours" at the same moment that I say "She's mine."

Doi grabs one of my skates, whips me around her in eight spins, and swings me into the air. Etsuko launches Suki up at me like a grimacing cannonball.

Suki and I clash up above, skate on skate. We sling ourselves in backward flips to stay aloft as long as possible and try to knock the other one out of bounds of the roof of the palace, but we're evenly matched. Our uniforms are black against the darkness above us, but we're illuminated by the rings of luminescent plant growth around our wrists, ankles, shoulders, and hips.

We must look from below like the constellations of two goddesses who have peeled themselves from the night sky to do battle.

On the roof far below, Doi and Etsuko look like swirling blossoms of cloth and metal as they spin and swipe their skates at each other.

Doi and I work in beautiful harmony. With every fling into the air, I'm saying I need her. With every kick off her skates, she's saying she needs me. I need her. She needs me.

As Suki is launched into the air, she reaches into the front of her robe and pulls out something colorful. When I fly up to meet her, she flings it at me. I snatch it out of the air. It's a paper doll of me, toppling an entire pagoda with a flying side kick of my skates. The words *Peony-Level Brightstar, Unstoppable Secret Weapon of Shin!* are printed in gold logograms above my head, stamped with the imperial seal.

Aiyah! That's the new "secret weapon" evidence! Where did she find them? How is this going to look now? I know she's doing this to distract me, but I can't let anyone else see these.

Etsuko and Doi fling Suki and me back up into the sky. Suki whips two more paper dolls to either side of her. I air dash to the left and sweep kick to the right to snatch both of them. As Suki descends from her arc, she flings five more in all directions.

I come down and Doi kicks me hard back up. I pluck three of the paper dolls out of the air, but in my distraction, Suki manages to land a lightning squall chop on the side of my face and I go spiraling down. Doi has to race across the whole length of the roof to catch me in time.

Below us, everyone's looking up to see what Suki is throwing around in the air.

"Peasprout, focus!" Doi launches me back up and I reposition myself in midair so that I am flying straight at Suki's face.

Suki reaches into the front of her robe and flings fistful after fistful of the paper dolls in all directions. They flutter down around us in a cascade of color. Some of the students below are already picking them up and examining them.

Below me, I see Doi pick up one of the paper dolls as well. I hold my breath, but she merely looks at it, crushes it into a ball, and throws it aside before continuing to fight Etsuko.

I can hear from the change in the sound of Doi's and Etsuko's skates that the roof of the palace that they're skating on doesn't seem to be the same thickness everywhere. Some parts are thicker and some are thinner, like ice on a pond. As if New Deitsu didn't patch it as—

I cry out a warning, but it's too late. The roof caves in. Etsuko goes crashing into the interior of the palace. Doi hops aside to avoid falling in, but I'm plummeting toward the hole. Just before I disappear into the chasm, Doi hooks my foot with her foot and sends me flinging up again.

Suki's not so lucky and falls through the hole. I see her land with her knees on Etsuko's shoulders. Doi jumps into the hole to continue the battle, so I plummet down and land with my knees on Doi's shoulders.

The ceiling within is too low for Etsuko or Doi to launch Suki or me airborne, so we battle inside the palace stacked like giants from a legend, with Suki and me battling with our arms and Etsuko and Doi with their skates. We fight side to side as we race down the length of the great hall, but neither of us gains an advantage. We're too well matched.

Finally, Doi skates us under a beam and yells to me, "Grab it!" I hook my legs under her arms, then I grip the edge of the beam and pull up with all my strength, lifting both of us up.

We swing back and forth from the beam. Suki sways on top of Etsuko's shoulders and they both gape at us, unable to guess what we're about to do.

Doi and I collect our Chi and then, on the forward swing, I send my Chi into her and we explode apart. She hurtles skates-first like a spear flying toward the point where Suki's knees rest on Etsuko's shoulders.

Etsuko throws Suki forward across the length of the hall to avoid being struck and crouches to let Doi fly over her. However, Doi twists around in her flight, curbs her blades, lands on Etsuko's shoulders, and clamps tight onto her with her hands and legs.

Meanwhile, Suki comes shooting across the length of the palace at me, limbs spiraling wildly as she tries to grab anything to keep her from touching the floor and being disqualified. As she reaches for one of my dangling skates, I lift it ever so slightly out of her reach, like I'm letting an insect creep past.

She goes crashing onto the floor of the palace below me.

For the first time, I notice Sensei Madame Liao and the other girls crowded in the doorway of the palace, watching our final battle.

"Infuriate me to death!" spits Suki.

Doi pushes off of Etsuko as if she were covered with leeches.

I skate to Doi. I bow and say, "I couldn't have done that without you."

"You needed me," she says.

"And you needed me."

"No one can be in two places at the same time." And then she surprises me by nearly smiling. She looks almost like Hisashi at that moment.

CHAPTER
TWENTY-FIVE

My triumph at winning the fifth Motivation is brief. I have to get the wine for Chingu before the Chairman visits again. My Chi freezes every time I think of the pendant with the crushed body of a criminal inside. I suspect the Chairman isn't the type to wait for sufficient evidence before enacting punishment.

After bowing to Doi in gratitude, I leave the site of the fifth Motivation and race toward the rail-gondolas leading back to the city. I have to get out of the academy while everyone is distracted with the aftermath of the fifth Motivation. Then I have to find wine in the city and get back before tomorrow, while the academy is still sleeping. And all of it before the Chairman arrives again.

"Iwi, it's brushtime!" comes the call. The birds, wearing luminescent harnesses, take flight and begin writing logograms.

"Vicious. Third. Attack. On. Pearl. Famous. Inspires. Renewed. Calls. For. Arrest. Of. Chair—"

Suddenly, the words in the sky stop and the birds scatter, circling in confusion.

I don't have much time to spare, but I sense that something's wrong. I skate toward the spot on the campus over which the birds are swarming and squawking. When I pass under the Great Gate of Complete Centrality and Perfect Uprightness, I kick my heel to stop.

Near the rail-gondolas, Sensei Madame Phoenix is surrounded by the New Deitsu team. I duck behind an ornamental sculpture of the Enlightened One and peer around the corner. A man grips Sensei's arm tightly. I can see the long nail of his little finger pressing into the sleeve of her arm even from here. Chairman Niu.

I skate as hard as I can in the other direction and almost trip on my nicked and jagged skate blades.

I hide on the original Conservatory of Music islet, which partially sank after a tsunami but was left there because people found the sumptuous ruins to be picturesque. No one ever goes there, because you have to hop across a series of tiny humps that rise out of the sea to access it.

I need to get out of Pearl Famous, away from the Chairman, and into the city as quickly as I can, but I don't dare cross the campus and be seen in case he's searching for me. I skate back and forth across the decaying floor of the conservatory, counting down the time.

After two hours, the air splits with a great clap, the same sound that I heard when they completed repairs on the Palace of the Eighteen Outstanding Pieties.

I wait another hour to be safe and then skate back toward the rail-gondolas, staying close to the edge of the Principal Island. The fifth Motivation must be long completed by now. My plan to sneak off the campus while much of the academy was occupied with the Motivation is ruined. I just have to hide if I see anyone between here and the rail-gondolas.

When I near the landing, I see someone under the Great Gate of Complete Centrality and Perfect Uprightness. I skate to hide behind a copse of false ornamental trees, but it's too late. I'm spotted. Make me drink sand to death! The person is waving at me with both hands.

It's Cricket.

"Peasprout!"

I hop off and race to him.

"What's wrong?"

"I saw them restoring the temple!"

"Cricket! You broke the rules!"

"No! They only said that we may not face in the direction of the worksite. They didn't say that we couldn't see it. The third-year students who'd devoted to the Conservatory of Architecture were gathered on the edge of the Principal Island facing the worksite. They were given special permission to watch the temple being restored.

"One of them is named Deen Dei-Hwun. She's ashamed that one of her eyes wanders a little in the socket, so she wears smoked spectacles even at nighttime, which is ridiculous since she's the prettiest girl at Pearl Famous. She let me talk to her while she watched the work being done. And I realized that I could see everything that was happening reflected in her spectacles!"

"Cricket, what have you done?"

"The work team brought giant metal spoons," Cricket continues, his face glowing as if he can't hear me. "They used them to sling great white balls at the ruins of the temple. And I saw the balls strike and eat away the ruins.

"Then I saw eighteen workers carry that palanquin to the site. They set down something small, the size of a skate. They blasted it with water from the sea pumped through a hose. Then there was a great *crack* and suddenly, the temple was there! I could feel the force against my back. It pushed the air so hard that everyone had to take a step to balance. It was so fast, Peasprout!"

"Cricket, you fool!"

"I haven't done anything wrong! I didn't face northeast."

"How do you think it's going to look if people find out that you watched how the temple was rebuilt? Suki's going to say that the Empress Dowager sent me here to destroy the structures and that your job was to watch how they were being rebuilt to learn the secret of the pearl!"

"But we didn't do anything wrong."

"It doesn't matter! You have no idea how much danger we're in right now because of your stupid fascination with architecture. All I've done to keep us safe, and you just skate right over it, like a worthless, ignorant Shinian peasant!"

Cricket is silent, his chin buried in his bony chest. At last, he speaks. "Peabird, don't say I'm worthless."

"Stop with the baby talk!"

"I'm going to win the sculpture competition and—"

"Enough about architecture!"

I have to keep him safe. I reach out and pat roughly all over his body. He shrinks from my touch. He hates when anyone touches him, because he's ashamed of his body, and I understand why. His limbs are as skinny as a fawn's. Every hard angle that I feel poking out of his rickety body stabs into my heart.

"Where is it?" I demand.

"You can't have it! It's mine!"

I realize that he only has courage to say this to me because it's not here on his person. I turn and skate as hard as I can toward the dormitories.

"Wait, Peasprout!" he cries, skating after me. He almost catches me because I'm slowed by my ruined skate blades, but I arrive at his dormitory chamber first.

He has so little, but everything is arranged with such care. The little cloth adorned with images of blue turtles that our mother used to wash his face when he was a baby is folded crisply into the shape of a blossom and placed on his pillow. The sight of that thin rag from Mother turned by his little hands into a thing of fineness cuts me.

But I can't hesitate now. I rummage through his things.

"Peasprout, please!" pleads Cricket, arriving breathless at the door.

I find it hidden behind the roll of his futon, gently wrapped in his sleeping garments. His entry for the architecture contest is a

241

sculpture in miniature of the Temple of Heroes of Superlative Character. The likeness is remarkable. The detail is so fine that I can see through the arch of the doorway the individual hairs that he's carved on the bare arm of Lim Tian-Tai. And it's not even completed. It's astonishing.

"Please, Peasprout!"

He looks up at me with those shining, frightened eyes.

I look at this work in my hand into which he's poured his whole heart.

I can't do this.

"Peasprout, I've spent over a hundred hours on it!"

I have to cut him down to stand him up. For his own good. For his own safety.

I know I have to do what I think I can't do.

I drop the sculpture to the floor, lift my skate, and stamp my blade down on it, slicing it in two.

I chop the pieces with my blade, ten, twenty, thirty times until everything is slivers and powder.

I push past Cricket and skate out of his dormitory chamber. I wait for the howls but hear only silence.

My little Cricket.

I cover my mouth with my hands to seal in the sobs as I skate away so quickly that the wind shearing against my face sweeps a shimmer of tears in the air behind me.

CHAPTER
TWENTY-SIX

*P*easprout, focus.

I can't think about Cricket. Or Suki. Or the Chairman. Everything depends on getting the wine. If only Hisashi had agreed to help me. I'm so hurt that he wouldn't—

Focus.

I hop off the rails on the city side. The sun has risen and the city is waking up. I have to make my way back toward the markets near where we first disembarked from Shin.

I skate past great ceremonial gates, plazas terraced into the sides of hills of the pearl, gazebos perched atop outcrops, and cupolas carved so exquisitely that they look like lace brocades. There are shops and teahouses atop impossibly delicate arches. The sides of great public edifices bulge with rounded balconies in which I see officials at their desks.

Everywhere, there are fragile half-moon bridges spanning

sculpted rivers. Many are topped with tiny tea pavilions wide enough to seat only two. The half-moons reflect in the water to form perfect moons everywhere. The whole city shimmers with the rivulets and waterfalls that spill from every structure.

The light from all the whiteness is starting to sting my eyes as the sun climbs in the sky. Ten thousand years of stomach gas, I forgot my smoked spectacles. I'll have to hurry before it becomes so bright that it'll be impossible for me to navigate through the city.

I arrive at a central market square ringed with tented kiosks opening for business. I have seven taels that I've saved up over the years doing wu liu performances at the street market. It should be plenty of money to buy a little wine. I find a few merchants carrying wine, but no one will sell it to a luckyteen-year-old girl. They ask me if my parents know where I am. One of them even threatens to report me to the police.

"You look for buy wine?"

I turn and see an old woman. I instantly recognize her accent as Shinian. She has a mole on her face the size of a fat tick. Three wiry hairs as long as my forearm sprout out of the mole.

"I make you best price!" she says in her broken Pearlian.

She chews betel nut. She blows the contents of her nostril onto the pearl. She lifts an earthen wine vessel.

"How much?" I ask.

"Two tael." She looks me up and down and adds in perfect Shinian, "You're a long way from home, young miss."

How can she know I'm from Shin? There's nothing Shinian in my speech, dress, or skating.

"I'll take it," I answer in perfect Pearlian.

The merchant sneers, switching back to her broken Pearlian. "You like speak Pearlian so much, we speak Pearlian. You think Pearl so fine and high. Don't trust them. They love lie. They lie so much."

I take out my small purse and count my seven taels.

When she sees the money, she says, "You look buy anything else? Betel nut? Sinkweed?" She looks at me harder, then recognition fills her face. "You Brightstar skater from Shin. You girl in *Pearl Shining Sun* newspaper."

"I don't know what you're talking about."

She looks around to see if anyone can hear her. "You like buy nice salt?"

I'm about to wave her off when I think of Cricket and how little he seems to eat these days. It must be because of the lack of salt in the dining-hall food. If I could just get him a little salt, maybe he'd understand that I'm always thinking of him, no matter how my actions must seem sometimes.

"Pearlian so scare of salt. From children time they teach should very be scare of salt. They put little salt in children eye. Teach them salt terrible. Salt burn. Salt eat like fire."

"How much is the salt?"

"Two tael one cup."

Merchants back home in Shui Shan sold a whole bowl of salt for one tael. But what is there to spend my money on, anyway? Seven taels wouldn't be enough to buy even one skate blade.

I drop lucky taels into her hand.

"Where you cup?"

"I don't have a cup."

"I sell you cup." She lifts a rough, dented vessel. "Three tael."

"Two taels for salt, and one tael for an old cup?"

"No. Three tael for cup. Two tael for salt. Two tael for wine. Seven tael total."

"I'll go buy my own cup."

"No. You buy salt in my cup or no sell salt. Or wine. And I call police."

At this point, other people and merchants are beginning to watch us, so I relent again and pay this vile creature her seven taels.

"Pearlian no use salt," she says. "You Shinian. You use salt. You burn all down." Hatred fills her face, but it's not for me. She's not even looking at me. She's looking at this city of Pearlians circling us two villagers from Shin.

I tie the wine with a sash around my waist, take the cup of salt, and leave her, but her words follow me.

I hear a voice, and by the time I hear "That's the girl!" I'm already performing the single-toe fire dolphin flip. I land, ready to meet them, with one hand pulled behind me holding the cup of salt and the other extended toward them like a blade.

It's the two boys who harassed Cricket and me when we first arrived from Shin. From Number-One Best Discount Noodle Academy or whatever it's called.

"You made us smell like stinky tofu for two weeks!" says the square-shaped boy. "We almost got kicked out because of you!"

"We weren't allowed to serve customers on the floor because of you," says the slimmer boy. "You made us late with our tuition."

They're vile boys. But they're poor. They work to pay for their wu liu schooling. I used to be them. I could soon be them, if I don't get to Chingu in time. Thus, I hold back.

"What're you doing outside of Pearl Famous?" says the square-shaped boy. "A little shopping, neh?"

Together, they lunge forward. My response is slowed by my jagged skate blades and the glare in my unprotected eyes. I block one boy, but the other one snatches my cup of salt. Ten thousand years of stomach gas!

"What is this?" says the square-shaped boy. He sticks his finger into the salt.

"Don't touch it!" I cry.

He grins at me, deliberately stirs his fingers around in the salt, and wipes it on his tongue. When he tastes the flavor, his eyes widen. He spits and gapes at me.

"Where did you get this?" he asks.

"Give it back!"

"We should report you!"

They leap onto the edges of one of the open chutes that carry the cargo sledges and speed deep into the harborside marketplace.

I'll be arrested for illegally buying wine and salt! I pump my skates hard and chase after them.

These boys aren't academy-level skaters. I quickly catch them on a stretch of the chute high above a busy street. When they see that they can't outskate me, they turn and come at me with not just chops and knees but open blades. They hop and flip back and forth between the thin edges of the chute, their moves made inaccurate by their fury. I have to be careful here. I don't want them to strike me, but I also don't want them to spill my cup of salt for Cricket.

I block each of their strikes successfully, but I fail to disarm them. They should be no match for me, but the brightness of the white city stings my unshielded eyes and my blades make my steps uneven.

I see how to win. We're high above the city on a chute. My opponents can only balance on its left edge or its right edge. And they can only be behind me or in front of me.

I don't need my eyes. I close them and let the sound of the boys' skates and hands cutting through the air show me where they are. Their reflexes are mediocre. Within five moves, I've sliced the straps from their skates and snatched the cup of salt back from the boys.

As they fall out of their skates and begin plummeting to the pearl below, I feel the square-shaped boy's unskated foot kick the cup of salt out of my hands. I open my eyes to see the salt shoot out of the cup and scatter in the chute behind me.

The cup lands on top of the salt. Then it disappears.

I scrape to a stop. Below me, the boys bounce as they hit the pearl on their socks, then continue shouting insults at me. I grab their skates from the chute and fling them in opposite directions as hard as I can.

I skate back to where the salt and the cup were.

There's a hole in the pearl of the chute. Through it, I squint and see the city street below. The faint sparkle of my metal cup against the whiteness down there catches my attention.

The edges of the hole are sending up tendrils of vapor. It looks like flesh that has been turned to liquid and healed over in smooth pink scars. It looks just like the damage done to the academy buildings.

Salt!

It eats through the pearl!

That's how Suki's been doing it. She must have placed great blocks of salt on the buildings. Where did she get it? Suki has plenty of money, but salt's not just expensive, it's forbidden.

It's like plants that die if the water is too salty or not salty enough. Or like the rice stalks that were killed when the fields in Pearl became salted after the Great Leap. Is the pearl some strange giant vegetable, like bamboo?

That must be why Pearlians don't use salt in their food and why they teach their children to fear salt. The pearl can't burn, but salt could destroy their whole city like fire could destroy other cities.

With this information, and Chingu's oracle, I'm going to prove that Suki caused the destruction and finally end her hold over me. I just have to get back into my dormitory chamber without being seen.

Luckily, it's still midday, so the whole academy is sleeping. As I ride the final stretch of the gondola rails back to the campus, I skate through a tumbling cloud enveloping the path.

I come out and scrape to a stop at the shore of the Principal Island.

In front of me, under the Gate of Complete Centrality and Perfect Uprightness, are all the senseis.

They have their backs to me.

They're carrying someone up the incline leading past the Gallery of Paragons of Honor toward the Hall of Benevolent Healing.

At the sound of my skates skidding on the gondola rail, Sensei Madame Yao turns and sees me.

"Chen Peasprout, what are you doing violating curfew?"

She pushes the sleeves of her robe up above her muscled forearms and pulls me off the rail. Her fingers embed in my arm and haul me up the incline.

"Sensei, I can explain! I was just running an errand—"

She plucks the vessel of wine from my sash, smells it, and fumes.

As she yanks me past, I look to see whom the other senseis are carrying.

It's a boy with eyebrows as thick as stage makeup, dressed in what used to be a fine embroidered robe. He's older. Not a student. He's dressed like a professional Pearlian opera company performer. I realize I recognize him from somewhere. But he's not wearing skates. What happened to his skates?

I turn back and look again.

Something's wrong with him.

Where are his feet?

The ends of the boy's legs are bundled in pink silk half the length of feet.

They're exactly the size and shape of lotus blossoms, bound tightly shut.

CHAPTER
TWENTY-SEVEN

Sensei Madame Yao takes me to the nearest structure, the Gallery of Paragons of Honor. She pushes me onto a bench in the middle of the hall and says, "Don't you dare step outside until we come back for you."

The portraits of the academy's paragons of honor stare down at me. All the first-ranked skaters in academy history. All the past leads in the Drift Season Pageant. All the graduates of Pearl Famous who died in the Bamboo Invasion and other wars against Shin.

"Dyun Bee-Chyin. Died Valiantly in Battle Defending Pearl, Bamboo Invasion, Second Year."

"Lao Ying-Lian. Died Valiantly in Battle Defending Pearl, Bamboo Invasion, Second Year."

They didn't even get to graduate. Their young faces stare blankly ahead, unaware that I'm here.

I remember now where I've seen the boy that the senseis were carrying, the boy with the bound feet. I look for his name and find it. His eyebrows weren't stage makeup, as his portrait has them as well.

"Zan Kenji. Wu Liu First Ranking, First and Third Years; New Deitsu Opera Company First Recruit."

He thought he was going to Shin as a goodwill ambassador. Instead, he went there as a hostage and came back as a sacrifice. All those years of training. All that work and talent and dedication. One of the greatest living skaters in Pearl. He's never going to skate again. He'll barely even be able to walk.

The Empress Dowager did this to him.

And this is just a warning.

She still has the other performer, Aki. Not a performer. A hostage.

If binding Kenji's feet doesn't get her the pearl, what's she going to do to his little brother until she gets it?

And now that she's mutilated Kenji, what are the Pearlians going to do to me and my little brother? We're just two children from Shin. Just because she chose me as the Peony-Level Brightstar doesn't mean we approve of the Empress Dowager's actions.

We didn't choose the Empress Dowager as our ruler any more than people choose for winter to be cold. But I don't know if Pearlians would understand this because they elect their leaders. Of all the strange privileges they have here, this is the strangest of them all.

I realize that the Empress Dowager sent Cricket and me here in exchange, even though she was already planning to use Kenji and Aki as hostages. She never cared what might happen to Cricket and me. She sent us right into the mouth of the tiger. All this time, some part of me wanted to believe that no matter what the Chairman or Suki or *Pearl Shining Sun* threatened, the Empress Dowager would use her power to protect us. Now I know that I'm truly on my own.

The door slides open. It's Doi.

"My father is on his way here," she says, closing the door. "I'm going to try to talk to him."

"I know how Suki destroyed the buildings! With salt! It melts the pearl!"

"How did you find that out?"

"I went into the city to buy wine for Chingu, and I bought some salt and it spilled."

"I see." Doi's expression is unreadable. "Peasprout, don't say anything about that to my father."

"Why not?"

"Because you don't want to look like you know how to destroy a building!"

"But I have to if I want to prove how Suki did it!"

"Suki's going to say that you found this out so you could teach the Empress Dowager how to destroy our city if we won't share the secret of the pearl with her."

"Then I have to get to Chingu. She's never wrong! She'll name Suki as the criminal. You have to convince your father to let me consult Chingu."

"Peasprout, just stay out of this. All you did was violate curfew and leave campus without permission and buy some wine. Maybe the senseis will still let you participate in the sixth Motivation."

"Your father threatened to have me crushed alive! That's why I have to prove that I'm innocent."

Doi pulls away. "He wouldn't do that."

"He showed me the shrunken trinket," I say.

She stiffens.

"Help me, Doi. I don't have anyone else. If you don't help me, I'm *on my own*. Don't let me down! Like your brother did!"

"I'm not Hisashi." Doi refuses to look at me. She cradles an elbow in her hand and presses her fist to her lips. There is so much struggle on her face that she looks as if she would rip in two down the middle. What would it cost her to help me?

At last, she says, "I'll help you."

The door slams open and the Chairman thunders in. He looks at me, then at Doi.

"What are you doing here?" he says to her.

Doi drops to her knees and lays her forehead to the pearl.

"Venerable and esteemed Father. I humbly beg you to listen to my worthless entreaty on behalf—"

"Get out!"

"Father, I beg you. Chen Peasprout needs to consult Chingu, the oracular monkey. Chingu will be able to prove that Chen Peasprout is not the criminal."

"I have all the proof I need."

Doi stands up, skates under one of the portraits, and kneels.

"Father, my request is worthless, but I beg you to indulge it, as a paragon of honor."

She puts her head down to the pearl again.

The portrait is of a young man, as handsome as Hisashi.

"Niu Kazuhiro. Architecture First Ranking, First, Second, and Third Years; New Deitsu Pearlworks Company First Recruit."

He was just like me once. Filled with pride for his achievements, hope for his future, and dedication to his honor. I turn my face away when the Chairman sees me looking at him.

The silence stretches through the gallery.

At last, the Chairman says, "Be quick about it."

The Chairman, Doi, and I arrive at Sagacious Monk Goom's little temple on pillars, along with Sensei Madame Yao. She insisted on coming when I asked for the wine back. I'm glad because I want as many witnesses there as possible when Chingu names Suki.

Sagacious Monk Goom looks at the vessel of wine and says, "Is that all?" When I tell him yes, his sighs could fill sails.

He takes the vessel from me. He pulls out the stopper and skates over to Chingu. He holds out the vessel warily and says, "Chingu! Look what I have. I have the nice nice! Very nice nice!"

Chingu's screeches have not stopped piercing the air since we entered the temple. When she sees the vessel, she begins to alternate her cries with grunts and she hacks with even greater force at the lacquered box on which she squats. When the vessel comes within reach, Chingu claws it from Sagacious Monk Goom's hand, plugs it into her mouth, sucks it empty, and flings it to the floor, smashing it into pieces.

Within moments, she goes slack and slumps down, her eyes roll back in their sockets, the lids close.

"Quickly!" says Sagacious Monk Goom. He scoops up Chingu. Her fist still squeezes the handle of the cleaver, but everything else is limp.

I help him open the lid of the lacquered box. Inside, it's like a little sedan with two seats facing each other. The walls are composed of intricate latticework that lets in light but keeps the faces of the sitters veiled from the outside. He slides Chingu into one seat and places a tray on her lap with sixty-lucky tiles. He looks at me and points to the other seat.

"Get in."

"Me?"

"You're the one with the question, aren't you?"

"What if she wakes up with me in there?"

"Ah, that would not be very nice. That would be very *not* nice. So quickly!"

I slip into the seat, and he closes the lid above us.

"Hurry, hold her hand and ask her your question."

I grab Chingu's hand without the cleaver. It's padded and soft and leathery and cold.

I close my eyes and grip her hand and say the question silently in my mind: *Who is responsible for harming Pearl Famous?*

At that, Chingu's eyes pop open. She starts screeching and hacking at the sides of the box with her cleaver, her eyes rolling.

I scream and drop her hand. She immediately stops and her eyes close again.

Sagacious Monk Goom opens the lid. "You asked her something too general, didn't you? Ask something precise."

He closes the lid on us, and I take Chingu's hand again and silently ask her: *Who attacked the structures of Pearl Famous Academy of Skate and Sword?*

Chingu begins shrieking again. She hacks the walls of the box so hard that the box jumps and almost rolls onto its side.

Sagacious Monk Goom opens the lid and cries, "What did you ask her?"

"I asked her something precise!"

"Did you ask her about the future?"

"Yes. I mean, no. . . ."

"She can only answer questions about the future. She's an oracular monkey. Phrase your question into something about the future." He closes the lid on us again.

I take Chingu's hand, close my eyes, and ask her: *Who will be discovered as the criminal who attacked the structures of Pearl Famous Academy of Skate and Sword?*

Chingu's hand falls from mine. She runs her fingertips in circles over the tray of sixty-lucky tiles, making them click and shuffle as her head lolls wildly on its stem.

She quickly grabs one tile as if she's catching a fly in the air, flips it over, and stabs it into my palm, facing up. Then a second. Then a third.

I read them. At first, they don't make any more sense than Supreme Sensei Master Jio's gibberish sayings.

Then I understand.

My Chi freezes all the way through my being.

I close my hand around the tiles, throw the lid of the box open, and jump out.

When Doi sees my face, she quickly turns to her father and says, "Oracles can be difficult to interpret. They might not really be saying what they—"

"Give them to me," says the Chairman.

"Peasprout . . ."

I have no choice. I lift my hand, open my palm, and show the three tiles to the Chairman.

He takes them and reads the logograms written on them.

Sister.

Boy.

Heart.

In classical Pearlian, *heart* is pronounced "shin."

"Sister of boy in Shin?" he says. "Sister of boy of Shin? The sister of the boy *from* Shin."

I watch the Chairman's eyes widen, then narrow as he arrives at the truth.

"There's only one boy from Shin here at Pearl Famous." He looks up at me.

"And he has only one sister."

CHAPTER
TWENTY-EIGHT

"I had nothing to do with it!" I cry.

The Chairman grasps one of my arms and Sensei Madame Yao, the other.

"Let me see Sensei Madame Liao!" I plead.

"This has nothing to do with wu liu," says Sensei Madame Yao. "She has no jurisdiction over this. You might be surprised to learn that wu liu isn't everything."

"Foundational principle of values number thirty-nine states that the interpretation of the oracles is sometimes incorrect!" I say. "Maybe 'heart' didn't refer to Shin at all. Maybe it's just a coincidence."

"Tell that to the Chiologists," says the Chairman.

"Where are you taking me?"

"You'll be detained until your trial for crimes against Pearl."

"Detained where? What does that mean?"

"It means," says Sensei Madame Yao, "as you students say, that you have seriously failed to keep the monkey pleased."

They take me to the central court of the Principal Island, where the morning assemblies are held.

In the center is a small pavilion of the pearl that was not there before. I tremble when I see the pavilion is in the same shape as the trinket.

"You can't put me in that!" I try to tear away from them, but it just gives Sensei Madame Yao an excuse to crush my arm even harder with her muscled grip.

"Doi, help me!" Where did she go?

She abandoned me! Just like her brother.

They haul me harder toward the pavilion. I try to dig my skates in. The chips nicked into the blades during the fifth Motivation are helping them dig into the pearl.

"What is going on here?"

We turn and see Sensei Madame Liao skating toward us. Beside her skates Supreme Sensei Master Jio.

And Doi. She must have fetched them. *Thank you, Doi!*

"We're detaining her for trial," says the Chairman.

"Chingu named her as the vandal," says Sensei Madame Yao.

"You're not using one of those on her," says Sensei Madame Liao.

"It's for her own protection," says the Chairman.

"You're not putting her in that *thing*," says Sensei Madame Liao. "This is an academy matter first. New Deitsu doesn't have jurisdiction until we determine that she has committed a crime. She will be confined to her dormitory chamber until trial."

"She attacked three academy structures," Sensei Madame Yao says. "This has nothing to do with wu liu. You don't have jurisdiction here."

"If she's accused of attacking structures, then this is an architecture matter. And those incidents delayed the Motivations. So this is also a wu liu matter. And you don't teach architecture or wu liu, do you?"

Sensei Madame Yao glares at her.

"Supreme Sensei?" asks Sensei Madame Liao.

Supreme Sensei Master Jio looks at all of us with sad eyes. He closes them and nods.

"You can't just trust her to stay in her dormitory chamber!" says Sensei Madame Yao.

"I will ensure that she does not leave her chamber," replies Sensei Madame Liao.

"How are you going to do that?"

"Are you questioning my judgment?"

"Supreme Sensei, you can't let this happen!"

Supreme Sensei Master Jio says nothing. Sensei Madame Yao throws my arm aside and skates off toward Eastern Heaven Dining Hall in a fury.

Sensei Madame Liao bows to Supreme Sensei Master Jio. She places her hand on my shoulder and leads me away. We skate past Eastern Heaven Dining Hall. The sounds of violent clanging emanate from within, as if someone were trying to batter a gong to death.

As Sensei Madame Liao leads me toward the dormitories, I start blathering, "Sensei, I swear, I'm innocent! I know who's behind this. Maybe she has a secret half brother from Shin or something. Or maybe the Chairman's interpretation is incorrect. *Heart* is pronounced 'shin' only in classical Pearlian; it's 'shim' in modern Pearlian. Or maybe it's just a coincidence. Oracles are misinterpreted all the time."

Sensei Madame Liao remains silent, but I can't stop the words from spilling out. "When I was not even five, my parents took me to an oracle who said that our whole family's destiny lay in my feet. They thought that meant that they should bind my feet so they could sell me to a noble house. But my parents didn't have the heart to do it. It turned out that our destiny *was* in my feet, because my future was to become a legend of wu liu, which I would never have been able to do if they'd bound my feet. That's why you can't assume an oracle is saying what it seems to be saying!"

Sensei Madame Liao doesn't reply.

When we reach my dormitory chamber, she accompanies me inside and slides the shoji door closed.

"Chen Peasprout," she says slowly. "The steps of an honorable person lead through walls; the steps of a dishonorable person become a prison."

She makes a hollow fist and strikes me in the five essential meridian points.

The Dian Mai.

My own body has become a prison.

CHAPTER
TWENTY-NINE

The flakes float upward like snow cascading in reverse.

The pearl in the courtyard of the girls' dormitory has been shedding flakes for days, lifted by the gaseous substances issuing from the pearl now that it is the Season of Drifts.

It must be distracting to do wu liu in these drifts.

The birds must not like them, either. I wonder if they have to write their headlines differently to compensate. I hear them crying as they must do two headlines a day now to keep up with the news. I could see them if I stood in the center of the courtyard.

But that would require me to take more than five steps outside of my dormitory chamber.

Today, two girls skating down the hall stop as they hear the birds. They stand in the courtyard and read aloud what they see in the sky.

"Mutilated. Hostage. Sent. Back. By. Empress. Dowager. Tells.

Of. Mysterious. Third. Skater. Sent. In. Failed. Plot. To. Free.
Them. Buy. Pearl. Shining. Sun. News. To. Get. Whole. Story."

I should be paying attention to this because it could be true and it could affect me. The newspaper was right about the Empress Dowager binding her hostage's feet, after all. Who is this third skater? Did the Empress Dowager capture him or her?

However, I can't summon the energy to care. Exhaustion pours through me. I close my shoji and crawl back to my futon.

My body feels torn. I've never been more depleted in my life. I've never been more agitated. At some point, I just go numb. I scoop my spirit and set it in a bowl floating beside my body.

Look at that girl, kneeling on her futon for the last five days so that she doesn't accidentally take five steps. Trapped in a space that any baby could cross.

She once said that she is the smartest, most capable person she knows.

She's been wrong about so many things and so many people.

But she was right about some things and some people.

If she can't keep her brother safe, no one can.

If she can't save herself, no one can.

And she is truly on her own.

In the evening, there is a knock on my shoji. I collect my used dishes and chamber pot and bowl of bathing water for one of the Shinian servant girls to clear. None of them ever speaks to me. I keep wondering if one of them is the girl who tried to teach me how to eat the Cave of Jade during the Osmanthus Banquet, whom I was so cold to. However, I never got a good look at her face. Every servant girl who comes in could be that girl, could spit in the food she brings me.

"Enter," I say.

It's not the Shinian servant girl.

Hisashi skates in. He kneels in front of me.

"They said you could have visitors now."

I don't say anything.

"Do you want me to leave?"

I say nothing.

"I blame myself. I should have tried harder to convince you not to—"

The emotions I've been holding away begin slamming into my stomach again. I can feel the shape of their fists as if they're screaming their names with every punch to make sure that I never forget them.

I double over. "Just . . . go."

Some time later, there is another knock on my shoji.

When I do not answer, the door slides open slowly.

It's Doi.

She does not kneel down to me.

"Stand up," she says.

I don't look at her.

"Peasprout. Stand. Up."

I'm so weary.

"Peasprout, don't you see?" She comes closer and kneels next to me. "This is the best thing that could have happened. If there's another attack while you're imprisoned in the Dian Mai, you'll be proven innocent."

She's right. If I weren't so weary, I might have thought of this. I get up. I make sure to plant my socks firmly on the pearl and not move them so as not to take any steps.

"How do we know that another one's going to happen?" I ask. "Why would Suki do that when she knows I'm trapped in here? She's already won."

"Forget about Suki! Every mistake you've made this whole year has been because you were focused on Suki. Focus on your own safety."

"What does it matter anymore?"

"Then focus on Cricket's safety."

At the sound of his name, I straighten up. Doi is right. I don't have the luxury to feel discouraged. They could still charge Cricket as an accomplice. His safety depends on my finding out who the true criminal is. "All right. I have noticed a pattern. The attacks always happen at the site of the boys' Motivations. The night before they're to take place. Doi, what if someone wants to prevent the boys' Motivations from proceeding?"

I look to see if Doi shares my excitement about this revelation. She looks as if she's so intensely bored that her heart might stop beating.

"That's silly. Why would anyone want to do that? New Deitsu just repairs the damage and the boys' Motivation goes forward in a day or two."

"That's true. Well, it doesn't matter anyway because I can't wait until the sixth Motivation. The tribunal of Chiologists is going to hold my trial in two days."

"Maybe another attack will happen sooner. Don't worry about that. Just stay here. That's the best thing you can do for yourself and Cricket."

"But I can't count on another attack happening! And without that, I don't have any evidence to disprove the Chairman's interpretation of Chingu's oracle! And even if another attack happens before my trial, I can't just let Suki get away with it."

"So you're just going to skate out of this chamber and confront Suki, and she's going to break down and confess? As you're writhing in pain with every bone in your body broken to bits."

"You want me to just await my fate and hope the tribunal won't agree with the Chairman's interpretation? I can't just stand by and do nothing! I'm going to find a way to get out of this Dian Mai."

Fury flashes on Doi's face before she pushes it down. She calmly turns and skates away from me to the shoji.

She hesitates there and looks back. Her eye is twitching. I can feel the tremendous pressure coming off her Chi. With a cry, she chops her hand down on my desk, splitting it in two and sending the halves crashing into each other.

I'm shocked by her violence.

"Why did you even come here?" I say. "Why are you so upset? Because I'm willing to take a risk to find the truth? I'm taking more of a risk by sitting here and letting other people decide my fate. I thought you, of all people, would understand that."

Doi flings the shoji open and skates out.

I thought Doi was different. But in the end, she's just another rich girl from Pearl who hasn't had to do the things that I've had to do to take care of Cricket and keep us safe.

I look at the desk, split cleanly in half. It makes me think of the exquisiteness of the sculpture Cricket created, and his shining eyes, and the dull sickening *snick* that my skate made as I stamped down, and the silence behind me as I fled away.

That evening, shortly before the hour of sleep, there is another knock on my door.

"Enter."

I'm so surprised to see Cricket that all the words that I had been practicing to say to him fly out of my head. He sees my skates set next to my futon and picks them up.

"I need to file the surface of the blades," he tells me without meeting my gaze. "I noticed something when we were doing some of those fine-vision exercises during architecture class—"

"I don't want to hear any more about architecture!" The words come out more sharply than I intended.

"Fine!" he yells. "You never listen to me. Even when it's for your own good!"

"How dare you talk to me like that? I don't know you. You are not my little Cricket."

"That's right," he shouts as he flings my skates at my feet. "I'm not your little Cricket! I'm not anyone's little Cricket!"

I'm so stunned and wounded that I can't speak.

He says nothing. At last, he kneels down and picks up the skates.

He works at the bottom of my blades with a file. Slowly, the nicks in them grow smaller and smaller until the notches completely disappear.

Cricket turns the file. He takes the sharp edge and scores one deft, long stroke after another on the bottom edge of the blade. Between strokes, he tests the blade, running it back and forth on the pearl like a child with a toy chariot.

As he works, he loses himself in the task, and some of his anger fades, and some of my little brother returns. The surface of the blade is so narrow but he's able to work lines into the hard metal that are impossibly perfect. He always had eyes as sharp as an owl's and hands as precise as the needles of a spider knitting its silk.

Cricket hands the skates to me. I feel them with my thumb. The blades are straight, but on the bottom side, there are now incredibly fine, regular ridges running along their lengths.

"I noticed that the pearl is formed with an almost invisible grain in it when we were examining it under lenses in architecture class." Cricket makes a point of neither swallowing nor swelling the word *architecture*. "When you skate, you need to find the grain in the pearl and skate with it. You'll know when you've found your grain."

He stands up without meeting my gaze and skates to the door. Without turning to look at me, he says, "Architecture and wu liu have more in common than you might see. Architects often build secret doors for themselves into their buildings. If you don't know how to look, they appear like mistakes or deficiencies. But if you learn how, you can glide right through them."

As he is sliding the door closed, Cricket says, "To see things differently, sometimes all you need is to retune your Chi. Like how we would kick the Blame Tree when we were little and we would feel better."

He leaves.

He was speaking to me in code.

He was telling me secrets in plain view, as if they were laid in marks on a grid. Is this something to do with the Dian Mai, and how to escape from it?

Deficiency.

Secret door.

Glide.

Retune Chi.

The Blame Tree.

Yes, we felt better after kicking the Blame Tree. I'm sure it helped us retune our Chi. But the Blame Tree was in Shin, thousands of li away, and it died years ago, and there's nothing like it here at Pearl Famous that could retune our—

The Arch of Chi Retuning! Where the weird healer sent Mole Girl after her accident. In the Garden of Whispering Arches. That's the most powerful antidote for Chi disturbances. But it's all the way across the Principal Island. As soon as I took my sixth step toward the Arch of Chi Retuning, my bones would shatter inside me. It might as well be thousands of li away; it's all the same to me here in the Dian Mai.

Is there a way for me to get out of the Dian Mai? I think of

Cricket's other clues. Architecture and wu liu. Where have I heard them mentioned together?

Sensei Madame Liao's words come back to me. *The steps of an honorable person lead through walls; the steps of a dishonorable person become a prison.*

The five-point bone-shatterer hollow fist is a prison. But perhaps my steps can lead through its walls.

Do not be so quick to judge deficiencies, Sensei Madame Liao had said. *Sometimes, they are just advantages that are interpreted incorrectly, like trying to read a logogram turned upside down.*

Where everyone else sees a deficiency in a building, the architect who built it sees a secret door and can glide right through.

Your ability to glide on one step. You could cross five li in five steps. No one else here can do that.

I learned to glide because I couldn't afford to replace my skate blades and because I relied on moves that travel farther to conserve my steps.

The clues are crying out at me like a silent word that I can't read because I'm looking at it upside down.

The Dian Mai imprisons me within the walls of my own body. But the steps of an honorable person can lead through walls. I thought that my reliance on gliding on one foot was a deficiency. But perhaps it is an advantage that will allow me to step out of this—

My ability to glide will allow me to skate all the way to the Arch of Chi Retuning as long as I stretch my five steps into five glides!

Sensei Madame Liao must have sent Cricket. She couldn't be

seen coming here herself. She had Cricket speak to me in code in case anyone overheard so that he wouldn't be implicated. She convinced Supreme Sensei Master Jio to let her use a Dian Mai on me instead of the shrinking pavilion. She knew that I was the only person here who could make it to the Arch of Chi Retuning in less than six steps.

She built a prison with a secret door for me, knowing that I would be the only person who could glide through it. I just needed Cricket to teach me how to see.

I'm not alone in this after all. Sensei Madame Liao was always there. And Cricket. I was just so busy facing forward toward my future that I couldn't see who was standing behind me.

There's only one reason why Sensei Madame Liao would risk this to get me out. She wants me to find the proof that Suki has been behind the attacks and disprove the Chairman's interpretation of the oracle.

How many steps would it normally take to travel five li? A hundred? Five hundred? Just the sharp corners and turns between here and the Arch of Chi Retuning would eat up so many steps. And I can't just cross the Principal Island in a straight line because of the older students patrolling the campus. I'd have to take the longer route along the northern perimeter. It's not possible.

I put on my skates. The woven reed fibers of the boots are stiff. I've never gone so long without wearing them.

Five li in five steps.

I stand. I can feel that Cricket's done a beautiful job of filing away the damage on the blades.

Five steps. That's all I get.

I stretch toward the shoji and slide it open. Outside, the pearl rises in silent drifts from the sleeping academy.

Five steps, and I need to have passed under the Arch of Chi Retuning.

I reach my left skate back and brace it against the wall. I am grateful that our dormitory chambers are so small.

If I make it in five steps, I take the sixth step a free person.

I crouch back on my skate pushed up against the back wall.

If I don't, the sixth step will be my last.

But I crossed three thousand li to come here. I can cross five more.

I explode out of the chamber.

I land on my right skate and careen down the dormitory corridor.

I have to fight the instinct to put my other skate down. I can do this. For Cricket.

This first step is for him. Thank you, Cricket, for coming to me and restoring my skates and bringing the message. I approach the first bend of the hallway and take the corner without slowing. I speed out of the ornamental gate of the girls' dormitory and across the complex of bridges dividing the dormitory areas. The rise and fall of bridges cuts down on my momentum and I leap forward onto my other skate.

This second step is for Sensei Madame Liao. Thank you,

Sensei. For teaching me what I needed to learn, both the skills that I didn't have and the value of the skills I had. Thank you for teaching me about deficiencies and heroes and myself. I swoop on my left leg and whip myself around the first corner of the Courtyard of Supreme Placidness. I take the second corner to clear the palace. I come around it and leap onto my right skate.

This third step is for Hisashi. I thought I knew you. You hurt me, but I can see now that you were trying to save me. I skate past the islet of the Temple of Heroes of Superlative Character. I can see the arch where I leaped off with Hisashi, hand in hand, trusting this beautiful boy whom I didn't really know but cared about, still care about. The drifts rising up from the pearl catch on my wet cheeks before they dissolve. My momentum slows, and I savor the moment as I pass by the temple, pass through my memories, until my right knee begins to throb with the sustained pressure. I pull out of it with a triple flying crane leap onto my left skate.

This luckieth step is for Doi. I needed you. You needed me. Thank you for being my partner, thank you for defending me, thank you for pleading with your father for me, thank you for trying to stop me from pursuing this, thank you for caring, and thank you for understanding that I have to do this. I leap over the false moats of pearlsilk ribbon and land on my right skate as I enter the Garden of Whispering Arches.

This final step is for you, Father and Mother, for all that you didn't do. You didn't bind my feet, like you thought the oracle meant when she said that our family's destiny lay in my feet. You didn't stay to raise Cricket and me. You didn't take care of us and shield us from so many things that children shouldn't have to face alone. But because you didn't do that, I'm strong enough now to take care of myself and Cricket. I'm certain enough now to take these five steps toward my destiny, even if my destiny is uncertain. I'm brave enough now to do what I have to do. So thank you, Father and Mother. It is only because of what you didn't do that I am now Chen Peasprout, and being Chen Peasprout is the truest gift you could have granted me.

The paths here in the Garden of Whispering Arches are laid in curves that weave back and forth, and there is not a single straight path in it. I've already lost half the momentum of my fifth step and I can't even see the Arch of Chi Retuning yet.

I finally sight it. At the crest of the highest hill in the garden.

I sling my center of gravity in loops, extending my left leg and swooping in one pestle windmill after another, whipping my leg as hard as I can to push me forward farther, a little farther, just a little, on my right skate. Daggers shoot through my knee, as if someone were trying to pry off the bone of my kneecap.

At last, I arrive at the Arch of Chi Retuning, curving like a rib bone in the moonlight. I hold my position on my right knee and glide into the shadow underneath it.

I come to a stop just before passing fully clear of it. I look up. Half of my vision is the dark underside of the arch. Half of it is the night sky above me.

Is this enough? Has it retuned my Chi?

Or will my bones shatter when I take the sixth step?

I try to twist and sling my arms to nudge myself all the way through the arch, but every movement sends spears of pain through my knee that almost cause me to trip and step forward.

What if I come down and crawl the rest of the way out from under the arch? No, it can't be that easy to defeat a Dian Mai. Any criminal could escape.

There's no other way.

I have to take the sixth step.

I lift my left skate.

I place it on the pearl in front of me and step out from under the arch.

The stabbing in my knee stops.

I hear a great crack, as of bones breaking. I close my eyes and wait for my body to shatter.

Something strikes my shoulder, then pounds to the pearl behind me. Pain lances through me. I open my eyes to see a great chunk of bone-white pearl lying on the ground.

I look up at the underside of the arch and see a missing section where the chunk of pearl used to be. Fissures begin racing across the whole of the structure.

I burst forward as hard as I can, skid to a stop, and turn just in time to see the Arch of Chi Retuning collapse into rubble and send up a bloom of dust that sparkles like crystals in the moonlight.

The strain of absorbing the Dian Mai destroyed the Arch of Chi Retuning. Like all our kicking killed the Blame Tree back in Shin.

I turn back and look out across the campus of Pearl Famous. I didn't know that I would ever gaze on this scene again. As I skated toward the Arch of Chi Retuning, I could have been skating past all these structures for the last time, because I could have been skating to my death.

But there they are all laid out before me now, like a landscape that I fully comprehend, a map that I know how to read to find what I'm looking for.

And what I'm looking for is justice.

"I know you're out there, Suki, and I'm coming for you."

CHAPTER
THIRTY

I race through the campus. During the days that I was imprisoned in the Dian Mai, great spinning fans on poles as large as windmills were placed along the perimeter of every islet near the water to suck the drifts of the pearl out toward the sea. They're churning so fast that anything that gets caught in them would be tugged up and chewed to pieces. What powers them? I'd better keep my robes and braids far away so that they don't end up sprayed in bits over the sea.

In the distance, I see someone hopping up the tiers of the Pagoda of Filial Sacrifice, slinging some sort of bag. My Chi quakes. The vandal!

I race toward the figure. It's definitely not Suki. She leads with her right leg. This person leads with the left, like most boys trained in Pearl. Could Suki have a male accomplice?

He turns to me but his hood hides his face in black. When he sees me, he abandons his ascent of the pagoda and backflips away, using the weight of his sack to launch himself into an open-toed scythe spin onto the roof of the Palace of the Eighteen Outstanding Pieties.

I pursue him at full speed. Cricket's modification of my skates is miraculous. It feels like they're locked on to rails when I find the grain in the pearl. I quickly shrink the distance between the figure and me. As hard as he skates, he's weighed down by the heavy sack he carries. When he lunges, I can see from the jostling of the sack that it contains several round objects. He sees me gaining on him, reaches into his sack, and tosses what looks like a snowball as large as a melon right into my path.

I leap forward and catch the snowball before it can hit the roof. It's heavier than I expected, and I almost drop it. The white ball is coarse and grainy, not like snow after all. As I continue racing after the boy, I touch my fingers to my lips.

Salt! It's a ball of salt, so dense that its weight is slowing me down.

"Stop!" I say.

The figure pumps his skates even harder. I can tell that he's an outstanding practitioner of wu liu to center his Chi so perfectly and move with such speed while carrying these salt balls.

"Stop! Who are you? Are you working for Suki?" As I grow closer, he throws another ball, aiming for the roof in front of me. If the salt touches the pearl, it'll eat away the roof from under my skates. I quickly throw my cloak out to catch the second ball, then snap the cloth with a flourish so that it ties itself around my shoulder in a sling. I toss both balls in it.

He throws another ball at my skates, and again, I catch it before it meets the pearl.

He's faster now that he's only carrying five balls, and I'm slower now that I'm carrying three. If it weren't for Cricket's modifications, I'd have lost him already. I gather all my remaining Chi into forward momentum, swing the bag of salt balls around me, and use it to launch myself into an east-directional, sixth-gate flying heron hook.

I land behind the boy and yank at his hood, releasing a length of beautiful waterfall hair.

No.

Doi. Why? You have so much to lose.

We stare at each other, and the look in her eyes is pitiable, her hair lashing across her face in the wind produced by the churning fans. Doi takes another ball and attempts to drop it on the short span of roof between us, but I grab the ball. We push against each other. For a moment, we're balanced so perfectly that we threaten to crush the ball between our hands.

I twist the ball away from her, then perform the same two-heeled sesame-seed pestle jump that won me the first Motivation. As I sweep over Doi's head, I reach out and grasp her waterfall hair to startle her just like she herself did to her attackers during the luckieth Motivation.

Her hair comes away in my hand.

I'm holding a wig of fine, black threads of pearlsilk.

We both scrape to a stop, and I look into the face of the person before me: those big, soft eyes; that short, dense hair; those cheeks where I know dimples lie dormant.

Not Doi. Hisashi.

No. It can't be. Not my Hisashi. He's not the vandal, because he can't be the sister of the boy from Shin. And because . . . because he's good. I need him to be good.

I stagger back a few steps and then slump with shock.

"Hisashi, why?"

He lunges for the wig, but I lift it up close to the spinning fan near us. The blades slap against the tips of the tendrils of pearlsilk hair.

"Why did you do this?" I demand. "Why were you pretending to be Doi?"

"Peasprout, I need that!"

"Answer me, Hisashi!"

"I'm not Hisashi!"

"What?"

"There is no Hisashi here."

"What do you mean?"

"Peasprout . . ."

I lift the wig even closer to the fan. The blades snag on a lock of hair and I tug back. With a whine, the fan pulls the lock out by its roots.

"Peasprout, I'm not pretending to be Doi. I am Doi. It was always me. Both of us."

Both of them. The same person.

That's why they never appeared together. That's why she had to sabotage the boys' Motivations. So that they wouldn't take place at the same time as the girls'. I think of Doi's smile when she said, "No one can be in two places at the same time." My hand is trembling so fiercely that I almost lose my grip on the wig. All those things that we said to each other when I thought she was Hisashi. At the Arch of the Sixteenth Whisper. On the dragon-phoenix boat during the Festival of Lanterns. I squeeze my eyes shut to force the tears of confusion and shock back down inside me.

She swipes at the wig again, but I open my eyes and tug it back behind me with a *snap*.

"Peasprout, I need that!"

"Why did you have to pretend to be two people?"

She tries to lunge around me, but I block her by hooking my leg around hers.

"Where is Hisashi? Do you really even have a brother? Answer me!"

She scissors her legs around mine and twists in midair, sending me spinning. I fly onto my rear and slide across the path from her.

"Were you disguising yourself as Hisashi to get close to me?" I ask. "So you could spy on me for your father? Is that whom you were talking to in the Courtyard of Supreme Placidness?"

Doi lunges at me. While she's in flight, I whip the wig behind her. She snatches at it but misses. I spring forward in a double somersault leap as she tumbles to the ground and snatch the wig out of the air.

"Peasprout, someone will hear us!"

"Tell me the truth!" I cry and lift the wig to the spinning fan again.

She leaps with both hands stretched like claws to snatch the wig from me. I flick the wig onto my head to free both arms to fight her, then crouch with my fists extended to meet Doi.

Seeing this, Doi changes the position of her leap midair. She rams her skates hard under the broken blade of my right skate, sending me hurtling into the air. The wig goes flying off my head.

She leaps up and plucks it from the air. She lands, clutching it to her chest, then turns to skate away.

With a yell, I yank at the strands of hair that trail behind her and haul her back like a horse on reins.

A sound rises across the campus. Someone has seen our battle and pulled an alarm.

"Please let go of the wig!" Doi says. "We have to get back before they find us out of the dormitory! I'll explain everything."

She's right. I can't be caught outside of the Dian Mai. I let go of the wig and we race back to the girls' dormitory.

When we skate into the central courtyard of the girls' dormitory, Sensei Madame Yao is standing there, waiting for us. Her muscles bulge through her little night undershirt. Suki stands next to Sensei, holding the cord of the alarm. The House of Flowering Blossoms girls flank her in formation, shoulder to shoulder, all of them in their night-robes, with their hair clamped in wooden straightening paddles. Suki stands next to Sensei, holding the cord of the alarm.

Sensei Madame Yao skates to Doi and me. She reaches into the sacks that we have slung around our shoulders and pulls out the balls of salt. For the first time I have ever seen, she smiles.

CHAPTER
THIRTY-ONE

First, Sensei Madame Yao brings us to Supreme Sensei Master Jio's chambers, then the two of them take us to a tower I have never been inside along the edge of the Principal Island. Doi and I are placed in a round chamber at the top of the tower.

Sensei Madame Yao commands, "Kneel on the pearl. Do not speak to each other. Speak into this if you have a confession to make about your crimes." She places a letter orb on the pearl between us. "Or about each other's crimes." She exits.

Supreme Sensei Master Jio looks at us with his hands folded up in his sleeves. I expect him to spout some useless, shaming nonsense. Instead, he says, "This hurts me, my little embryos. You have done something so extreme. People do not do something so extreme unless they are really suffering. My heart hurts because I failed to help you through that. I failed even to see that. I apologize." He bows to us.

And I thought he was a fool.

He leaves, closing the shoji.

"You owe me some answers," I say. "Start talking now, or I'll tell the senseis everything."

"I didn't want you to get involved. I was trying to protect you."

"Do you even have a brother named Hisashi?"

"Yes. But he's in Shin."

Chingu's oracle was correct after all. We just interpreted it incorrectly. If Doi's brother is in Shin, then the criminal responsible for attacking the buildings is not me, the sister of the boy from Shin. The criminal is Doi, the sister of the boy *in* Shin.

"Why isn't he here?"

"Hisashi went to try to bring back the New Deitsu skaters. He pretended to be a third wu liu skater from Pearl Famous. He brought some of the pearl to create a skating court for them to perform on for the Empress Dowager. They were going to invite her to sit in the place of honor, in a little structure in the center of the court."

"Just like Lim Tian-Tai got the eunuch Mu Haichen to do," I say.

"Yes. Once the Empress Dowager stepped in it, Hisashi would trap her and threaten to shrink her into a trinket unless she gave him and the New Deitsu skaters safe passage out of Shin. My task was to stay here and pretend to be both of us so that nobody would know he wasn't at Pearl Famous. But the Empress Dowager wouldn't step into the little structure."

"How did you know what he was doing in Shin?" I ask, but

then I realize I already know the answer. "You were communicating through the Chi pulse messages."

"Yes."

Someone comes skating up the ramp to our chamber at the top of the tower. The shoji door is unbolted and flung open so hard that the entire chamber shudders with the force. Chairman Niu's silhouette towers like a monster in a shadow-puppet play. He sees me, hisses, and grabs a fistful of my robe. He hauls me up so forcefully that both my skates leave the pearl for an instant.

"Let me go!" I pull my arm back to deliver a three-fingered gouging phoenix strike at his face.

"Don't hurt him!" Doi cries. Her arm shoots out at my head, but her fist stops short of my ear.

How dare she! I launch my other fist at her and stop just short of the Chi spot between her eyes.

The three of us stand there locked in this ridiculous triangle, our arms unmoving, all of us darting our eyes from one person to the other.

Finally, the Chairman releases his fist from my robe with a shove of his palm. I drop my arms only when Doi drops hers.

"I'm innocent," I tell him. "You have no right to detain me here."

"I owe you an apology, Father," Doi says. "Hisashi and I were just trying to help you. But I was careless, and I got caught."

The Chairman's head whips toward Doi when he hears Hisashi's name. "What does your brother have to do with this?" He turns to me. "Did you drag him into the Empress Dowager's plans?"

I open my mouth to tell him the truth, but I pause. Doi came up with this plan that could have gotten me imprisoned. But she also convinced her father to let me consult Chingu. When she knew that Chingu would name her. She couldn't have counted on the oracle being misinterpreted. She risked herself for me.

I fall silent. I can't tell the Chairman that Doi was responsible for all of this. It has to be her decision to do so.

"You Shinian snake," the Chairman spits, reaching for me.

"No, Father!" Doi says, shifting in front of me. "I'm the one who's been attacking the structures."

The Chairman stares at her. When it comes out, it's almost a bellow. "Why?"

"The boys' Motivations were at the same time as the girls'. I couldn't be in two places at the same time, so I had to find a way to delay the boys' Motivations."

"Two plac— Where is Hisashi?"

"He's in Shin. That's why I had to pretend to be both of us. So no one would know about our plan."

"What plan?" he roars.

"To show you how much we love you."

I look at this girl, with her shorn hair and her arms at her side, looking down at her father's feet.

"You're not making any sense," he says. "What plan? Why did you do this? Answer me!"

Doi still says nothing.

"Do you want me to tell him?" I ask her.

She looks at me and nods.

I take a deep breath and slip from behind her so that we're standing side by side. I look steadily into the Chairman's eyes.

"Hisashi went to the court of the Empress Dowager to bring back your hostages for you. He was going to trap her in one of the shrinking pavilions. Doi's role was to stay here and pretend to be both your daughter and your son so no one would know. They did this for you, so that you wouldn't have to give up the secret of the pearl to get back the hostages."

I watch the Chairman carefully. He can't be unmoved by this.

He glares at his daughter.

"You fool!" he spits out. "What if the Empress Dowager figures out that she has the son of the Chairman of New Deitsu in her custody?"

"We were just trying to help you."

His hand lifts to strike her.

I ready to block it.

Doi lifts her chin and says, "Hit me. I deserve it."

He pauses.

His towering outline quivers over her. Then it seems as if all the air is let out of him. The Chairman wipes his brow, chest rising and falling. He turns his own palms up and studies the lines on them.

"I blame myself," he says to her. "But you're done here, and you're done with your plan. You're going back to Pearl Colony. I'm going to commit you as a novice nun. You're done with wu liu. You will never compete again. And you're going to say that you found Peasprout attacking the structures."

I look at Doi. She is being forced to choose between her own future and mine. I always knew we were rivals and that one of us must suffer for the other to prevail. Destiny just found another way to pit us against each other.

"We'll imprison her and offer her up in exchange for your brother," the Chairman says.

"No!" Doi cries.

"How else do you think I'm going to clean up this disaster?"

"You can't do this to her!" shouts Doi.

"*You* did this to her. It's her or your brother."

How did I get caught in this dangerous game? I'm just a girl from Shin.

But so was Little Pi Bao Gu. And she came here to Pearl and was asked to use her talents to protect her new home from Shin.

Heroes come in all shapes and sizes, but so do traitors.

Doi and Hisashi—the real Hisashi—and I are trapped between tigers. The Empress Dowager. The Chairman. We cannot fight. We cannot run.

The only way out is to grab one of the tigers by the tail.

I pick up the letter orb that Sensei Madame Yao left in the cell in case Doi and I wanted to confess or accuse each other. I twist apart the two halves.

I speak into it, "Divine and Calm Mother Empress Dowager of the Great Shin Imperium, your worthless servant Chen Peasprout has just learned how to discover the secret of the pearl. The third skater from Pearl brought a pavilion. If you sleep inside it, it will produce in your dreams a Bai Lou Meng, which is an oracle that will tell you any secret you wish. Please hurry. The future of Shin depends on it. Your undeserving emissary, Chen Peasprout."

I close the orb, pull out the pearlsilk membrane.

The Chairman says, "Is that true?"

"No," I say. "But the Empress Dowager does extreme things when she doesn't get what she wants. She won't be able to resist stepping inside, and Hisashi can trap her and demand safe passage out of Shin for your skater and himself."

Doi wraps her hands around my hands folded around the orb.

"Peasprout, you can't do this! You'll never be able to go back to Shin," she says. "Or Cricket! You'll never be safe there."

I push her hands away and hold the letter orb toward the Chairman.

"We've never been safe anywhere."

"But the Empress Dowager's Chiologists will analyze the orb and know it's a lie!" Doi argues. "They'll hear the blockage."

"Chiologists can only hear if the speaker is speaking against her will. I'm not saying this against my will."

"I'm not going to let you do this. I've pulled you into enough trouble."

"Be silent, you stupid girl!" the Chairman says.

"This isn't her problem," she replies. "This is our family problem. I won't let you bring her into this."

"Don't talk to me like that, you worthless child."

He lifts his hand again.

My palm flashes out to stop him from striking Doi, but the blow never comes. Instead, the Chairman pulls back his hand. He covers his mouth, but not before I see the corners tug down as he tries not to cry.

He straightens and collects himself. Then the Chairman takes the orb from my open palm.

He skates to the door leading out of the chamber.

"Father," cries Doi, rubbing her chest as if to squeeze the pain out of it. "Don't leave angry with me. I was just trying to unbreak our family. That's all I've ever wanted."

He hesitates there and turns back. His eye is twitching. I can feel the tremendous effort coming off his Chi in waves, but he's unable to contain his emotion.

He returns to Doi and looks as if he's struggling to find words.

Say something to your daughter, I silently beg. Before I can reach them, he slaps her across the face so hard that he has to take two steps to keep from toppling forward with the force. Doi slides across the floor of the chamber and collides with the bags of salt balls.

The Chairman is crying, a grotesque keening sound. He says, "I should never have listened to your mother. I should never have chosen the two of you over her."

He exits the chamber, looking only at the broken long nail on his small finger, and bolts the door behind him.

CHAPTER
THIRTY-TWO

Doi's heaving as hard as if she just skated a Motivation.

"Are you hurt?" I skate over and kneel by her side.

"It's nothing."

"You're bleeding." I reach to wipe the corner of her mouth with my cuff, but she flicks my hand away.

"Just leave it."

I let her collect her Chi.

"I'm not going to let you send the orb to the Empress Dowager," she says.

"Your father already has the orb. It's too late."

"I'm never going to put you in danger again. I'm going to keep you safe."

Doi pushes herself up and kneels facing me, too close. She says, "Because all we have is each other."

Her eyes are soft and needing and familiar. Hisashi's eyes.

All those deeply private things that she got me to share with her while she was disguised as Hisashi. She deceived me. She tried to kiss me.

Doi reaches out to touch my face.

The thought of her touching my skin repels me. I feel so betrayed. I slap her hand away.

Doi's expression swells with hurt.

She touches my arm, and I can't help it. I shrink back. "Don't touch me!"

"Peasprout—"

"Stop it! It was all lies!"

"It was never a lie. It was real. It wasn't Hisashi; it was me."

"It could never be real."

"Why?"

I say nothing. I've said enough. I don't want to be cruel, but Doi understands as if I've spoken every thought aloud.

"Because I'm a girl," Doi says quietly.

She gets up, picks up one of the bags, and plucks out a salt ball from it.

"Fine; it could never be real. But now I'm going to do something so real, you'll never forget me." Doi hurls the salt ball at the floor beneath her skates. The pearl begins to steam and sizzle.

She stamps on the ball and the salt sprays outward. She brings down the other skate onto the material and with a *crack*, she disappears through the hole in the floor.

"Doi!" I cry.

I need to stop whatever she's going to do, but I've struck a pact with the Chairman. I can't go breaking out of imprisonment again. Not with my record.

But I also can't let Doi do whatever it is she's planning on doing.

I grab the other sack of salt balls and drop through the floor.

I spot Doi on the floor of the tower below.

"Doi, stop!" I cry again. But she leaps out through an arch and is gone. I lean hard and skate after her.

It's dark and my vision is obscured by the drifts of pearl flake rising up all around me toward the night sky.

I see her. Doi is skating toward the Palace of the Eighteen Outstanding Pieties with the bag of salt balls swinging behind her.

She's going to destroy as many structures on the campus as she can. She only has three salt balls left, but three can cause plenty of devastation.

"Doi, stop! Please don't do this!"

"What do you care?"

"Your father could do something even worse to you!"

"Oh, I know what he could do to me that would be worse." She skids to a stop, faces me, and spits, "Nothing! Nothing he could do would be worse!"

She skates off. We hurtle on the rails down curving narrow alleys with the tall academy structures crowding above our heads. We wend around pillars and leap over arches. Bridges suspended with pearlcord sway as we race under them.

Doi nears the Palace of the Eighteen Outstanding Pieties and does a double-sleeved heron flip onto the spine of the roof. She lands sideways, and her skates catch on a bump in the roof. I use her stumble to catch up. She regains her balance and flings a salt ball down onto the roof behind her, but I do a backward tornado mallet and send it flying into the sky before it touches the roof. I hear it splash into the sea behind us. She has two salt balls left; I have four.

As she leaps off to a retaining wall beside the palace, I throw a ball at her feet to stop her. She catches the ball and turns to me. Now we both have three balls. "Peasprout, don't! They'll say the Empress Dowager made you do it."

"You stop and I'll stop."

I fling myself in a triple-toe nightingale spin and try to seize the sack from her. I purposefully don't curb my kick coming out of the spin so that I nick her shoulder with the edge of my skate blade to startle her. Doi drops a ball between us, leaving her two, but I crouch and kick the one she dropped aside with an inverted iron parasol sweep. I hear the ball splash far to the right. Doi whips away and hops on the rail leading to the Conservatory of Wu Liu.

She races away from me on the outer rails, over open water. If I can knock her into the water, all the salt balls will melt. I hope that the senseis will be merciful if I only attack a stretch of rail and not an actual structure.

Cricket's modification of my skates is even more apparent here on the rails, which are carved to follow the natural grain. I shoot forward as if the pearl were propelling me.

As the length of rail between Doi and me closes and the path takes a sharp turn, I reach in my sack and fling one ball at the rail in front of her and one behind.

She leaps high and blocks them before they strike the rails, catching one and knocking one into the sea, giving her three balls and leaving me with just one. However, by the time she comes down, I've lunged forward and am there waiting for her. Before her skates touch the rails, I knee her into the sea.

Doi goes plummeting into the ocean with the sack. As it's about to fall into the water, she kicks the sack so that her three remaining salt balls bump up. One ball comes flying back toward me, and I catch it. She juggles the remaining two in the air, alternating swimming strokes with kicks and elbow bumps to keep them from touching the water.

Doi does a flying golden dolphin flipper kick and flings herself up backward onto a rail. She tosses the last two salt balls into her cloak and wraps the fabric to form a sack around her body as she races forward.

The rails divide into two tracks, and we race alongside each other. Now that we both have two salt balls left, we're willing to risk throwing them at the rails. We each hurl a ball at the track in front of the other and leap over the explosion of salt, vapor, and the pearl.

We shoot together in an arc toward the Principal Island, our arms and skates locked in a lucky-fisted palanquin formation. We each only have one salt ball left, and we can't let the other steal it. Doi and I are hurtling toward the hard pearl, and we'll be injured if we don't break apart, but I don't let go. She'll have to be the one to let go.

Doi does, and she comes slinging out of the lock in a brilliant half spin that carves a crescent into the pearl. I land harder.

"Why are you doing this?" Doi says, her voice breaking. "Why are you trying to stop me?"

"Because I'm your friend!"

"I never wanted you as a friend!"

I don't know what to say to this.

"Do you know," she says, her chest heaving, "what it's like to want something? And then learn that you can never have what you want? Do you have any idea how that feels?"

"Yes, I do! He was good and kind, and he made me feel something I'd never felt before, but I'm never going to see him again, because he never existed!"

Now Doi's the one who doesn't know what to say. She turns and skates hard, clutching her last salt ball.

I follow her through the Garden of Whispering Arches, but she's starting to get away from me. With a pang, I remember the last time I was here with Hisashi—no, Doi. My knee flashes with pain. She continues to skate through and under and over the arches at full speed, and I'm starting to slow. I skate over an arch and my broken skate heel catches on some ornamental filigree. I nearly trip and drop my last ball.

She turns back, sees me, and cries, "Peasprout, not there!"

"Why?" I say. The tablet on the arch says that it's the Arch of Buried Whispers. "What are you hiding here?"

"I can't tell you."

"Haven't you lied to me enough?"

"There's something irreplaceable here!"

"Tell me!" I cry, and I swing my arm back, ready to send the ball flying at the arch.

Doi's face crumples, then she skates over to the structure. With a nod, she indicates that I should skate to the other end and place my ear to it. She gently taps with the heel of her hand and the tips of her fingers in a rhythm.

One, two, three, lucky.

One, two, three, lucky.

One, two, three, one, two, three, one, two, three, lucky.

Each beat of lucky ends with the gentle pressure of her full palm on the arch. And then the arch begins to ring with a high hum.

As I crouch next to it, I hear a voice in my ear, stale and thin, like a sound from long ago but bright and joyous. It's whispered, and it's hard to tell whether it's a boy's or a girl's voice.

It says, "Today, on the thirtieth day of the sixth month, the last day of the Season of Spouts . . . I finally found what I thought I'd never find."

I press my hand over my mouth. The voice is the same voice that I heard whispering into my ear from an arch so long ago. Like a voice from the dead. Which it might as well be. That boy who whispered words that lifted me so is gone now, forever.

I turn to look at Doi far away at the other end of the arch.

"See," she says. "I told you. Something irreplaceable."

And as the pearl rises from the ground in silent drifts around her, Doi falls to her knees, buries her face in her hands, and weeps.

THIRTY-THREE

The senseis find both of us guilty of violating curfew. The only destruction we caused was to the outer rails. No structures were damaged. We could have been expelled and maybe arrested if there were.

The damage from the prior attacks can't legally be used against Doi because it was covered by the contract for service with New Deitsu, so it cost Pearl Famous nothing. The academy suffered no legal harm and any claim it had was transferred to New Deitsu when they repaired the damage. The last thing that the Chairman wants is more attention to this matter, so he's unlikely to press charges against his own daughter.

Our sentencing session is all smeared in my memory, but I remember many of the senseis being vicious toward us. I wrinkle into ash at the memory, because we deserved their anger. However, I also remember Sensei Madame Liao staring them down, stabbing her finger at clauses on the scrolls of academy rules. The other sen-seis raged when they couldn't find a path around her logic. I recall Supreme Sensei Master Jio saying that when they attain sagehood, they'll understand the justice in mercy, and Sensei Madame Yao punching a hole in a table, and at the end of it, Sensei Madame Liao proclaiming, "That is final!"

Our punishment is harsh but less harsh than we deserve. Doi and I are both required to surrender our skates for the rest of the term. We'll both forfeit the last Motivation.

I am grateful that no mention is made of Cricket in all of this. No one suspects him of having any part in the vandal attacks. Further, his speaking in code to help me escape out of the Dian Mai pro-tected him from being implicated after all.

I have so many things I want to say to Cricket, but when he sees me, he skates away. That is probably for the best. He shouldn't be associated with me.

New Deitsu comes to the campus and does its work quickly, since all they have to do is replace the rails. When they're finished, Chairman Niu doesn't follow it with another visit. I wonder if I'll ever know if he sent my letter orb. I wonder if the Empress Dowa-ger will ever receive it. If she'll be fooled by it. If she'll realize I tricked her. If I'll ever be able to return to Shin. All I know is that I never wanted to choose between Shin and Pearl. But the Empress

Dowager's own actions forced me to. And when I had to choose, I chose my new home.

I chose Pearl.

Sensei Madame Liao and Supreme Sensei Master Jio command Doi and me not to talk to any of the other students about why we've been unskated. But it's not going to matter whether we talk about it or not. The two best girl skaters in our class got eliminated from the final Motivation after all these attacks on the campus. No one is going to fail to put it together.

But it seems like the excitement of the final Motivation, and the upcoming Drift Season Pageant and Beautymarch, and maybe even a bit of satisfaction that two leading girls got kicked out of the running, mean that most of the students leave us alone more than I expected. I think that all the students can sense that we're damaged, we're trouble, we're unlucky to know. Our spectacular downfall makes Suki as happy as if she had been anointed Empress Dowager.

Doi stops pretending to be Hisashi. She appears on campus as herself, with her close-cropped hair. The student known as Niu Hisashi simply disappears from the life of Pearl Famous. But then again, he never went to classes, never appeared in crowds, never seemed to have any more friends than I did.

You'd think that the son of the Chairman of New Deitsu would have a lot of friends. Perhaps he does.

I wouldn't know.

I've never met him.

The secret of the pearl and the salt seems to be intact. As everyone said, the pearl comes from the sea. The sea is salty but only so salty. Everyone here seems to grow up accepting the danger of salt without asking why it destroys the pearl. That must be why no one uses anything saltier than seawater to season their food. That must be why none of the merchants at the market except for the Shinian woman had any salt to sell. She probably smuggled it in from Shin. She only sold it to me because she hates Pearl. She knew the destruction it could cause. I remember how she told me to burn everything down with it.

Why would they build a city that can be destroyed by so common and useful a thing? And not ask more questions about it? But then again, fire is common and useful, too. No one asks why fire burns. It's just something that people are taught to be afraid of from when they're little without needing more explanation. I'm starting to learn that there are a lot of things like that that we're taught.

Now that I know, it seems so obvious. Salt is prohibited because it destroys the pearl, which means the pearl is made from some living matter. It's probably a rare crop, just like bamboo. Shin invaded Pearl for its bamboo, and Pearl is afraid that Shin is going to invade again, this time for the pearl. Shin and Pearl are sending their most famous skaters as pawns in the fight for the pearl.

Salt. The pearl. My fame. All of them fine, sparkling things. All of them responsible for the position I'm in now. All of them leading me to my decision to become a traitor to Shin.

One evening, as I'm shuffling in my socks back to my dormitory chamber after evenmeal, I pass a gathering of students. The twilight has repainted the campus in hues of black and kingfisher blue. A cluster of boys huddles in a golden glow of lanterns under the Gate of Complete Centrality and Perfect Uprightness.

They're playing some sort of game. Each boy holds the carved wooden sculpture that he'll be submitting for the competition. There's a boy in the center of their circle with a band of cloth folded over his eyes. Cricket. One of the other boys holds out a sculpture. Cricket reaches out with just his thumb, his pointing finger, and his long finger.

As soon as his three fingers touch the sculpture, lightly, Cricket cries out, "The Pavilion of Dreams in Red!"

The boys around him laugh and demand, "How did you know?" And then, as if they're used to hearing the answer, they sing in chorus, "Proportions!"

Cricket looks as happy as a brightstar of wu liu, taking his place on the stage of an opera. He doesn't have to excel at wu liu now to prove that he's not a spy who is just decent enough to pass for a skater.

Architecture comes as naturally for him as wu liu does for me. When you're doing it, it feels as if all the forces within you are pushing you to your destiny. It doesn't matter whether I think he's good enough to succeed in architecture. It's not for me to decide.

With an indescribable heave in my breast, I say good-bye to the brother I have known.

"Farewell, my little Cricket," I whisper. "I release you. You have found your grain."

Doi and I each struggle alone across campus in our socks on the slick pearl. She won't speak to me. I'm not sure I want her to. She lied to me and made a fool out of me. She played me like a pearlflute.

Why did she do it? She must have known that it was pointless.

She created something, then let me start to like it, then destroyed it.

Not something, someone.

Not like, love.

I miss Hisashi. I miss the kind, strong, brave boy who showed so much heart and shared so much of his heart, who did so many things for me that I can never forget.

Except that boy didn't do those things.

That boy didn't suffer the punishment in Sensei Madame Yao's class.

That boy didn't patiently teach Cricket and choose him as his partner.

He didn't fight Suki for me over the pearlflute.

Or open my eyes to the cruelty we inflict on living creatures.

He never listened to me when I felt so lost here.

He wasn't the one who saw me and heard me and understood me.

Someone else did those things.

Someone who tried to help me, who stood against her father for me, and who lost her career in wu liu as a result. As well as everything else she cared about.

My anger fades.

Doi only wanted what everyone wants.

What I wanted.

I can't give her what she wants most.

But I can be her friend.

Watching the last Motivation take place without us is hard to describe. I know how I would once have described it. With grand statements and the sweeping, extreme language that I loved to use so much.

The girls' final Motivation is Drunken Grasshopper Dance. It's just a simple spinning and jumping exercise derived from an old Shinian children's game called hops-and-crosses. I was champion of hops-and-crosses for all of Shui Shan Province three times before the age of six, but I don't like to boast.

Suki takes first place in the sixth Motivation by completing ninety-seven continuous rotations. Doi did one hundred and sixty rotations during the "Dragon and the Phoenix" routine when she was only ten.

As I watch the girls compete and turn their bodies into those beautiful forms, a pain that I can't describe fills my breast. There's only one other person who knows how that pain feels. However, when I look over at Doi, she stares straight ahead at the girls on the pearl doing what we are not.

At the conclusion of the final Motivation, the final wu liu results are announced at an assembly of all the first-year students. My heart bursts when I learn that Cricket is in the top half of his class! Near the bottom of the top half but the top half, nonetheless.

Then the girls are announced. Suki takes first ranking. Etsuko and Chiriko take second and third. In fact, they've done so well that their final scores dwarf those of the boys. The three of them will be awarded the top roles in the Drift Season Pageant.

Doi ranks fifteenth. The hall hums with whispers when this is announced. We all know that she's the greatest practitioner of wu liu at Pearl Famous. I can admit that now.

My final points rank me sixteenth. Unlike Doi, I'll have next year to make up for my shortfall, and I know that I still have a chance to be asked to devote to the Conservatory of Wu Liu at the end of the second year. But who knows what's going to happen next year? I came here as part of a goodwill exchange. That goodwill has ended.

What's going to happen if my plan works and the Empress Dowager is tricked by the letter orb? She'll be furious. What if Shin decides to invade? Will that give the government here a legal right to take me as a prisoner of war? What about Cricket?

When I think of how I only cared about taking first ranking and the lead in the Drift Season Pageant as the first student from Shin, I burn with embarrassment. What a silly, self-involved girl I was.

As we leave the assembly, the students race out in a noisy flood, cheering the official end of the term.

They skate past me with unnecessary speed, but I don't blame them. They're just happy that the Motivations and rankings are done. Happy, because they have the Drift Season Pageant and Beautymarch to look forward to. Happy, because it's hard not to be happy when you're skating on the pearl.

When the crowd blows past, a figure remains on the pearl. She must have slipped as all the other students raced past. She's kneeling with her legs splayed out to keep her balance, like a fat goose. Niu Doi. Who has never once fallen down in the year that we've been here. Except for when she stood on her hands in Sensei Madame Yao's class. For me.

Two boys skate to her. Hong-Gee and Matsu. Whom Doi defeated at the boys' third Motivation. They both extend an arm to her. She hesitates. She must resent their pity. But then she reaches out her arms and they lift her to her feet with that grip, forearm to forearm, like pilots of battle-kites. She grasps the balustrade of the path beside them. They bow to her. Nothing comes out of her mouth; nothing expresses itself on her face. The boys leave her.

I take careful little steps over to her, holding on to the balustrade.

We must look pathetic together with our bare socks and our hands gripping the rail like drunkards.

"Why didn't you just let me do it?" Doi says. "Why didn't you let me destroy Pearl Famous?"

"I had to try to stop you from doing more harm to yourself."

"I was going to do it anyway."

"I couldn't stand by and do nothing."

"What does it matter? I'm done here."

"Who knows what the New Year will bring?"

"What do you care what happens to me?"

I don't say it. She needs to say it. If she doesn't say it, it's not true. I was wrong. It's not something that I can offer, whether she accepts it or not. That's not friendship. That's pity.

At last, she turns to me, her lips pressed together to hide their trembling. "You truly are my friend."

"It takes you a while, but you get there eventually."

"You're the friend I've waited my whole life to meet. I was stupid to push that away just because I couldn't have everything else that I wanted from you."

She places her hands on her chest to emphasize these last words. When she does so, her balance falters. Doi scrambles in her socks, and reaches out to grab the balustrade beside us. Her hand briefly brushes my hand, resting on it.

She snaps her whole arm back and takes two small steps away from me. Doi's gaze fixes on the pearl between us. Hot waves of shame roll off of her Chi. Her face burns with an expression of profound hate.

I realize that this hate is aimed wholly at herself.

She hates the strongest, bravest student here at Pearl Famous because of what that girl liked.

Whom, not what.

Loved, not liked.

I don't know much about these things. But it seems deeply wrong that love should ever be a reason for hate.

I take her hand in mine and fold my other hand over hers.

Doi looks at me with astonished eyes. It cuts slices into my heart to think that she, who defended me so many times and paid so high a price for it, should be so surprised at such a small kindness in return.

When she sees the tears on my cheeks, her heart at last caves in.

"I don't want to leave here, Peasprout! I'm frightened! And what's going to happen to you? What are we going to do?"

I have no answers for my friend, and the only thing that I can do is offer my hands and join my weeping with hers.

CHAPTER
THIRTY-LUCKY

The final weeks of the school year are filled with preparations for the Drift Season Pageant. The opera that the first-year students are going to perform is *The Great Leap of Shin*. Sensei Madame Phoenix selected a script written by two girls whose names I don't recognize. When the winning students are called to ascend to the front of the hall at the announcement ceremony, I see that it's the two silent girls whom I forced to partner with me in literature class. Good.

Mitsuko is chosen by Sensei Madame Yao for the score that she composed. Two first-year boys and one first-year girl are chosen for their sculptures. They'll assist the three third-year students who have devoted to the Conservatory of Architecture in designing and building the opera stage. I wonder how much the first-years are entrusted with the secrets of the pearl.

A great sheet of pearlsilk that's twice as tall as the Temple of Heroes of Superlative Character encircles the site of the construction on the central performing stage at the Conservatory of Music. Whatever they're building in there must be epic. The three students' winning sculptures are displayed on slender plinths in front of the site. They're fine works. However, it hurts to notice that none of them has an interior as Cricket's had, with two sculptures inside. He should be behind that sheet of pearlsilk now, helping to create the stage.

"Cricket, can you ever forgive me?" I cry at the wall of pearlsilk.

There's rustling behind it. I didn't realize that anyone was working there. The curtain parts and a head appears. It's Cricket!

When he sees me, he freezes. There are so many things I've wanted to say to him since I destroyed his sculpture, but the only words I get out are "What are you doing in there?"

"I'm helping with the creation of the stage."

"But . . . how?"

"I helped the three winning students carve their entries, so they asked me to help them as their assistant. And then Supreme Sensei Master Jio saw a design I drew and he liked it."

Two third-year students suddenly appear through the slit in the pearlsilk. One of them, a tall, bossy-looking girl, says, "Cricket, you promised to help—" She cuts herself short when she sees me there.

"I'm sorry, Peasprout. I have to go. I'm doing something

important." He says this without gloating. He smiles wanly and disappears behind the screen.

Since the Drift Season Pageant is cast according to wu liu rankings, Suki was given the lead role of the chief engineer, Mu Haichen, but refused it, because she found it "disgusting" to play a eunuch. The role went to Etsuko, who also was offended at playing this great hero. Suki instead chose to play the role of the boy Lim Tian-Tai. However, she threw a fit at playing a boy and insisted that the script be changed so that at one point, it's revealed that Lim Tian-Tai was only pretending to be a boy and was actually a classical beauty and a princess in disguise, and that at least half of her time onstage be spent in beautiful gowns. Sensei Madame Liao fired her from the production for insubordination, but Sensei Madame Yao and Sensei Madame Phoenix brought Suki back and insisted that her requested changes be made.

The two boys with the highest rankings in wu liu take the roles of the girl assassins Shok-Bee and Yumi. Suki and Etsuko were originally offered the roles, but they insisted it would be humiliating and morally outrageous to make them play supporting characters. Thus, the opera ultimately proceeds with two girls playing males and two boys playing females.

At last, the evening of the performance of the Drift Season Pageant arrives. We gather in Eastern Heaven Dining Hall for the End-of-Term Feast. Doi and I don't eat a single bite because everything has animal parts in it and Doi made dumpling soup and vegetable curry-fried rice for us beforehand. However, it's also because we're restless with anticipation to see the opera performed. At last the clarion formed by the tower on the eastern side of the Hall of Lilting Radiance sounds, and a great cheer rises up. We all proceed to the site of the performance at the Conservatory of Music, Doi and I rowing a small boat across the water so we don't have to navigate the rails in socks.

When we arrive and finally view what they've been building behind the great sheets of pearlsilk, we gape in shock and delight.

The entire stage is a vast structure of the pearl in the form of a massive tsunami wave. It curves over itself and reaches out toward the audience, looming over where we sit. The surface of the structure seems to indicate a riot of busy detail within the wave itself. However, the stage towers so high above us that, in the dim light, it's impossible to see what's embedded inside it.

When the sun has finally set, we take our seats. The lanterns lining the aisles are dimmed. A student skates onto the dark stage. She does a pinwheel flip ending in splits and flings two torches to either side of the stage. They strike twin fuses leading to strings of firecrackers. As the explosions race up the fuses, we see that the stage is braided with lattices of fireworks, lighting thousands of tiny candles strung through the interior of the wave to swell the whole structure with a sweep of golden light.

We gaze, dazzled. Then another gasp goes up as we see that the whole structure is translucent and deep inside are carved giant dolphins and sharks and whales and schools of fish and monstrous unnamed things churned up from the sea floor by the tsunami, all in living detail but far more massive than they would be in reality and all hanging above us instead of swimming below.

It's like something out of a fever dream, vivid, impossible, and so unbearably beautiful that it brands itself onto the sleeping mind and is wrenched with us into waking. The marvel on everyone's faces, bathed in golden light from the wave above us, tells us that we're all awake together and that tonight, reality is better than a dream.

As I stare up at the form of the wave bearing every wonder of the deep, I realize that there's only one person who has the skill to carve these sculptures within a sculpture. My heart's bursting so full of pride that I can't hold the tears back.

When the opera begins, it quickly becomes apparent that it bears only the most rudimentary resemblance to the true events of the Great Leap of Shin. If the boy Lim Tian-Tai had as many costume changes during his desperate race to the Imperial City as Suki has during the performance, he would still be only halfway there now. However, as pure spectacle, it's staggering.

As the dance battle between the armies of Lim Tian-Tai and Mu Haichen escalates, the skaters begin to skate round and round to gather speed. Several of them sweep up the half cylinder formed by the wave and use it to launch up and engage in aerial combat. Several battles end with the loser kicked through the air and flying over the audience.

The forms and the movements and the sounds are so striking, they impale themselves in your mind so that you quickly get to the point where you feel that there's no other form of fighting in the world, no other form of sport, no other form of dance. This is the only way to move. Everything else is just a pale shadow.

Watching this, I know that wu liu is all I've ever wanted to do. And I know that wu liu, and everything else that's important to me, might be taken away because I chose to help Pearl; I chose to help my friend.

I also know that I had to do what I did.

For I am Chen Peasprout. And being Chen Peasprout is more important to me than being a legend of wu liu.

I'm drawn out of contemplation as the opera hurtles toward its great finale. The eunuch Mu Haichen issues the command with a chop of his hand; the great fireworks cannons strike the beat for the leap; the Great Wall of two hundred million men stretching six hundred li across the vastness of Shin, represented by the army of skaters in black, leaps in unison on the central spine of the earth. At the seventy-eighth leap, the earth shudders and quakes and cracks and breaks.

A rumble rises behind the audience. We all turn to look. A phalanx of skaters in blue, trailing fluttering ribbons, washes down the aisles through the audience, representing the tsunami wave launched by the Great Leap of Shin. The skaters fling themselves into the half cylinder, take its curve hard, and come whipping up and back at us, soaring overhead and scattering petals of blue paper as we're all washed under by the tide that drowned the first city of Pearl. We roar as the structure is flushed with water, and the candles are put out, and we're plunged into darkness.

The cast, composer, author, and architects take their ovations. Afterward, the three stars come down from the stage to meet their fellow students and show their sumptuous costumes up close. The first-year students who won the sculpture competition are gathered with the third-year Conservatory of Architecture students on the stage, basking in the majesty of their handiwork.

"Where is Cricket?" I hear one of the stage design team say. They search in the audience and see him. They skate down together to bring him up on the stage.

I want to go to him, I want to say things to him, but I don't know if I have the right. I turn to Doi beside me. She nods toward the stage.

I shamble up the ramp at the side of the stage. When Cricket sees me, he is still. He doesn't look away or bury his chin in his breast. Is it his turn now to be ashamed of me, in my socks, with my sixteenth-place ranking? He nods his head slightly. I shuffle to him. His friends part to let me through.

I reach down and take his hands. I look at the wave yawning over us and say, "That came out of your hands? These little hands?" The tears trace down my cheeks. "Can you forgive me? I was so wrong." He turns his face up to me, weeping openly as well.

"How could I not see?" I say. "Those statues you carved inside your sculpture of the temple. They were just too small for me to see how beautiful they were." I look up at the giant dolphins and whales and other sea life teaming within the form of the wave hanging over me. "But now, you've made something so big that it fills the sky. And even someone as stupid as I am can see." I place my hands on his shoulders. "I see you, Cricket. And I'm so proud of you."

And there, in front of all those people, I open my arms to him. I don't embrace him; I don't wrap him up in my arms. I come toward him as he comes toward me, and we embrace each other.

When the Drift Season Pageant is over, the students all proceed to Divinity's Lap to participate in Beautymarch. No rankings. No competition. Just every student getting a turn to skate for everyone else, for the pure joy of skating. Doi and I row to the Principal Island and come ashore. We hold on to each other for steadiness as we follow the other students.

"Go get your skates." We turn to see Sensei Madame Liao.

"We've been unskated for the term," I say.

"The term is over," says Sensei Madame Liao. "Now, go get your skates. You are skating in Beautymarch."

We gape at her. I look at Doi. Her face is filled with doubt. The doubt is the shame of parading ourselves in front of our fellow students after our spectacular humiliation.

"You have paid what the law required you to pay," says Sensei Madame Liao. "Do not let anyone else make you pay more. Never let anyone do that to you."

Doi and I slip and stumble back to our dormitory chambers as quickly as we can, and every time we fall down, I laugh, knowing that we're about to skate again.

When we arrive at Divinity's Lap, Beautymarch is already

under way. All the first-year boys and girls are arrayed in a vast circle, each student playing an instrument. The sound of *erhus* and flutes and traveling zithers and *taiko* drums fills the air as the great sculpture of the Enlightened One towers over us, her hand resting on the roof of the Hall of Lilting Radiance, her smile sweeping over us all. Sensei Madame Phoenix skates about, directing her birds to spell out auspicious logograms over the Enlightened One's head. The luminescent harnesses crossing their green bellies spell out GENEROSITY! LOYALTY! FRIENDSHIP!

"Chen Cricket!" Sensei Madame Liao calls out.

Cricket tosses his *taiko* drum to the skater exiting the circle. He takes the center and skates strange little fidgets, doing no real wu liu, only fussy footwork, as he does when he's nervous. He's finding the grain in the pearl with his skates, working it with little twitches of his blades. As he does so, he's making the pearl change color! It turns blue and silver under his skates and then we see that he's making a figure in the pearl. He creates the image of the Temple of Heroes of Superlative Character. Everyone cries out with delight at his clever trick. The pearl quickly heals over and the image vanishes.

"Chen Peasprout!" calls out Sensei Madame Liao. I toss my *erhu* to Cricket as he exits the center. It doesn't matter how I skate. It doesn't matter what the other students think. I'm simply grateful for the joy of skating and for the honor of sharing a court with my friend Niu Doi one last time. There are cheers from some of the students as I give them one of my lifetime's 608 riven crane split jumps.

"'The Pearlian New Year's Song'!" calls out Sensei Madame Liao. I exit the center and go back to the circle of students as we begin to sing, joined by Sensei Madame Phoenix's birds.

If I learned just one thing, then the year has not been wasted.

If I traded one illusion for a revelation,

If I kept just one friend, then the year has not been wasted.

May we meet here in the New Year. May we meet here in Pearl!

"Captain!" calls out Sensei Madame Liao. Whom is she calling captain? It's a term of affection in Pearl. It means "the best," "the bravest," "the highest."

Suki makes to enter the center, but Sensei Madame Liao glares at her, turns away, and calls out, "Captain! Captain! Captain!"

Sensei Madame Liao stares down the length of the circle of students. As she beats on her drum and calls out "Captain!" it's clear that her stare isn't a challenge.

It's not a command.

It's an invitation.

She's inviting us all to support something.

A few students begin to take up the chant. "Captain! Captain!"

She's inviting us to put aside childish rivalries. She's inviting us to search within us for enough imagination and heart to become our next, better selves. She's inviting us to show that we're ready to advance to the next year.

The court resounds with chants of "Captain! Captain! Captain!"

We all look to where Sensei Madame Liao is looking.

She's looking at my friend.

Doi enters the center of the circle, her eyes shining with tears.

When she crosses her skates and rises on her toes and begins to wave her arms in wings, a cheer erupts from the crowd and the students cry out, "The Dragon and the Phoenix! The Dragon and the Phoenix!"

Doi begins to skate the length of the circle with her arms spread out behind her. She brushes her fingers lightly over the instruments of every student in the circle, inviting us to chase her.

Then she's off! She leaps out of the circle and races across the campus. We follow behind in a long train, drumming and playing like a great singing dragon.

She leads us atop the roof of Eastern Heaven Dining Hall and takes a spinning shadowless kick leap off the edge into the night sky. Everyone does the leap behind her, making a wave pass along the body of the dragon and flip out of its tail.

She leads us onto the outer rails, doing one single-footed twisting leap after another, and we all follow, making the body of the dragon seem to spiral in its flight over the dark water.

She leads us inside the Temple of Heroes of Superlative Character and bows down in a side split as she skates past the restored statues, and we all follow, making the body of the dragon seem to bow to the heroes of Pearl.

She skates up the ramp of the temple, and we follow, making the body of the dragon thread up the spiral.

She leaps out of the arch at the top, making the body of the dragon fly out of the temple. She lets out a roar, and we follow and holler our throats raw, making the air thunder with a terrible bellow.

She leads us back to the Principal Island and the assembly court. We form a circle around her, and as we pound on our drums and saw on our strings faster and faster, Doi launches into a brilliant, furious spin. Fifty rotations. One hundred rotations. One hundred and fifty rotations. Two hundred rotations!

She's done it! She's broken the record! She has once again made Pearl Famous Academy of Skate and Sword history! She ends the rotations with a hard skid, toes pointed on the pearl, one hand on her hip, the other spread in the air like a fan, head tossed back. The students scream with joy and the circle explodes in applause for this girl, the greatest artist of wu liu that Pearl Famous has ever known, for Niu Doi, my friend.

FINAL CHAPTER

I spend as much time as I can with Doi in the final days.
She's going to travel back to her aunt's in Tao-Ka several hundred li south of the city of Pearl. She'll spend the New Year's month there to await word of whether her father is truly going to send her back to Pearl Rehabilitative Colony to be committed as a novice nun.

Cricket and I are uncertain what our status here as exchange students is now, since the goodwill exchange between Shin and Pearl is clearly over. Sensei Madame Liao has temporarily arranged for Cricket and me to stay at a boardinghouse in the city during the holiday month. We can't stay at Pearl Famous because it undergoes "maintenance" during the recess. I guess they don't want students seeing what *maintenance* means.

The day before we are to leave, I hear a voice cry out, "Iwi, it's brushtime!" I turn to see logograms forming in the sky. The birds spell out: "Empress. Dowager. Mysteriously. Cuts. Off. All. Communications. With. Pearl. Buy. Pearl. Shining. Sun. News. To. Get. Whole. Story."

What can it mean? All I know is what the villagers below Tianshang Mountain learned the hard way: When the Empress Dowager goes silent, it's not the last time you will hear from her.

In the final days, I cross paths with Mole Girl.

"What's your name?" I ask her.

She laughs. "Gou Gee-Hong."

"Gou Gee-Hong, thank you."

She laughs again. "For what?"

"For being good luck," I say, and bow.

On the final day, when I'm finished with all I have to prepare, I skate to Doi's dormitory chamber. She's there with her few things bound in neat parcels of pearlsilk and string.

I can't help it. It's selfish of me. I should be brave for her now. But the tears come anyway.

"Don't cry, Peasprout."

"What are you going to do?"

"I don't know. I'm frightened. Do you believe I'll figure something out?"

"Yes! You're the bravest, most talented, truest person I've ever known. If anyone can figure something out, it's you."

"Then I'm not so frightened. It might sound strange, but this has been the happiest year of my life."

"What?"

"All those girlhood classics I read when I was young. I envied those girls so much. I wished for the friendships they found, which seemed more real than anything I'd ever known. Even though they were just imagined. And now, I've known friendship greater than anything anyone imagined. Thank you, my friend."

Then, for the first time, Doi smiles at me and I see that she, of course, has dimples. I'm unprepared to see them there. I'm thrown. She looks at me, the smile and the dimples suddenly gone. She's uncertain if she's said too much.

Doi wants to embrace me, but she doesn't. I feel, once again, the embarrassment and shame flash through her Chi.

So I open my arms and embrace her.

As I press her form against me, I smell that familiar scent, like plains sweetgrass, and it smells like someone I knew, but that person's gone now. Forever. My heart clenches. I realize that there's only one person who knows what I'm feeling right now, because she's feeling the same thing.

When we separate, I see my friend's face covered in tears that I caused.

And I know that she's seeing the exact same thing.

Doi bows to me and says, "May we meet here in the New Year."

I bow to her and say, through my tears, "May we meet here in Pearl."

I shoulder my belongings and exit my dormitory chamber. Cricket told me that he'd want to wait until the last moment to say goodbye to all his friends. Cricket. With friends.

At last, the time comes and we have to leave for the boardinghouse in the city. Cricket and I take our things and skate across the campus to the Great Gate of Complete Centrality and Perfect Uprightness at the entrance of Pearl Famous.

Something is happening at the bottom of the slope leading down toward the rail-gondolas that bridge Pearl Famous and the city.

Doi's down there. She has her back to me and her hands cupped to her mouth as she faces some sort of great round container on a sledge being hauled by someone.

"Doi, what's wrong?" I cry.

She turns around and lowers her hands with a look of profound emotion on her face, but I can't tell if that emotion is happiness or misery.

"Doi, what's happened? Is something wrong?"

"Yes. No. Yes."

"What have I missed?" says the person behind Doi.

Doi steps aside, and I see someone holding the rope pulling the

round container, dressed in the high collar and sweeping cloak of the Pearl Famous uniform.

I look into this face that my heart knows so well but that I'm seeing for the first time.

I cannot speak.

There is no air.

There is no time.

There is no world beneath my skates.

Or I am tumbling through all of it.

He smiles, and the dimples flash in his cheeks.

"Joyful fortune to make your acquaintance," he says. "I am called familial name Niu, personal name Hisashi."

ACKNOWLEDGMENTS

I, Disciple Lien Henry, author of this worthless novel, commence 10,000 bows of obeisance at the skates of these benevolent and sagacious persons, without whose assistance my work would be even more miserable and completely without qualities:

Fifty bows to my kindergarten teacher, Sensei Madame Sally McEachen, for seeing a light in a child who was not from here and didn't speak the language, and for surrounding that light with mirrors;

Fifty bows to each of my Clarion West instructors, Sensei Master George R. R. Martin, Sensei Master Chuck Palahniuk, and Sensei Madame Kelly Link, for enthusiasm and guidance regarding the material that would form the foundation for this novel and this world;

Fifty bows to Sensei Madame Sheila Williams, Supreme Editor at *Asimov's*, for giving a new writer his first story publication and embracing the ungrateful daughters of Pearl Rehabilitative Colony;

Fifty bows to Sensei Madame Sarah L. Thomson for early editorial wisdom that showed me what the next level of skill looked like;

Fifty bows to my mother, Shio-Mei Lien, for all the stories;

Fifty bows to my father, Fong-Chi Lien, for extensive insight on Chinese and Taiwanese language and culture;

Fifty bows to Jerry Lee Davis for encouragement to pursue writing;

Fifty bows to Gray Adams for unconditional support;

Fifty bows to Warwick Sims for telling me that birthing Pearl was the most important thing I could be doing with my life;

Fifty bows to Lian Hearn and Rachel Swirsky for inspiration and early affirmation;

Fifty bows to Ken Liu and Stephin Merritt for help with names;

Fifty bows to Miriam Spitzer Franklin and Linda Nagle for the perspectives of vegetarian and vegan figure skaters;

One hundred bows to my sister Ann Lien for early feedback and lifelong, belief in me;

One hundred bows to all at ICM for the thousand-armed defense, including Master of Statutes Colin Graham, Foreign Kingdoms Ambassador Hana Murrell, Lieutenant General Number-One Berni Barta, and Lieutenant General Number-Two Tamara Kawar;

One hundred bows to Peasprout's army at Houtu Famous House of Literature including Supreme and Final Sensei Madame Jean Feiwel, Supreme and Flawless Sensei Master Christian Trimmer, Publicity Mage Brittany Pearlman, Design Mage Carol Ly, Creativity Mage Patrick Collins, Artist of Superlative Characters Afu Chan, Artist of Surpassing Maps Elisabeth Alba, Production

Mage Thomas Nau, Managing Mage Hayley Jozwiak, Copy Mage Erica Ferguson, Logogram Neatener Number One Andrea Curley, and Logogram Neatener Number Two Kayla Overbey for their skill and talent;

One hundred twelve bows to my Clarion West classmates, our workshop director Les Howle, our workshop administrator Neile Graham, and the entire Clarion West community for the most important and transformative experience of my life; and

Eight thousand eighty-eight bows to my agent, the Mighty and Wise Sensei Madame Tina Dubois Wexler, and my editor, the Sage and Venerable Sensei Madame Tiffany Liao. Thank you, dear Senseis, for nurturing, cultivating, and growing me. Peasprout might or might not change the world as she hopes, but you have already changed mine.

All hail! All hail! All hail!

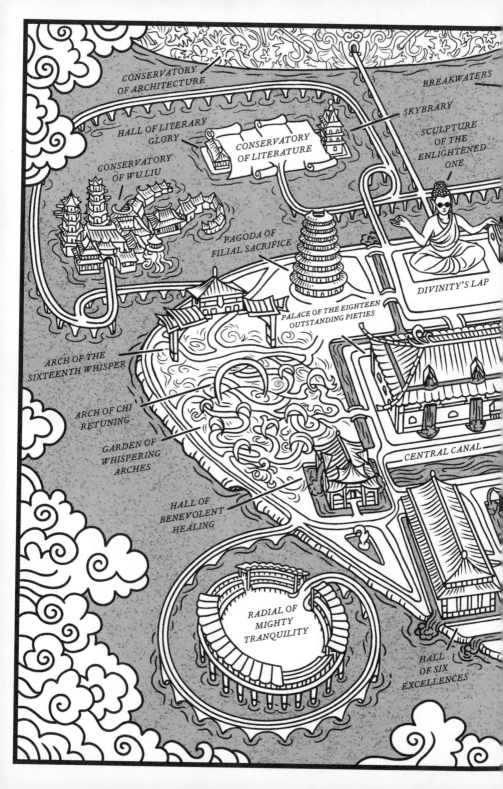